THEY ALL DIED SCREAMING

KRISTOPHER TRIANA

ISBN: 978-1-940250-45-8

Artwork by Don Noble
    www.roosterrepublicpress.com

Interior Layout by Lori Michelle
    www.theauthorsalley.com

Printed in the United States of America

First Edition

Visit us on the web at:
www.bloodboundbooks.net

PRAISE FOR KRISTOPHER TRIANA

"Whatever style or mode Triana is writing in, the voice matches it unfailingly . . . it's a safe bet we'll be seeing his name a lot in the years to come."

—**Cemetery Dance**

"Kristopher Triana is without question one of the very best of the new breed of horror writers."

—**Bryan Smith**,
author of *Depraved*

"Jesus! And I thought I was sick!"

—**Edward Lee**,
author of *Header*

"Kristopher Triana pens the most violent, depraved tales with the craft and care of a poet describing a sunset, only the sunset has been eviscerated, and dismembered, and it is screaming."

—**Wrath James White**,
author of *400 Days of Oppression*

"Body Art is the lost collaborative film from Larry Flynt and David Cronenberg. It's messy and brutal and a lot of goddamn fun."

—**Splatterpunk Zine**

"I've written that a way to judge the health of a genre is to gauge the number of emerging young, good writers. Kristopher Triana is one of the newest bumper crop of good ones . . . His prose is excellent, his plots compelling. Check out a rising star."

—**Gene O'Neill**,
author of *The Cal Wild Chronicles*

ALSO FROM KRISTOPHER TRIANA

Toxic Love

The Ivory Dealer

They All Died Screaming

Hell is Full of Palm Trees

Body Art The Coloring Book

Shepherd of the Black Sheep

MORE EXTREME HORROR FROM BLOOD BOUND BOOKS

#Horrible by KJ Moore

Welcome to The Splatter Club

Burnt Fur: Twisted Tails of Horror

Knuckle Supper by Drew Stepek

D.O.A. Anthology Series

The City by S.C. Mendes

Black Planet by Nikki Noir

Mother's Boys by Daniel I. Russell

Prince of Nightmares by John McNee

400 Days of Oppression by Wrath James White

Something Terrible by Wrath James & Sultan White

The Resurrectionist: Authors Preferred Edition by Wrath James White

This one is for C.V. Hunt

"We knew the world would not be the same. A few people laughed, a few people cried, most people were silent."

—Robert Oppenheimer
in an interview about the Trinity explosion, first broadcast in the television documentary *The Decision to Drop the Bomb* (1965)

"Flying towards me, wrapped in laughter
A woman's face, a terrible taste
of the morning after kisses and goodbyes
I can never seem to catch my footsteps
Have desires, they fly away
And every day I've got to fight the plague."

—Scott Walker

PROLOGUE

"I'M TOO DRUNK to dig this goddamned grave."

Still holding the bottle, the man cleared sweat from his brow with his forearm. In his other hand was the shovel he'd barely made a dent in the earth with. The hole was no bigger than a fish tank. The boy gazed into the grainy abyss, frowning. He knew what was coming.

The shovel was tossed to him.

The man snorted. "Best get started while there's still some light."

There was no sunshine here, just the muted glow of another overcast day. They were beneath concrete heavens, toiling in a hell of weeds, poison ivy, and fruitless bramble. The stench of pig feces dominated every other odor, canceling the fresh, spring scent of the woodland on the edge of the farm.

Blowing out a snot-rocket, the man stumbled to a tree stump and sat down slowly, holding his lower back. His vertebrae crackled like Jiffy Pop. The boy used to love popcorn. He missed it. He missed a lot of things. Settled, the man took another pull on the whiskey. Some trickled down his chin and his tongue darted out to lick it up, a frog after a fly. The boy watched him with tired eyes before turning back to the hole where a single worm wiggled at its newfound freedom. He wondered if the man would have killed it if he'd seen it, if the creature was worthy of the man's mercy, if it met the criteria of his aberrant morality.

Pushing the shovel into the dirt, the boy raised a small clump containing the worm, tossing it aside so it could live. On the ground beside it, the mildewed army bag was a grim reminder of those creatures who'd been far less fortunate.

CHAPTER ONE

THE BITCH WAS screaming.

Something about fucking every one of his friends—well, the friends of whoever she was yelling at. Chuck wasn't one to eavesdrop, but drunken hollering at three-thirty in the morning was just interesting enough to pull him away from his dog-eared paperback. It was just as well. Scotch had blurred his vision too far to continue reading.

"That's right!" the woman across the hall shouted. "You think those lowlife scumbags won't line up to fuck this?"

There was a slap. Chuck wondered if the guy had hit her or if she'd smacked her own backside for emphasis. He got out of his Schlitz-stained easy chair, took off his reading glasses, and went to the door. He heard a male voice, but the words were muffled and coming from further down the hall, fading. Chuck opened the door to see the woman in 213, the one he only saw at night, usually carrying a brown bag from Nishant's package store around the corner. She wore a faded Mötley Crüe t-shirt, sleeves ripped off so low he could see she was braless. Tangled hair, dyed red with dark, brunette roots. She was Chuck's age, maybe older. On the short side. Curvy. Thin lipped. Her nose turned up slightly, snout-like; all she needed was a pierced septum and she'd be like a skanky warthog.

She raged at her beau as he headed for the stairway. "You walk out now, Tony, and you can just keep on fuckin walkin'! Take a long walk off a short dock!"

But Tony said nothing, letting his footsteps on the stairs say it for him. One apartment down, another neighbor opened his door, called the woman a psycho cunt and told her to shut the fuck up, then slammed his door closed again. Another neighbor banged on

2

the ceiling from the floor below. The woman's chest rose and fell in deep, angry breaths. Noticing Chuck standing there, she yelled back at her boyfriend.

"Hey, Tony! My neighbor's out here now!" She turned her eyes back to Chuck, still shouting so Tony could hear. "Howdy, neighbor! How'd you like to get your dick sucked? Come on in!"

Chuck couldn't help but snicker. He was always up for a blowjob, but figured this lady's heart wasn't in it.

"I'm gonna let him stick it in my ass too, Tony!"

There was the sound of the bottom floor's door coming open, then the faint glow of streetlights bouncing off the walls of the stairwell. Then nothing at all. Tony had departed. The woman bared her teeth, a junkyard dog at the end of a chain.

She turned to Chuck with a sigh. "Wanna drink?"

Her apartment was even worse than his. The view from the doorway was of dirty dishes piled in the kitchen sink. Chuck stepped inside, and when the door swung closed, the domestic carnage of the living room presented itself. Clothes all over the floor and slung over the backs of chairs. Ashtrays overflowing with cigarette butts and joint roaches. The piercing stench of an ignored litter box. Unopened bills on the table stained with the crusty rings of a week's worth of coffee cups. One of the arms of the outdated, flower-patterned couch had no lining.

"Nice place ya got here," he said.

"Yeah, right."

The woman sat at the folding card table where a bottle of Evan Williams was whispering Chuck's name. She had a half-full tumbler of her own, so she took an overturned one and wiped it out with the end of her shirt. Chuck stared at the pale flesh of her exposed midsection and the empty hole of her belly button piercing. Stretch marks lined the divots of her hips, which jutted out of her cutoff jeans like tomahawks. Filling his tumbler to the brim, she slid the glass over as he sat down.

She held out a pack of cigarettes. "Smoke?"

"Sure."

She put two in her mouth, lit them, and then handed him one. It was slightly crushed. "Don't bother askin 'bout that blowjob."

"Wasn't gonna."

She smirked. "Yeah, sure."

"I'm too drunk to feel anythin'. Probably wouldn't stay hard."

"Well, I ain't drunk yet, but I aim to fix that." She shot back the tumbler and smacked her lips. "I'm Leslie."

"Chuck."

"You say *Chuck*?"

He nodded. "Chuck. Like ground beef. Like vomit."

"Well, ain't you a charming one."

"Nope. Just a dirty old man."

"Can't be that old from the looks of ya."

"Just turned forty-two."

"Yeah, well, I'm forty-fuckin-four. Don't wanna think of that as old. When'd ya turn forty-two?"

"Around three hours ago."

She smiled. "It's your fuckin birthday? No shit?"

"No shit."

"Fuck, man. Let's toast."

She poured herself another and topped his off. They raised the glasses in a swaying salutation.

Leslie said, "Happy fuckin birthday."

They slammed back their drinks as if in triumph. Leslie puffed on her Lucky, hot-boxing it, the long turd of ash refusing to drop off. Chuck looked at the spattering of scars on the insides of her arms, some masked by tattoos, others fresh enough to still be scabby. There were a couple of faint scars on her forehead where the flesh met the hairline, and other on her chin. It made him want to see her naked almost as much as her big breasts did, but for different reasons.

"So what're ya doin for the big day?" she asked.

"Nothin."

Chuck didn't care to elaborate. He wondered why he'd even told her it was his birthday. He always tried to ignore them.

"Birthdays used to mean cake and spankins," she said. "Now it's just another fuckin notch on the lids of our coffins. In a few months, I'll be forty-five. Halfway to fifty and alone. No family. No real career. Not even a lousy boyfriend now that fuckface walked out."

"So it's really over?"

"Hell, it was fuckin over with Tony even before tonight. He's been hintin at seein other people."

Chuck nodded. "In my experience, when somebody starts talkin 'bout leavin, they're already gone. But to hell with it, there's more to life than love."

"*Love* my ass. All I've got is a shit job runnin a fuckin cash register and a filthy cat who hides more than he does anythin else. Who'd want to celebrate a birthday when your life's like that, huh? Be like swimmin in a septic tank."

Chuck scratched at his two days' growth of beard. "Could be worse."

"I don't need cheerin up."

"A job's a job."

"Until the store closes, and it's likely to any day. Nobody fuckin shops anymore, man. They do it all online. Sales bein what they are, the company done froze everyone's wages. No raises, no Christmas bonuses. I can barely afford this one-bedroom shithole as it is. Half my income goes to the fuckin rent. I'd go be a waitress, but everybody wants young chicks with higher asses." She bounced one breast with her hand. "Even these big ol' titties don't benefit me as much as they did when I was, like, twenty-two. Ya'll men are lucky. Ya don't age out like us broads."

She puffed until she hit the filter. Chuck noticed her eyes were deep chocolate, the pupils like pinpoints. Not the bright, rainbow eyes of a girl but the hard, truck exhaust eyes of a woman who'd seen too much too often. When those eyes fell upon him, he shifted in his seat and looked down into the swirl of his drink to escape their intensity.

"So whadda ya do, Chuck?"

He slid the tumbler to her for a refill. "Nothin."

She made a *pffft* sound with her lips. "Whadda ya mean *nothin*?"

"Was workin at an electronics warehouse. Unloadin pallets. But they fired me last week."

"Laid off?"

"Nah. I was drinkin on the job. That and they caught me stealin a hi-def TV."

"Clear picture mean that much to you?"

"Nah. I don't watch TV. I was gonna pawn it."

She leaned forward. "I'm actually charmed by your honesty. It's rare in a man."

"Dishonest enough to steal."

"Everyone makes mistakes."

"Wasn't no mistake. Never had a job I didn't swipe stuff from."

"You some kinda klepto?"

"Nah. I do it on principal."

Leslie snickered.

Chuck continued. "I mean, hell, I break my back loadin trucks or scrubbin toilets or whatever, and get paid shit wages to do it. All these jobs nobody wants. I take 'em and what's my thanks? Minimum wage I can't live on. The scraps of scraps. So I steal things to make up for it. Fuck 'em."

Leslie reached for her cigarettes. In the moment she looked away, Chuck squeezed the zit on his jaw, releasing its white innards. Clear liquid followed, tailed by a drop of blood. He drew back his finger and looked at the Silly String of pus before wiping it on his jeans.

"You're not gonna rip *me* off are ya?" Leslie said.

"I don't steal from people, just big businesses."

"Shit, I ain't got nothin worth stealin no ways. Might as well rob a dumpster."

Chuck rolled his shoulders. "So you got no beefs drinkin with a thief?"

"Not unless you got beefs drinkin with an alcoholic tramp."

He shrugged. "Never have before."

Leslie poured him another.

CHAPTER TWO

PANIC SEIZED THE BOY. Though his instincts told him to run and find her, he froze in place. Looking around at the wishing fountain, then back to the arcade behind him, then the Camelot Music and Payless Shoe Store on either side, the mall seemed suddenly bigger. A massive, endless labyrinth he could never find his way through without Mom.

He'd only let go of her hand for a moment to look at the coins in the fountain, thinking if he could gather enough quarters he could play some video games in the arcade. Mom had told him to stay close as she'd browsed the display windows of Casual Corner, but the boy had gone completely around the fountain, looking for quarters close enough for his short arms to reach. When he'd come around again to where he'd started, his mother was gone.

The boy forced himself to move. He sprinted to Causal Corner, putting his palms on the wood paneling of the exterior as he peered inside, somehow afraid to enter. The racks of women's clothing created another intimidating maze. He found himself wishing he'd been allowed to bring his Rambo toy machine gun or plastic He-Man sword. Maybe it would have given him courage to imagine he was bigger, stronger, a man instead of a boy. Thinking of his muscle-bound heroes, he took a deep breath and stood up straight, but deflated easily. Still shaking, he entered the store, scanning each woman's face, praying for his mother's. Every woman with auburn hair offered hope until she turned around, revealing disappointing faces.

"Mom?" he called out, barely more than a whisper. He didn't want these adults looking at him. He didn't want them to know he was *alone*. "Mom?"

Fear pummeled his innards, drying out his mouth, blurring his vision with tears.

It's all your fault, he thought. *You should've stayed close like Mom said to!*

But he was almost ten now, too embarrassed to walk around holding his mother's hand. The boy darted out of the store and back into the cool vestibule of the mall, his senses heightened by desperation. He stretched his ears for the sound of her voice, but could not break through the chatter of the patrons and droning Muzak. He sniffed for his mother's perfume, but the recirculated air offered only the smell of hot pretzels from the concession stand and sweet smoke wafting from the cigar shop. He scanned the area again, racing around the wishing fountain, whispering her name, on the verge of sobbing and ashamed to be so.

When backed into something, a hand fell on his shoulder.

"Whoa there, son."

The boy turned to see a middle-aged man with slicked-back hair and a smile that revealed small, yellow teeth. There were spaces between each one, like the mouth of a jack-o-lantern, but while this frightened the boy the man's security guard uniform offered a surge of relief.

"Can't be runnin 'round like that in my mall," the guard said. "Could slip by this fountain. The water sprinkles out, ya know."

The boy tried to speak but choked on heaving breaths. The man bent down to his level.

"Ya okay, kid?"

The boy shook his head.

"Look lost. Ya lost? Where's your parents?"

The boy whimpered. "I can't find my mom."

The guard smiled and the boy had to look away from his fish teeth. He squeezed the boy's shoulder a little too hard.

"Thought so," he said. "What's your mama look like?"

"Um, she's got red hair and brown eyes. She has on a red coat and—"

"Yup. That nice redhead, I figured it. Don't worry, kid, your mama's waitin for ya at the office buildin! We've been lookin all over for you!"

The man laughed, the underside of his face flushing pink. His positivity made the boy smile a little. He would have felt bad if he hadn't, seeing how the man was offering such wonderful news. He was with an adult now, a man of authority there to protect and serve, just like it always said on cop cars, like they talked about on *CHiPs*. Mom and Dad always told him to find a policeman if ever he was in trouble. Now the boy had been rescued by a hero with a paunch instead of a muscular movie idol.

"Come on," the guard said. "I'll drive ya on over."

He offered his hand. It was clammy, as if it had just been washed. He walked the boy away from the fountain and toward the sliding glass doors leading to the parking lot.

"Don't worry now, kid. Everything's gonna be alright. Gonna be just fine, you'll see."

"Um, sir . . . where we goin?"

"Like I told ya, your mommy's in the manager's office buildin 'round the other side of the mall. We'll drive on over to save the long walk through the lot."

They stopped in front of a brown pickup truck with rusty sores and a green replacement door on the passenger's side. There were no hubcaps and the windshield had a small spider web of cracks along the bottom. The boy's brow furrowed when the man opened the door for him. He'd been expecting a slick, white car with *mall police* or something like that written on it in shiny letters, not this sorry hunk of junk. There was a foul, organic odor to the truck's interior too. It reminded the boy of the petting zoo Mom and Dad had taken him to, where he'd played in the barn hay and fed the calves and ewes.

"Well, come on," the man said. "Let's go to mommy."

The man helped him climb into the cabin and closed the door behind him. The boy had a moment alone to examine the inside of the truck, noting the overflowing ashtray and wet, stained magazines on the floor. Their covers showed pictures of tractors, guns and men fishing. A rack behind the boy's head cradled a hunting rifle. His fingers started trembling again. The driver's door swung open and the man got in, the boy flinching at the *thunk* of metal on metal as the door slammed shut. He looked all around the parking lot as they drove, uncertain what he was scanning for, uncertain of everything. Neither of them spoke until they'd gone around the back of the building where there were few cars and no people in sight. The man put the truck in park but kept it running.

"Just need my medicine real quick," he said.

He reached across the boy, causing him to push back against his seat, giving the arm a wide birth. Beneath the thick hair, the flesh was discolored with pink blotches. The man opened the glove compartment and retrieved a brown bottle and small rag. When he opened the cap, a sweet, chemical odor filled the cabin as he dabbed some of the clear liquid onto the cloth.

"Okay, kid, so—"

The man came at the boy in a sweaty lunge, beast-like as he pressed the rag over the boy's nose and mouth, muffling his shrieks. The boy tried to squirm away but the man was too powerful and the seat belt kept him in place. Gapped, stained teeth sprinkled spittle across the boy's brow as he was pushed down, deep into the cushions, deep into the black embrace of a forced sleep.

CHAPTER THREE

"**SEE,**" **EUGENE SAID,** pointing at his phone's screen. "Right, there. All these caller IDs have the number six in them. Just like I told ya."

Chuck put his beer on the bar and leaned closer, having to squint without his reading glasses. Eugene scrolled, showing him all the phone numbers. They all, indeed, had at least one six in them.

"So what?" Chuck said. "There's only ten numbers to choose from. Six is bound to pop up a lot. It's just a game of odds."

"What?" Eugene's bug eyes went impossibly wider. They were bloodshot tonight, twitchy. Chuck figured it was more a lack of sleep than anything else, though Eugene was a known drug user. "Nah, man, nah. This ain't no coincidence. This is *harassment.*"

"How so?"

Eugene shook his head. "Six is the number of the beast, man! Shit, don't you know that? Six-six-six equals *Satan.* They're putting six in each of these numbers on purpose. It's a threat to my freedom."

Chuck took one long pull from the bottle. He'd need more beer for this conversation, so he motioned to Barman for another. The big bastard waved a finger in acknowledgement while serving his current customer, a skinny blonde Chuck had been ogling out of the corner of his eye. More and more he was drawn to these younger women. Now that he was past forty, he was haunted by the realization he'd probably fucked his last teenager. It made him want one all the more. This one was in her twenties (close enough) and wore a skintight, strapless dress and heels. He wondered if she was one of the hookers from down by the docks. He couldn't be sure, despite how many of them he'd fucked.

"They're screwing around with my freedom!" Eugene said.

11

"How is callin you fuckin with your freedom? I don't get it."

"Don't get it? Can you be this thick?"

The short man was sweaty and his messy hair seemed thinner ever day. Chuck wondered if he was plucking them out one by one or if this pending baldness was yet another side effect of years of chomping down on hallucinogenic mushrooms in a misguided effort to expand his mind, an effort that had effectively ruined it.

"Chuck, these Satanists are trying to scare me because they know I'm an herbalist. Big pharma is always trying to stop us from natural living and healing. They hate our earth remedies, our crystals and our—"

"Big pharma? I thought it was Satanists."

Eugene's eyes darted, lost in the holes of his own conspiracy theory. "It's the same thing, really. They're all tied in—like fucking Nazis, like the fucking billionaires who own this country, the world. The ones leading us into the apoca—"

"They're just sales calls, Gene. Everybody gets these automatic robo calls from numbers they don't know."

Eugene smiled, uglier in smugness. "That's what they've got everybody believing."

"No, that's what they *are*. If you picked up the phone for once, you'd see that."

"Are you kidding? I can't pick it up! Then they'll know they've got the right number for sure. If they're not certain it's me, then they can't get to me. They can't get to my family if we stay private and I'm there to protect them."

As usual with Eugene, Chuck could have laughed, and might have if the whole thing wasn't so pathetic. Eugene's family wasn't a wife and kids. He still lived with his mother in the apartment at the end of the hall, four doors down from Chuck. *That* was his family. But Eugene didn't see it as his mother taking care of him, even though she was the only one bringing in any real income. He saw it as him taking on the role of man of the house after his father died, that he was the protector and provider, a responsibility passed down to him via the patriarch's untimely death. But the old man had passed of pancreatic cancer over a decade ago and Eugene was still there, living in the spare bedroom where he smoked pot and argued conspiracy theories online with strangers. Chuck had known him for more than two years and in that time Eugene had had as many jobs as he'd had girlfriends—*zero*. He was a paranoid burnout, hurtling through his thirties while still living at home, but he saw himself as some sort of crusader for the rights of herbalists, which was an overly prestigious title for people who grew plants with black lights in their bedrooms.

A beer slid down the bar. Chuck snatched it.

"Thanks, Barman."

Chuck wasn't being rude. That was the name the grim barkeep preferred. Chuck doubted any of the patrons knew the man's real name, even the other regulars. It was easy to imagine him with a twisted past, maybe a former Hell's Angel who had gone into hiding or a mafia hit man turned snitch and forced into witness protection.

"Anyway," Eugene went on, "my incoming call history is *proof* of harassment."

Chuck wished he could still smoke indoors. Without a cigarette every hour or so, his nerves became too sensitive to tolerate other people for very long, especially when they were even crazier than he was.

"Sure, Gene. If you say so."

Eugene grinned. "You'll see one day. Everyone will. I'm just ahead of the game is all."

Chuck allowed his neighbor this delusion. He'd long ago tried to convince Eugene to seek therapy, but the man believed psychiatrists to be government brainwashers, warping minds to their will and poisoning people with meds that were nothing more than big pharma toxins. He claimed to get all the mental healing he needed by aligning his chakras with dandelion powder, goldenseal root tincture and three tablespoons of kratom each morning, which he sprinkled over jackfruit patties. But in the afternoons, he self-medicated just as Chuck did—with round after round of sweet, obliterating alcohol.

"I saw you the other night," Eugene said. "You know, talking to that girl in 213."

"Oh yeah?"

"Saw you go into her place too."

"Yeah?"

"Uh huh. Just be careful, man. You know."

"No. I don't. Whadda ya mean *careful*?"

Eugene raised his eyebrows. "She's got a revolving door for a pussy. You know I monitor the halls, to protect my family, and I've seen a lot of guys in and out of her place after dark. Last night wasn't the first guy who left her screaming in the hall."

Chuck shrugged. "So what?"

"*So what*—what is that? Your new catch phrase? *So what* is she's dirty. She could have all kinds of STDs, man."

"I don't catch diseases, STDs or otherwise."

"That pussy must be like a biohazard dumpster. I wouldn't fuck her with my worst enemy's dick."

Somehow Chuck doubted that. If *any* woman showed sexual interest in a cracked wallflower like Eugene he'd probably worship at the altar of her snatch the rest of his life, loyal and subservient to his queen. Chuck often wondered if the poor schmuck had even lost his virginity, if he'd always been like this or once had some semblance of a man's life before everything deteriorated, melting him down into the pitiful paranoid who now slouched on the barstool beside him.

"Don't be such a chauvinist," Chuck said.

"Hey! I'm no chauvinist, man. I love women."

"Then don't treat women who like sex like they're some kinda walkin disease bag."

"So you *did* fuck her?"

"No, but I ain't sayin I wouldn't."

"Even though she sleeps around?"

"Look—*I* sleep around. And a male tramp is no cleaner than a female tramp. Besides, Gene, you're too much of a germaphobe for your own good."

"No I'm not."

"Ya put on gloves before pumpin gas."

"Those things are filthy."

"Ya don't even carry cash for Christ's sake, only a credit card you insist on doin the swipin with so no cashier has to touch it. You've sterilized life so much you're never gonna enjoy it. Don't you ever wanna launch?"

"You mean . . . *cum*?"

"I ain't talkin 'bout fuckin. Well, that's part of it but that ain't the whole thing. I mean launch into life, into real fuckin manhood instead of this childish, life-on-hold existence you got goin."

Eugene looked at him blankly and in that instant Chuck held a morsel of hope he'd broken through. But then Eugene scoffed, the superior smirk returning. "I'm more alive than anyone in this whole bar. I don't need to *launch* because I'm *awake*. Really awake."

Standing up, he slammed back the rest of his whiskey sour and clapped the bar.

Barman approached. "Heading out, Gene?"

"Yes, sir. Put it on the tab, my good man."

Eugene put his chest out as if he'd accomplished something.

Barman sighed, showing teeth. "I'm gonna need something from you next time; something in the form of payment. Got me?"

Eugene's smile fell away. He nodded at Barman but didn't speak as he slinked toward the exit.

"See ya, Gene," Chuck said.

Barman made a notation at the register and came back with a wet rag, wiping down and picking up Eugene's pile of crumpled napkins. Chuck glanced at one of the TVs mounted high on the wall behind the bar, an image of a glacier followed by the depressing sight of scrawny polar bears. The legend on the bottom of the screen read: MORE POLAR ICE CAPS SNAP FREE AFTER MASS MELTING. Chuck yawned.

"Hey, Barman. Ya lookin for anybody?"

"You asking me out?"

Chuck snorted a laugh. Barman was a miserable bastard, but the two men shared in the humor of busting each other's balls.

"No, you dumb ape. I mean are ya lookin for any help 'round the bar."

Now it was Barman's turn to laugh. "You got fired *again*? Jesus, that has to be some kind of record. What's it been, five jobs so far this year?"

"Six if ya count that day pickin up trash on the highway."

"*Day*? That's a stretch. You came to the bar after only a couple of hours, you lazy prick."

"It was too hot out."

"Shit, man. Why the fuck would I wanna hire you? I'd have to be the stupidest businessman in the world."

"Come on. I'm no employee-of-the-month, but I can bust my ass good as anybody. I can clean up 'round here, get the floors mopped, get rid of the graffiti in the men's room."

"I like that graffiti. It's like local color. Gives the place charm."

"They're jokes about takin a shit, man. That and phone numbers for them dock whores and a couple of cocksuckin queers from downtown."

"Poetry of the streets, Chucky. Poetry of the streets." The big man slung his bar rag over the sink behind him. "Anyway, I don't do the hiring 'round here. Says *Rudy's Place* on the sign out front, last I checked."

"Alright, well, where is he?"

"You want an interview *now*? You're eight beers in, dipshit."

"Yeah, but I'm not drunk."

"You look like a pile of sun-baked dog shit. You haven't shaved in days and you look pale, despite it being summer. Looks like you haven't slept either."

"Meh. I always look like this."

"Well, the boss ain't here anyway. Usually isn't."

"Then where is he?"

"I don't fucking know. I don't keep tabs on him, I keep tabs on the bar."

Chuck put his head in his hand and leaned on the bar. He looked at the television to get a break from Barman's scowl. On the screen, people wearing medical masks were walking down city streets. The legend read: MORE SUICIDES IN CANADA.

Barman went on. "And speaking of tabs, if you ain't working how're you gonna pay for all the booze you belt down every goddamn night?"

"That's why I need a fuckin job."

"To keep yourself alive or just keep yourself drunk?"

"Same fuckin thing."

Chuck looked away. The young blonde at the end of the bar had vaporized while he was listening to Eugene's loony bullshit, replaced by some portly bastard with a backwards baseball cap and a t-shirt that read *I'm Fat, Let's Party*, his attire twenty years younger than he was.

"Look at this asshole," Barman said. "A walking mid-life crisis.

Can't accept the crippling blow of time. The call of the void is just too scary for some people."

Barman approached the newcomer, leaving Chuck with the last beer he'd be drinking here tonight. He felt suddenly exhausted even though it was only nine and he hadn't done jack shit with the day.

Leaving Rudy's, Chuck was smacked across the face by the city's heat and the smell of the trash that had been piling in the streets since the garbage strike began two weeks ago. The August night was oppressive, moist in the worst way, enhancing the stink of the ghetto. He thought of it as moving through a pond of menstrual blood. Just another sweaty drunk stumbling toward the next drink, the next brain-melt, the next escape from the shit-stained jaws of life. The streets were raw tonight, cracked under the weight of the collective desperation of its people. Pain seemed to burst from the lines in their faces as they crept away from the streetlights' glow, searching for darker, quieter, more familiar hells. Chuck undid the buttons of his guayabera shirt, unashamed. Retrieving a pack of cigarettes from his front pocket, he took out the final one, which he'd already smoked halfway down. He tossed the pack into the alley, lit up, then stepped beside the dumpster to take a piss. It foamed at the base of the alley wall, sousing a fat cockroach. It writhed on its back, helpless, dying. Chuck thought killing another living thing with your piss had to be the ultimate dominance of another species.

These days it was rare for him to feel dominant of anything, even vermin. Eugene's sense of superiority was a delusion, but at least it gave him some form of pride, which was more than Chuck had. Broke again, unemployed again, drunk again. He cycled through the fetid failure of his life like shoes tumbling in a dryer, going around only to end up right back where he'd started every damn time. If it wasn't for the work-related back injury he'd faked down at the packing plant he wouldn't even have the remains of his settlement money, which was all he was getting by on. That was two jobs ago. Part of the agreement was he had to quit the plant, which he did without regrets after a month of monotonous labor under the kind of boss who never stops reminding you that nothing is ever good enough. Familiar with his own fuckups, Chuck knew he'd just blow the ten grand on old pulp novels, cigarettes, and endless rounds at Rudy's, so in a rare moment of foresight he'd paid for nine months' rent in advance. He may have only four hundred dollars to his name, but at least he had a place to stay.

By the time he made it back to his building his shirt was sticking to him, his graying chest hair matted down. The heat had to be some kind of record. Chuck's balls swam in their own furry soup, his feet steam-cooked in his shoes. The elevator was more like a sauna, so he took the stairs. That's when he heard her. She was as loud as last night but jovial instead of raging. Her voice was raspy, words a little slurred.

"Make it a large with pepperoni! Yeah . . . and some fries! You guys got any beer? No? Well, can ya pick some up on the way over?"

Chuck reached the landing. Leslie was standing in the hallway, dressed in a thin, white nightgown that ended mid-thigh and a pair of pink flip-flops. Her hair was a tangled briar. She leaned against the wall for support as she spoke into the phone, the dim light of the hall revealing her age.

"Alright, fuck it, then," she said. "Just bring the food fast as ya can. I'm starved over here and it's too fuckin hot to cook . . . yeah . . . yeah, okay, bye."

She hung up, spotted Chuck, and waved. "Hey, wazzup?"

"Same shit."

Leslie threw her arms around his neck and hugged him like long lost family.

"It's so good to see you!" she slurred. "What's your name again?"

"Chuck."

"Oh, right. Like puke or whatever. Shit, man, I just ordered some pizza. Wanna hang out?"

"Sure."

"Got any beer?"

"Got some scotch."

"Even better."

She'd clearly had enough, but Chuck was in no condition to criticize. He was buzzed enough that a glass or two of that Johnny Walker would hit his head like a sock full of quarters. Besides, he didn't really care if she caved in to her alcoholism, as long as he could get sloshed right along with her. He was in a state of loneliness uncommon for him, and the feel of the woman's breasts squishing against his body as they hugged had lured him like a hundred fishhooks. He went to his room, snagged the bottle, and joined Leslie in her apartment, closing the door to give the neighbors a break from her big mouth. He put the scotch on the counter and reached for her pack of Lucky Strikes.

"You're in better spirits tonight," he said.

"Tony can go to hell. He's not gonna shit all over my life no more. 'Sides, I had today off. I'm always in a better mood when I ain't gotta deal with no customers. I hate every one of their guts, even the nice ones."

"I feel ya there."

"Oh, do ya? You *feel* me?"

She'd twisted the meaning of his words, flirting, her eyes swimming in drunkenness.

Chuck said, "Dealin with other people all day long is a special kind of hell."

Leslie groaned. "Tell me about it. When the demo lady calls out sick—and the cunt does it all the time—I have to run her table. Ain't nothin worse than givin out little sample cups to people. They always say the same shit: *Oh, what do we have here?* So you tell the fucks, describing the food over and over. Then they stand there, eating in front of you, and as if that's not fuckin disgusting enough, then they talk with their mouths full. God, I hate that. Buncha fuckin vultures. Buncha pigs."

Chuck winced and tried to hide it by smoking.

"But the worst," Leslie continued, "is when ya get stuck with some fuckin old person. They always think you're interested in their life story, so ya end up in a one-sided conversation that couldn't be more boring. Their lives, their kids, their former jobs, their health. Like anyone gives a flyin fuck. And you're stuck there 'cause you can't leave the table."

"Jesus, that *is* awful."

"I tell ya, sometimes I wish they'd all just fuckin die."

"The customers."

"Nah, everyone."

"What about your friends and relatives?' Chuck asked. "And your neighbors?"

"Don't have any friends or relatives. Not no more." She sniffed and cleared her throat. "And neighbors? Shit. Have you seen these freaks? You seem alright, Chucky, but these other motherfuckers, my sweet Christ. Ya know I hear the guy in 220 is a shut-in, so fat he hardly ever leaves his apartment. Probably ain't seen his dick since the '90s. And the rest are all broke-ass losers like us. Why else would anyone live in this dump?"

Leslie poured drinks they finished almost instantly. She looked off, staring at nothing, her eyes a little misty. "Can't believe that asshole left me."

Chuck wasn't surprised by Leslie's sudden change. It was the old seesaw of the alcoholic, a metronome swing between dizzy elation and toxic depression. He just hoped she wasn't about to cry. He wasn't in the mood to console someone and was never any good at it when he tried. But there was one thing he knew from experience always cheered a woman up, especially a drunk one, the only solace he had to offer.

"You know," he said, "the best way to get over one man is to get under another."

They'd forgotten about the pizza.

When the doorbell rang, Leslie was bent over the kitchen counter, one leg up on it, her nightgown high around her waist. Chuck was pulling her ponytail back, stretching her neck, stretching her everything, and she was even louder in sex than she'd been while screaming in the hallway, as if she were being hit by an axe instead of a dick. The doorbell hushed her.

"Hold on," she told Chuck.

"To hell with 'em."

"Fuck that, I'm hungry."

She scooted off and Chuck braced himself against the fridge. His shirt was gone and his jeans were around his ankles, shoes still on. He briefly thought about offering to pay for the pizza but decided against it. He resented it too much. It's arrival was turning his balls as blue as curaçao. Leslie pushed her gown back into place, but it was tight and didn't make it all the way over her hips. She failed to notice this before opening the door, accidentally giving the delivery boy a glimpse of her bush. The stunned young man glanced at it whenever Leslie wasn't making eye contact. Before he could tell her the total, she took the twenty from the end table and pushed it into his hand, snatching the food and closing the door without a goodbye. She placed the box and bag on the kitchen counter, fries spilling out, and wiggled a slice free. Bending over the box, she took her gown completely off now, breasts dropping, nipples grazing the top layer of grease on the pizza.

She looked over her shoulder at Chuck and said, "Come on."

She finished three slices before they climaxed, moaning along with Chuck's animal grunts, the smell of sauce and fried potatoes mixing with the raw, gym-locker stink of summer sex and booze sweat. As they screwed, her chest and face and hair collided with the pizza, the cheese sticking to her body, grease pouring down her chin and neck, orange pizza juice spilling over her breasts and belly.

"I needed that," she said when they were through.

"Me or the pizza?"

She rose from the counter and stretched her back, a crooked smile her only reply.

CHAPTER FOUR

THE **CAGE WAS** meant for dogs. The boy knew that, just as he knew his mother must be frantic in the mall, searching for him with the same panic he'd felt upon losing sight of her. He shuddered against the bars of the dog crate, wiping away tears to better see where he was. A basement or cellar. Something underground. Cracks in concrete walls revealed dirt and packed clay. The temperature here was lower than outside, the air musky, and cobwebs reached up a moldy staircase, their fat-bottomed owners wrapping victims in little, silken coffins. A small snakeskin lay a few feet from the boy's prison. The bowl at his feet was empty. Though he hadn't been hungry, he'd eaten the mac and cheese so not to anger his kidnapper.

Kidnapped.

The word turned the boy's stomach like a corkscrew. He was just like those black-and-white pictures on milk cartons, the ones that always made him look away. As much as he'd been working toward independence, excited to be inching closer to his teenage years, now the boy had been diminished back into a child, weeping for his parents to save him, his love for them suddenly enormous, enriched by the terrible potential of never seeing them again.

What was the man going to do with him? Was he to be kept as a pet? A P.O.W like Rambo? A slave? Or was he going to be hurt—maybe even killed?

The sound of a door opening made the boy jolt and he banged the top of his head against the crate. A black ghost of shadow stretched across the concrete, the sound of footsteps stinging the boy's every nerve. His mouth went dry, his gulps like swallowing steel wool. The man pulled the string on the light bulb suspended from the ceiling. He was out of his guard uniform, dressed down in scuffed cowboy boots, slacks, and tank top.

"Don't worry, kid. I ain't gonna rape ya. Ain't no pervert. Ya won't have to do nothin sexual."

The boy closed his eyes tight.

"And I ain't gonna hurt ya, 'less ya make me. Now, ya gonna be a good boy or a bad boy?"

The boy sniffled, tucking his head into his chest. The man kicked the cage and the boy jolted back, but there was nowhere to go. The cage's limited height kept him in a near fetal sitting position.

"Best answer me, kid."

Getting the words out felt like drowning. "I'll . . . I'll be g-g-good."

"That's what I wanna hear. But it takes more than words." The man squatted down on his haunches, face close to the bars. "What I wanna see outta ya is the same obedience I gave my old man when I was your age and—how old are ya? Twelve?"

"Nine."

"Wow. You're big for your age, huh? That'll do nicely. Like I was sayin, when I was nine, ten, and on up to a teenager, I always did what my old man told me, even when I didn't wanna, even when I was feelin rode hard and put away wet and every bone in my body felt like broken glass. I tell ya, I did more chores than a mule and worked twice as hard. Had to keep the farm goin strong. I'd dig ditches, fix fences, chop off chicken heads . . . "

The boy closed his eyes again, holding sobs inside his chest.

"If I complained, I'd get the belt." The man leaned in further. "Ya don't want the belt, boy. Believe me. I've got bumps on my ass that ain't never gonna heal. I don't wanna be hard on ya the way Pa was me. Don't wanna hurt ya. But ya gotta 'member you're here for a reason. You're here to *work*. Not cry, not argue, not try an run away. Just work."

The boy embraced the darkness behind his eyes. He would gladly go blind and deaf, anything to escape this man's presence.

"We understand each other, kid?"

The boy's mouth failed him. When he tried to speak, all that came out was whimpers. He expected the man to rage at this, but his tone became gentle, almost fatherly.

"Now, now. I know you're scared, this bein your first day here an all. Just nod if'n ya agree."

The boy did.

"Good. Just relax and calm down. Won't be no chores today. Ya show me you're gonna behave and I'll bring down a cot for ya to sleep on, get ya outta this here cage. But we have to grow a trust, you and me. That starts today."

Pigs.

They were everywhere. Rolling, snorting. Squealing in a black pit of mud and waste. The stink was monstrous, reminding the boy of a campground's portable toilet he'd once stepped into only to find a pyramid of feces rising out of the bowl, several inches above the seat, a temple for a hundred flies. He'd gagged then and almost gagged now, swallowing it back so the man wouldn't notice.

Leading him around the wooden fence that boxed the hogs and sows in their play area, the man's boots made wet pops as they sloshed through the mud. It had poured rain last night. The boy had heard the storm from the cellar. Now, at daybreak, the clouds hung low and ashen. The house was smaller than the boy had expected based on the size of the cellar. There was also a tin shack, a pen of rotten wood, and a maroon barn at the edge of the farm where dense thicket warned against any effort to escape. The boy was confident he could outrun the man, but there was nothing but forest for as far as he could see. He didn't even hear cars in the distance. He'd be lost and alone in those woods if he managed to make it off the farm. And the man would come after him; of that the boy was certain. The rifle would come out of the truck. It meant the man was a hunter. He knew these woods. They boy knew nothing, nothing but fear.

The truck sat along a dirt road leading to the farmhouse. It wound through the woods in a vein of mud and rock, its path disappearing into brush and shadows. The boy could follow it, but it would leave him exposed. Unless he could break out of the cellar and flee while the man was sleeping, the path was not as promising as it appeared. There was no escape plan that didn't suffocate him. He didn't want to die in those woods. He just wanted to go home. He wanted Mom. Maybe if he were good, as he promised his captor he would be, the man would let him go once all the chores were done. It didn't occur to him that a farm's chores are ongoing, that maintenance was never completed.

They stepped around a generator and went inside the tin shack. It was cool, damp, the silvery sheen reflecting their warped images back at them. The boy dropped his eyes so not to see his own face. It would look too much like the kids on the milk cartons. Against the wall were two machines with chords that ran out to the generator. One was a steel tub with a pipe extending from the bottom, the end of which was capped by a grate with small holes. Beneath the pipe was a bucket. The other machine was a metal table with a steel bar above it like a gallows. Running down from it was a saw blade connected to the table, pieces of dried meat still clinging to the menace of its teeth.

"This here's the bone saw," the man said, slapping the table. He pointed to the tub. "And there's the meat grinder. Today I'm gonna teach ya to take 'em apart, clean 'em and put 'em back together again. That's where this'll begin."

CHAPTER FIVE

HOW HAD HE not noticed her before?

She couldn't have been older than eighteen, seeing as she was getting off the school bus. Barely legal or jailbait. Hard to know for sure. Chuck watched her from his living room window, blowing smoke through the parted curtains. He was in his underwear, a sheet of sweat on his belly and boiling in his hair. He touched his crotch as the girl got closer to the building. Blonde, skinny. No tits but a pretty face. She briefly turned around to wave at someone inside the bus, her skirt fluttering, revealing an ass that broke Chuck's heart. One ripe piece of lady fruit. He sucked his teeth, wincing from a desire that would never be fulfilled. He was middle-aged, a gray compost of a man. He wasn't even a sexual being to women this young. To them he may as well be a mummified eunuch shitting himself in a wheelchair.

But they couldn't stop him from looking.

She *had* to be new. He would've noticed her before. But she was still in high school, so she couldn't be living on her own. Maybe she and her mother had moved in after the family broke up, the old man running off with a cheap bimbo young enough to be his daughter. *The American dream*, Chuck thought. How easy it is to be a man, to be completely void of responsibility. To be shameless, even cruel. It was a luxury he knew too well. He also knew why he enjoyed watching girls like the teenager below. It was more than dirty-old-man syndrome. These girls were the ones he'd known so intimately in his youth, the ones who'd made him a man. He only wanted to touch them again, to brush their hair as he once had and caress them until the sorrow seeped out of their flesh, freeing them for a brief but magic moment.

Chuck went into the bathroom and masturbated. Faces he hadn't seen since childhood flashed across his mind, but an orgasm was refusing to release so he gave up and got dressed. The arrival of the school bus was an alarm clock, reminding him it was almost happy hour down at Rudy's. He was still in yesterday's underpants. Might as well get another day out of yesterday's clothes.

As he left his apartment, one of the kids from a few doors down ran past in a blur, shouting at his friends to wait up. Chuck glowered at him, but the kid didn't notice as he swung down the stairs like a miniature Tarzan. Outside, the sunlight hurt Chuck's eyes even with sunglasses on. The plastic buds for the nose had broken off and the metal dug into his skin. The city was even more ugly during the day, this ash-colored sewer sprouting out of the ground like conqueror worms. The sidewalks blurred behind waves of searing heat, somewhat camouflaging the rats that scurried between the piles of bagged rubbish. When Chuck reached the alley, he spotted a still-smoking cigarette on the ground, barely a quarter of the way spent. He picked it up and puffed, leaning against the wall, the shaded concrete cool against his back, chilling the sweat.

A shadow caught his eye. Near the dumpster, a shape was stirring, too big to be a stray dog. The thing snorted as it scuffled away from the trash and scattered plastic bottles, knocking cans out of its path. There was a sound like a skateboard. Something was coming slow but steady, the roaming livestock of the streets. Chuck froze without knowing why.

"Ya gots any more smokes, buddy?"

The voice was raspy, as if the man had been talking all day. He emerged from the shadows rolling on a square, wooden plank with grocery cart wheels screwed in beneath it. He was a grown man, but his legs were like that of a six-year-old—small, thin, and useless. Despite the heat he was dressed in layers, a patchy winter coat and a trucker hat that read: *Date Sluts Cause That's All There Is.*

"Want this one?" Chuck asked, holding out the cigarette he'd just found. "Wasn't mine anyway."

The mongrel didn't ask what he meant, only snatched the butt away and put it in his mouth where it remained throughout their conversation. From inside his coat he retrieved a flask with a rebel flag on it.

Chuck said, "You're a long ways from Dixie."

"Don't give a fuck 'bout them rednecks. I took me a shit in Georgia once and it still smells like it. I just found this damn thing and, well, a flask's a flask. Wanna drink?"

Chuck bent over to take it. "Always."

"Heh! Good man."

Chuck was unable to tell what kind of booze it was. It tasted like soiled fire so he handed it back.

The man said, "Folks call me Shitty."

"That's your name? *Shitty*?"

"Has been longer than my birth name was."

"Mine's Chuck."

"Pleased to metcha."

Shitty held out his hand and it wasn't until Chuck shook it that he realized it wasn't complete. Fingers were missing, either mutated or mutilated. Shitty's smile was like a backed-up toilet, his brown teeth seeming to float in his mouth when he spoke.

"What's a fella like you doin in my alley?"

"Headed to Rudy's to get drunk. Wanna come?"

Shitty shook his head. "Ah, bars won't let me in no ways. Say I ugly up the joint. They're right too. Heh heh."

"Fuck that. I know the bartender. He'll let ya in long as you're with me."

"Well, hell. Guess I could come along with ya then. You buyin?"

Chuck felt suddenly charitable. He'd found someone in a worse state than he was and that made him feel pretty good.

"You got it, Shitty."

They walked and wheeled to the bar. Once inside, Chuck lifted Shitty under his armpits and plopped him down on a stool, putting his wheel board up against the bar. Face to face with the man, Chuck got a whiff of him and instantly wished he'd chosen a booth to keep Shitty away from the other regulars. They might get kicked out after all.

Barman's pitbull face glowered when he saw Shitty, but he glowered so often Chuck wasn't sure what it meant.

"Who's your new friend?" Barman asked.

"This here's Shitty."

"I know that. But what's his name?"

Shitty snorted a laugh. "That is my name."

"Shitty what? Shitty Smith? Shitty Johnson?"

"Just Shitty."

"Like Cher," Chuck said.

Barman remained stoic. "That's pretty funny. You know, Shitty, you smell like a dead skunk's cunt."

Shitty giggled.

"I've gotta spray ya."

Barman brought up an aerosol can from behind the bar, misting Shitty with citrus air freshener. Shitty giggled the whole time.

"Just don't get that stuff on me," Chuck said. "And bring me a double bourbon, would ya? And whatever Shitty wants."

"Gin and Tonic," Shitty said, "and a PBR chaser."

Barman nodded. "It's my pleasure to poison people a little at a time."

When the drinks arrived, Shitty sucked them down. Planning to be there all night, Chuck took things slower. When someone sat on the stool next to him, he wasn't surprised to see Eugene. His neighbor's eyes were even more frog-like than usual, swollen with a steady paranoia. He spoke only to Chuck, unaware Shitty was with him.

"People are dying," Eugene said.

"What's that now?"

"Upstate. It's a new sort of virus or something. It's come down from Canada like a swarm of locust. Now it's headed south."

"Ah, Jeez. Here we go . . . "

"Don't tell me it's just another one of my delusions, Chuck. This has been on the TV news. Ain't you seen it?"

"Don't have a TV."

"It's in the papers too."

"Don't read 'em."

Shitty laughed and Eugene looked at him, wincing at the man's disheveled appearance.

"This here's Shitty," Chuck said. "Shitty, this is Eugene."

Shitty reached across to shake Eugene's hand, but Eugene recoiled.

"Don't take it personally," Chuck explained. "Gene here is one of them germaphobes."

Shitty shrugged. "Whatever. How 'bout another round?"

Chuck motioned to Barman and he refilled their glasses. He shot Eugene a hard stare.

"You got money for me?"

Eugene reached into his pocket, opened a fresh Wet Nap, and used it to retrieve his wallet and two twenties.

Barman snatched them, turned around, and poured Eugene his usual.

"Mommy give you your allowance?"

Eugene's face reddened, but he said nothing. Barman was not the kind of guy you talked back to.

"I know 'bout that virus," Shitty said. "He ain't lyin."

Barman turned back to them. "The Scream?"

"Yeah, that's it," Eugene said. "That's what they're callin it now—The Scream."

Chuck sipped. "Sounds like a real gas."

"Might be a gas," Eugene said, "I wouldn't put it past the government to test out biochemical weapons on its own people."

"That's not what I meant by *gas*, but okay."

"I seen it," Shitty said.

The other men turned toward him.

"You've seen it?" Eugene asked. "Like, in person?"

"Shit, yeah. Week or so ago. Rita done got it. She's a bag lady, ya know. Hangs 'round downtown sellin friendship bracelets and—"

"Yeah, yeah," Barman interjected. "Fuck her life story. Just tell us what happened."

"Word was she was actin strange. Somebody said she done got the rabies, but that weren't it. When I saw her down on the Nickle, she was runnin. Now, this is an old broad who always done walked hunched over, and here she is haulin' ass like her pussy hair is on fire." Shitty snorted at his own joke. "Yes, sir, she was really movin. I figured she needed help, so I wheels out in front of her and put up my hands. But she don't stop. She done tripped over me instead. Fell down on the sidewalk—BAM! She rolls on her side, spittin up teeth from her busted lips. That's when I got a look at her face. It was all yellow. There were bits of pus in the corners of her eyes and they was all bloodshot. Like the white parts turned *completely* red. I asked her if'n she were okay and she got up and grabbed onto a parkin meter to keep standin. And that's when she got to screamin.

Put her hands to her head and pulled her hair out, just screamin and screamin like she was bein stabbed."

Shitty pushed aside his empty gin glass and sipped his beer.

Eugene hung on the man's words. "What happened then?"

"Dunno. She was still screamin when I rolled off. Nothin I could do, really, and she scared me a bitty bit."

"Did an ambulance come or anything?"

"You kiddin? She's homeless, man. People just kept walkin. Ain't nobody give two fucks 'bout people like us."

The men fell silent. Barman broke it. "Maybe they were right to. Maybe she's just crazy."

"Come on," Eugene said. "You heard him say she had the pus in her eyes and the jaundiced skin. Those are the symptoms."

Chuck put his drink down. "How have I not heard about this yet?"

"Because," Barman said, "you wouldn't know your dick was cut off unless you found it floating in a glass of booze."

"True, but still."

Eugene said, "Two hundred and fifty confirmed cases in the northeast alone. Not to mention thousands in Canada. It's becoming an epidemic—"

"Let's not go overboard."

"—but if it spreads in cities like this, where the population is much higher, it could become a *pandemic*. That's an epidemic, only on a much larger scale. A pandemic can go global."

"And this Rita lady has it. In our city."

Shitty nodded. "Yup yup."

Eugene's face had gone pale. "We need to be extra careful."

"So what the hell caused this thing?" Chuck asked.

"They don't know yet. They don't know if it's a contagious virus, if it's airborne or carried by insects, or if it's some sort of neurological phenomenon, like an aneurism or mental illness. And there's no cure."

"You mean . . ."

"Oh, yeah. It's fatal as fuck."

"Wait, it *kills* you?"

"In a matter of speaking."

Barman nodded. "For once Gene is right. They said on the news that once you start screaming you can't stop. You can't eat because you can't chew while you're screaming. And you can't go to sleep either. So you slowly go more insane until you just drop dead from exhaustion. But most cases end in suicide before that happens."

"Jesus Christ . . . "

Shitty clapped his hands. "Praise the lawd!"

CHAPTER SIX

THE MAN WAS in the mud pit, naked and covered in filth. All around him the pigs wiggled and writhed, playing. A crooked smile stretched across his face as he gazed upon the swine as if he were their creator rather than owner. The boy watched from the window of the barn's loft where he'd been put to work forking hay. He'd toiled so long and hard the palms of his hands had blistered and peeled. Every inch of him was dirty. His whole body ached for rest he dared not ask for. Seeing the man wade through mud and filth, the boy's fear only deepened.

Why is he naked?

The boy had witnessed bizarre behavior from the man over the past few weeks (maybe months, the boy had lost track of the days), but this was a new level of disturbing. Particularly alarming was the mold-like discoloration of the man's feet and calves. The skin there had a green hue and was peppered with small, open sores. Wouldn't they get infected if he kept frolicking through hog waste? The thought made the boy feel queasy.

He went back to piling hay, sweating though the afternoon was cold and damp. Murk hung in the sky, thick and immobile misery. It seemed to rain every day on this farm, a grim reminder of the ruin his life had become. He would never see Mom and Dad again. Never ride bikes with Shawn and Amos as the sun went down. Never play fetch with Rocky or feed him bits of people food when his parents weren't looking. Here, there was only grayness and shadow, sweat and heartache and decay. The boy cried often, but never when the man might see. He kept his sorrow hidden, whether from fear or pride he couldn't say.

A horrible squeal snapped him out of his revere. The roar of the pig grew louder and the boy looked out the window again, spotting the shrieking sow. The man was crouched behind it, his pasty arms wrapped completely around the animal's body, hands clenched together at the swollen underbelly. The man's head was titled back, eyes closed, his rictus grin pointing to the sorrow of the sky. And he was moving. Thrusting. Slamming his nakedness into the sow's back end. The boy covered his mouth to hold in a scream. He didn't know much about sex but knew it when he saw it. The man squealed in reply to the sow's bleats, a deranged love cry that chilled the boy's flesh. He didn't want to see this, but kept looking, hoping he'd been mistaken, that the man wasn't really doing this awful thing. But when the sow scooted forward, the man's erection popped free, slick and exposed, removing all doubt before it was shoved back into the pig's gaping, black hole.

The man laughed and turned his head back and forth, clearly enjoying himself. The boy gasped when their eyes met. He backed away, but the man had already spotted him in the window. It didn't stop him from raping the sow as it struggled in the fecal matter beneath them. He waved at the boy, and then locked his hands again to keep the pig in thrall.

"Love!" he shouted.

CHAPTER SEVEN

LESLIE WAS TOO drunk to fuck.

She refused to even get off the couch when Chuck tried to get her to bed.

"Eat shit!" she said. "Leave me the fuck alone you fuckin asshole."

Chuck let go of her wrist and she collapsed into the cushions. He took his cigarette back from the ancient McDonald's ashtray and blew smoke out of his nostrils.

"Thought we was gonna get wild tonight," he said. "I even got that toy ya wanted."

Leslie groaned. Her face turned into the torn arm of the sofa, her bare back showing off all the little scars. She wore only a pair of men's gym shorts. They were too big so she'd rolled the waistband and they hung on her hips, threatening to fall off at the slightest touch. Chuck had the urge to yank them down and expose her ass but he didn't want to get into an argument. Booze had turned Leslie sour tonight. It was probably best to just go back to his apartment and let her sleep it off. He reached for the half-empty bottle of Scotch on the table, but Leslie snatched it away before he could.

"That's mine," Chuck said. "I bought it."

"Fuck you!"

"Fuck me?" He took down her shorts after all and spanked her, hard. "Fuck you."

Leslie shot up but stumbled. Unable to stand she fell back to the sofa, her rage tapping out.

"I'm hungry," she said.

"So make yourself somethin."

"I fuckin can't. You do it."

"I ain't makin you shit."

"Come on, Chucky. Don't be an asshole!"

"You're the fuckin asshole. You've been yellin at me half the night."

"*I'm not fuckin yellin!*"

As if on cue, the neighbor below banged on the ceiling. Leslie looked all around, unsure where the noise was even coming from.

Chuck lit a cigarette off the butt of his last one. "You keep it up the whole complex is gonna bitch to the landlord and he'll kick your sorry ass out."

Leslie rose, pulling up her shorts and leaning on the couch for support. She stuck her head out the window. "Go ahead! Call the cops!"

A voice called out from the darkness of the complex. "Shut the hell up! People are tryin to sleep!"

"You shut the hell up! This is my motherfuckin house! I do whatevah I want so fuck you, dickhead!"

"Fuck you too!" yelled another voice, a female. "Shut up you drunken slut!"

Leslie leaned further out the window, bare breasts passing over the edge. "Suck my dick, you fuckin cunt!"

Chuck took Leslie by the waist, pulling her back in so she wouldn't fall over the sill. He closed the window as yet another voice called her a stupid whore. She leaned in to Chuck, draping her arms around his neck, going from raging to snuggling in less than a second.

"Take me to dinner," she said. "I want French fries."

"It's late. Everything's closed."

"Nu-uh. The diner's open til, like, two."

"Christ, Les."

Chuck sighed. She'd stumble her way there on her own if he didn't go with her. Probably get hit by a car or fall in the alley and pass out. In this neighborhood, doped-up teenagers could come along and play with her tits and jerk off in her face while she lied there unconscious. Bums could snatch her purse, piss on her, and run. Grade school punks would throw bottles at her for laughs. It all had happened before with other hopeless women foolish enough to be intoxicated and alone on these mean streets after dark.

"Get dressed," he said.

He helped her to the bedroom and she picked a man-sized shirt off the floor. When she put it on, he saw it was a *Texas Chainsaw Massacre* t-shirt with Leatherface waving his saw in the air.

"The fuck you have that for?"

Leslie looked down at it. "It belonged to what's-his-name. He was a movie buff."

She stepped into her flip-flops, pulled her hair back in a messy ponytail and looked for her purse on the way out, but Chuck kept her moving.

"Forget it. I'll buy."

"Such a gentleman."

"Just walk before I come to my senses."

Out on the street, the night had cooled the city down into the eighties, but the humidity was unforgiving, thick enough to drink. Leslie complained about it the whole way, leaning against Chuck as a crutch to keep her upright. A gaggle of rats scurried from an alleyway. Leslie flinched at first but then snickered as they passed.

"They're takin over," Chuck said. "Fuckin things are everywhere."

She stopped once in front of Nishant's package store, not realizing it was closed and saying they should pick up some vodka, but Chuck tugged her along. He was coming down from a day long drunk while Leslie was still drowning in hers. Food was the best thing for her. Food and water, if he could get her to drink it.

They took a booth at the back of the diner. For this late on a weeknight, there was a good amount of patrons, including a group of young women laughing jovially in the booth farthest away from them. One of them wore a beaded necklace with tiny dicks on it, a sash that read *Bride 2 Be,* and a plastic tiara. A bachelorette party in its final hours. The bachelorette was homely and most of the girls were overweight, but Chuck would have fucked them just for their youth.

An exhausted-looking waitress took their order, eyeing Leslie who had leaned her head against the window. For a moment Chuck thought she'd fallen asleep until she yelled out "French fries!" and chuckled. The waitress frowned and an old man at the counter turned to look at Leslie, but when his gaze met Chuck's he looked away.

"I just wanna be filled up," Leslie said once the waitress had gone.

"With fries?"

"Nah, I mean all filled up, everywhere. Not just my stomach."

"I'm not sure what you're . . ."

Under the table, her hand slid across his leg and up his inner thigh, inching toward his crotch.

"I want my belly and mouth full of food," she said. "My pussy full of cock. I mean *completely* full. A fuckin huge dick. Two or three dicks up in me at once if that's what it takes. And I want that toy you bought wedged up in my asshole and my bladder full of vodka, my lungs fulla smoke."

Chuck nodded though he didn't quite get it. "Full."

"All filled up. No more holes, Chucky. No more voids. No more fuckin emptiness."

There was a quiver in her voice, a soft sadness hidden beneath the vulgarity. She squeezed the lump in his jeans and leaned into him, breathing in his ear.

"Wanna fuck me in the bathroom?" she asked with foul breath. "I've done it before."

"Our food's about to come out."

"French fries," she said, as if she'd just remembered.

She continued rubbing his crotch, even when the waitress came with their plates. Luckily the woman didn't notice. Leslie dove into her plate of fries with one hand and started unzipping Chuck's fly with the other, hiding it all beneath the table. He bit into his burger and stared at the party girls, watching them giggle and snap pictures of each other with their phones. Leslie had his dick out of his jeans now and was stroking him, still shoveling fries into her mouth.

"Tell me when," she said.

Chuck watched the girls even when they noticed he was staring at them. The look of discomfort on their faces only heightened his arousal. Soon his dick was pulsing.

"Now," he said.

Leslie grabbed a large fistful of fries and brought them under the table, catching Chuck's cum with them. Once he was empty, she put the fries back on the plate, eating them with a fresh dressing of semen. She put her head on his shoulder like they were teenagers and Chuck put himself back into his jeans, finishing his burger as the girls left the diner with their heads down, avoiding any possibility of making eye contact with him.

It was Saturday when Chuck saw the blonde again. He was headed downstairs to collect his mail and she was sitting at the bottom of the stairs, texting on her phone. Her shorts were so high cut he could see a bit of the underside of her buttocks. Pink toenail polish matched her shirt, and she wore too much makeup but somehow made it work. He stopped on the staircase when he saw her and she looked up at him, smirking as if she knew all the filthy things that sprung to his mind at the mere sight of her.

"Hey," she said.

Her voice was a butterscotch kiss, her batting eyelashes the soft teeth of a Venus fly trap sucking him in to be devoured. Chuck nodded. She didn't move from where she sat so he stepped over her, very aware that for just one brief moment his genitals were level with her mouth. He wanted to grab two fistfuls of those blonde locks and smack her face with his cock until her lips swelled, but instead he kept moving, glad he wasn't drunk yet, for he might have been incapable of resisting such hardwired urges.

"You smoke?" she asked.

He reached for his pack of cigarettes.

"Nah," she said. "I mean, like, do you *smoke*. Like, weed."

When she leaned forward Chuck tried to look down her shirt, but it was too tight and there was nothing there to produce cleavage.

"No, I don't smoke pot," he said. "Why? Need some?"

"I'm dying for a joint. Like, literally dying."

Chuck almost laughed. This chick made pot sound like heroin.

The beauty sighed. "Ever since my folks sent me here, I haven't been able to score anything but dirt weed. See, there was, like, a big bust at school not too long ago, so now anyone whose got the good shit is really careful about who they give it to. I'm new. No one trusts me yet."

Chuck had trouble believing a girl this cute couldn't get whatever she wanted, but he let it slide. She was talking to him. It didn't matter what about. The sound of children yelling, running and laughing echoed from the floor above them, the same brats who always raised Cain in the halls.

"I can get ya some grass," he said.

"Really?"

"Yeah, I know a guy."

"Cool! Can we meet him today?"

"Nah. He's kinda paranoid. Best if I get it from him and then get it to you."

She stood up, bouncing with youth, all sunshine on daffodils. She was everything he wasn't, a kitten in a picnic basket to his mangy bobcat living in a shithouse. He could never hope to fuck her, but maybe if he became her dope hookup he could talk her into letting him jerk off in front of her. Maybe get her to take a few nude pics for him or at least let him squeeze that incredible ass just once. It was still too early to tell how she'd react to such requests, but her bluntness in asking a total stranger for drugs (and the revelation she had been sent away to live here) gave Chuck hope she was a lost youth fresh out of a juvenile detention center, that there was a bad girl hiding beneath her rosy appearance. Troubled girls were always easier.

"How much will it cost?" she asked.

He stepped forward, sniffing the air around her, tasting her essence at the back of his throat. "Ain't ya ever seen an after school special?"

She looked at him blankly.

Chuck said, "You should know the first one's always free."

"Who's at the door?"

It was an old woman's voice; frightened, nagging.

Chuck heard her and Eugene too. "I got it, Ma."

"Tell 'em to go away."

"I said I got it."

"I don't like no visitors."

"I know, Ma."

"Who is it? Who—"

"Shut up, Ma! *God!*"

Multiple bolts and locks tumbled and the door cracked open, still attached to one of those small chains. Eugene smiled, relieved. "It's just my friend, Chuck, Ma. Calm down."

The woman said nothing.

"What's up, buddy?"

Chuck blew smoke. "Not much."

"Not supposed to smoke in the halls."

"Yeah."

"Some people are allergic."

"You're allergic to everything."

His mother called from somewhere within. "Close the door!"

"Alright, Ma! Christ Almighty!"

He undid the chain and slipped through the crack, not opening the door all the way.

"I need some dope."

Eugene scanned the hallway. "Shit, man! Keep it down, would ya? They could be listening."

"Who? The neighbors?"

"No. The feds. The DEA. Any government agency could have this place tapped."

Chuck didn't argue. He needed something from Eugene, so he played nice.

"Fine, let's go to my place."

Eugene mulled this over. "One sec."

He went back into the apartment, closing the door and mumbling back and forth with his mother, then came back out. The men walked down the hall and Chuck opened his door. A wave of cigarette stench (among other odors) hit Eugene and he recoiled. Chuck took him by the arm and pulled him in before he could run back to his mommy.

"Yikes," Eugene said, looking around.

The apartment was no messier than usual. Empty liquor bottles on every table and counter. Old paperbacks with yellowed pages stacked on the floor. An overflowing garbage bin filled with takeout food wrappers and a crushed pizza box.

"Yeah," Chuck said. "I've been meanin to fire that maid."

"You have a maid?"

Chucked rolled his eyes. "Jesus, Gene. No, of course not."

"You should get one. This place is a pig sty."

Chuck grimaced.

"Just saying," Eugene continued, "unsanitary conditions like this will attract roaches and other disease carrying vermin. You know, rats have become a big problem in the city lately. Read about it online. Because we had such a warm winter and a hot-as-balls spring, the rats were able to stay active longer and reproduced more frequently. Now with this garbage strike the little fuckers are having a field day."

Chuck shrugged. "Let 'em."

"Some say they could be carriers of The Scream."

"Why? Have there been rats that actually can't stop screaming?"

"No, but they don't have to show signs to carry the virus, if that's what this thing is. I think it's viral, don't you?"

"I think I want my weed."

"Okay, well, I got the stuff. How much you want?"

"I dunno. Couple of joints."

Eugene reached into the pocket of his jeans and pulled out what looked to be an ounce of marijuana, bright green with red streaks running through it, the buds hard and tight.

"Looks nuclear," Chuck said.

"Oh yeah. It'll blow your head off and fill it with stars. Better take it real easy with this stuff. Since when do you smoke, anyway?"

"I don't."

"So whadda ya want with it?"

"It's for a friend."

Eugene grinned. "That chick you been bangin across the hall?"

"Yeah."

"She's nuts you know. Makes more noise than a dump truck. Drives my Ma right up the wall."

"Leslie has . . . problems."

"She's a raging alcoholic—that's her problem. That or she's diseased, like most people. They were saying online that this *Scream* thing is like the bubonic plague, that it's a long lost disease come back to haunt us. Making everybody crazy." Eugene put the bag on the counter and took out his rolling papers. "Broads are nuts anyway, though. They've always gotta make drama, be the star of their own little soap opera. That's why I don't date."

Chuck allowed his friend this delusion of grandeur, despite knowing it was women who refused to date Eugene, not the other way around. With four joints rolled, Eugene put his baggie back in his pocket.

"Got a drink?" he asked.

"Always."

As Chuck went to the cabinet to fetch the remaining bottle of Evan Williams, the sound of a door slamming echoed up the hallway, immediately followed by yelling. It was a man. Not yelling *at* someone. Not even making words. He was just screaming, as if he'd just witnessed the ultimate terror. His cries were raw and guttural, fierce enough to make Chuck's skin prickle.

"The fuck?"

Footsteps followed, sounding like bison thundering across an open range. Pounding shook the walls.

Eugene paled. "Oh my god . . . "

Something glass shattered in the hall. A woman shouted but her words were unintelligible beneath the roar of the man. More slamming. More stomping. Endless screaming.

Chuck headed to the door. "This fuckin complex. It's always someth—"

"Don't open it!"

"I wanna know what the hell's goin on."

"That guy out there must be diseased! *The Scream*, dude!"

Chuck's hand stayed on the doorknob, but he didn't open it. "I dunno, Gene. People in this place are always makin noise. You know that."

"But listen to that, man! That's not the normal yelling of fighting spouses or some shit. That guy's screaming like all hell's breaking loose."

Maybe it is, Chuck thought, not knowing why. "This I gotta see."

"Don't! I mean, what if it really is a virus? You could get infected."

But Chuck had already opened the door. Eugene ran backward, ducking behind the counter that separated the living room from the kitchen. He put the neck of his t-shirt over his nose and mouth like a mask. Chuck stuck only his head out, turning toward the noise. At the end of the hall, a heavyset black man in his underwear was rampaging, kicking holes in the walls, not seeming angry but rather in a state of pure horror. A hint of yellow was visible on his flesh, as if he'd been sprayed with pollen. Blood ran from his knuckles and dribbled down the dents he'd made in the drywall. A small, skinny woman was pleading with him to stop but was too frightened to get close.

Chuck stepped out into the hall. "What's the problem here?"

The woman looked at him with teary eyes. "My husband ain't slept in days. He won't stop screamin."

Chuck had to get close to her. The husband was making it hard for them to hear each other.

"You call the cops?" he asked.

"Hell no. He gots two priors for bein drunk n' disorderly. He ain't had no drink in almost a year now, but them pigs'll throw him in the slammer and swallow the key."

"Maybe we oughta call the paramedics."

"He's just . . . *tired*."

"Lady," he said, gesturing toward the husband as he slammed his forehead on the handrail of the stairwell. "He's gone berserk."

"He ain't crazy, he's just—"

A deafening howl cut her off as the man dove down the staircase as if into a swimming pool, headfirst, arms out at his sides like wings.

Now it was the wife who screamed.

The sound had been so gentle, like an egg hitting a tile floor. The man's skull opened, releasing a stream of brains and skull fragments. Blood poured from every hole in his face, nostrils gushing, dislodged eyes bubbling with pink pus. The mangled morsels of the man's gray matter oozed from his ears. His boxers had exploded with voided bowels and one leg was snapped backward at the knee, the cap jutting out of the torn flesh of his leg.

The wife sobbed at the bottom of the staircase as the body was hauled away in a zippered bag. Chuck sat on the bottom step behind her, watching the scene, listening to the questions and hollow condolences of the officers, photographers and coroners. Half the complex had come out to see what had happened but were roped off by caution tape. Eugene was among the gawkers.

A medic who looked fresh out of school crouched beside the widow. "It may have been an aneurism. They can be so painful the sufferer will bang their head on things. We'll know more later."

As the medic rose to his feet, Chuck followed him outside.

"It wasn't an aneurism," Chuck said. "That guy had gone apeshit."

"It's hard to know the cause at this point."

But the young medic's eyes betrayed him. He knew damn well what had happened.

Chucked leaned in, keeping his voice low. "It's The Scream, ain't it?"

The medic looked away, neither confirming nor denying.

"You been seein it a lot?" Chuck asked.

"I'm really not sure what it is."

"But these symptoms. Screaming, unable to stop. Yellow skin and fucked up eyes. Seen this a lot recently, aint'cha? Shit, I can see it in your face."

"Mister, I—"

"Come on, man. I ain't tryin to bust balls. I just wanna know if it's safe to stay here. If this shit is spreadin then I need to get the fuck outta this—"

"And go where?" the medic interjected. "There've been reports coming in from north *and* south of here. Maine to the Carolinas. The worst of it is up north but it's still spreading."

"This is becoming a . . . " Chuck strained for the word Eugene had used. " . . . a pandemic?"

The young man sighed with exhaustion. Chuck wondered how long he'd been on duty, if cases were popping up enough to warrant forced overtime. He offered him a cigarette and to Chuck's surprise the medic accepted. They lit up together.

"It might not be all that bad," the medic said. "There's no reason to panic."

"You seem pretty nervous to me."

"My mother called this morning. Her best friend came down with this same thing and they live all the way out in *Montana*. They put her in a behavioral health center, and she screamed non-stop throughout her entire stay. Never stopped, not even to sleep. Then died suddenly."

"That's how it works, right?"

"This recent phenomenon, yes. But normally it takes far longer for someone to actually *die* from insomnia. But my mother's friend died in less than two weeks. This has been the case with most sufferers. That, or they commit suicide." He looked to the ambulance where the body had been loaded. "And the craziest part is, the suicides are always by extreme measures. No simple gunshots to the head or overdose on pills. These people jump in front of buses and slit their own throats."

"Jesus. So this Scream, it must be contagious, right?"

"I don't know. But there have been no cases of it taking over whole families or workplaces. No community spread. It's just one person at a time, at random."

"My friend saw on the internet that this thing might be like the bubonic plague. That true?"

"The symptoms are totally different."

"I don't think he meant it like that. He said somethin 'bout it bein an old disease come back."

The medic sighed smoke. "If someone does have the answers, they sure haven't shared them with us."

CHAPTER EIGHT

THE LOCKS ON the door turned one by one, waking the boy from bad dreams in which he was alone at a mall inhabited solely by pigs.

No light shone through the cellar's only window, a square of sealed glass too small for anyone to pass through, but still barred, inside and out. It wasn't dawn yet. The boy sat up as the man came down the staircase, the boards bending from his burden.

"Rise n' shine, kid. There's chores to be done."

The boy slid off the cot. He was not allowed to groan so the springs groaned for him. He was still wearing his flannel and jeans. He just needed to put on his work boots, all clothes that had been provided for him.

The man scratched his armpit. "I'll take care of the hogs. I want ya to feed the veal."

The boy shot up, posture suddenly erect, testicles drawing tight to his body. The cellar felt colder now, the damp earth of the walls like an igloo.

"I ain't never fed them yet," the boy said. "I dunno how to do it."

The man smiled. "Ain't nothin' to it, kid. Just give 'em the formula."

"I just don't think I can—"

"Well, you're gonna. Gotta learn sometime. Gotta earn your keep 'round here, ya know."

The boy struggled to speak against the lump in his throat. "I'll do anything else. I'll clean out the hog house and—"

The man's hand rose into the air and the boy shut his mouth and closed his eyes, bracing for the hit. But the sting never came. Just a warning this time.

"Now get yer skinny ass upstairs 'fore I lose my temper."

The boy took the stairs two at a time. In the hall, he stepped into his muck boots, pulled the bandana from his back pocket and tied it around his face like a bandit in an old western movie. It smelled of mildew and dried mucus. The bottom was still damp from where he chewed on it to soothe his nerves.

The man followed, picking at his ass as he leaned into the fridge, pulling out two bottles with rubber nipples.

"Take a look here, kid. This is a special solution just for the veal. It's sort of an artificial milk, low in iron and other nutrients. That keeps 'em anemic, see? Keeps the meat tender. They each get one full bottle. Make sure they finish the whole thing. Probably won't be an issue 'cause they ain't eaten since yesterday's lunch. You'll have to hold it up to their mouths though."

The boy winced and shivered, instantly regretting it though he'd been unable to prevent it. The man's face grew dim, the glowering of a dominate male.

"Don't go sissy on me, now. Ya know I need help. That's why you're here. I can't keep this place runnin on my own. Now, ya do a good job and I might letcha retire a lil' early today. Give ya some time to play with the hogs and read your comics n' such." He handed the boy the bottles. "Now get on to the pen and don't come back 'til the feedin's done with. No breakfast for ya 'til the veal has got theirs."

The man took a box of generic Captain Crunch from the cupboard as incentive and poured himself a bowl, sitting down as the boy placed the bottles into the satchel and slung it over his shoulder. He opened the front door, stepping out into grievous nothingness. The farm's darkness was as deep as it had been in his nightmares, an uncompromising eternity of dread. Livestock croaked from the shadows. Though only five acres, this land housed nine sows, five boars and almost a dozen piglets. The boy strode by their free-range mud pit and the few hogs that were out snorted in excitement at his approach, expecting an early dose of feed. Despite his bandana, the horrid odor of fresh shit punched at the back of the boy's throat, making him waiver on his way across the field. It must have rained last night. The ground sucked at his boots, making him think of the quicksand that always appeared in *Choose Your Own Adventure* books. The boy almost wished there really was quicksand he could spiral down into. Anything to get out of here, out of what he was about to do.

He heard them whimpering before he even opened the door to the pen, crying in the darkness of their cages somewhere behind the moldy plywood walls. The boy took a deep breath and stood before the door, staring at the rusty handle, afraid to touch it, fearing even that would hurt him somehow, as if the horror of what lied within had boiled down into a concentrated, purer evil just waiting for the boy's hand. It would enter through the soft meat of his palms and poison his heart forever.

The bray of the veal snapped him out of his thoughts. Navy blue light was splitting the horizon now, the small mercy of a coming dawn. The symphony of crickets had quieted, not yet replaced by morning birds. How long had he been standing there? How long before the man would come to check on him, only to find he hadn't even entered the pen? He didn't want to enrage the man, especially not after forgetting to close the latch to the barn the other day. No livestock had escaped, but they could have, and that was enough to warrant so many belt whips the boy had trouble sitting down.

Finally, he took the handle, surprised by its warmth, and inserted the key into the padlock. The door wasn't even open before the veal starting screaming. The boy hesitated before flicking on the 40-watt bulb that swung from the low ceiling like a pendulum's blade. He brought the lock in with him, shut the door behind him, and sealed the interior latch with it, just in case.

It stank in here. Piss and feces, vomit and sweat. It was uncomfortably warm inside this condensed pen, the insufferable heat of day having lingered even after night had cooled down the earth. It was a wonder the veal could survive such extreme temperatures, a wonder they could survive at all, given the hellish living conditions.

The boy tried to ignore them but was unable to tune them out. The blonde one shook against her chains.

"Please help us!" she cried. "Please, little boy, you have to get us out of here!"

He could not look the blonde one in the eye, and the brunette in the next cage was chained so tightly she couldn't roll over to see him. She cried out blindly, pleading like the blonde. But what could the boy do? Though better off than they were, the boy was in a similar position of imprisonment, of helplessness. He put down the satchel, removed one of the milk bottles, and moved toward the blonde. Her cage was so small she had to tuck down into a cannon ball to fit into it. Her wrists and ankles were pinned to the grated, concrete floor by chains only three links long. The man had explained that demobilizing them diminished their muscle mass, which would keep the meat tender. The veal was not to be starved, but it was never to get any exercise. Because of their prisons, the veal couldn't even stretch, lie down or turn over. Judging by the dried clumps of feces that had yet to sluice through the grate beneath them, they were never allowed out of these cages at all.

"You have to help me," the blonde whispered as he drew near with her feed.

The boy's eyes watered. "I can't."

He stuck the nipple through the bars and the girl, no older than fifteen, caved to her hunger and pressed her face against the cage so closely her cheeks indented against the bars. They were smooth and brown. She must have been tanning all summer, enjoying the beaches now that school was out, her young flesh bronzing under a sun she would never see again. The flesh, unaware of what it was now deprived, still reflected those sunnier days, days only recently taken away, traded in for these final days of pain.

The veal suckled at the nipple, an infant again. And like an infant, all she could do was drink the milk, then shit and piss herself later, and cry until her lungs could burst.

The boy shivered in his seat, not wanting to say anything. The man stood beside him at the kitchen table, his greasy apron giving off a sour smell. He put his hands on his waist, nose twitching with impatience.

"I'm tryin to show my gratitude here, kid," he said. "Ya done a good day's work, and a workin man should have a good dinner. Now tell me whatcha want."

It'd been canned vegetable soup and PB&J sandwiches for so long. Well water to drink and bananas for snacks. The boy wanted his favorite dish, the one his mother used to make for breakfast. Something he hadn't had since he'd been brought here.

"Some bacon and eggs would be—"

The man slammed both fists on the table, bending over so his face was inches from the boy's. His rotted teeth hissed.

"No pork will *ever* touch your fork," the man said. "You understand me, boy?"

The boy closed his eyes and nodded.

"Shit," the man said. "Ya think 'cause this here's a pig farm I'm gonna serve up bacon n' pork chops? Yeah, that's what everybody thinks, don't they. 'Cause they don't know the kinda man I am." He pulled out a chair and sat down, making the boy recoil. "I spent years—ya hear me—*years* in the business. 'Fore I owned this here farm I worked at the processin plant up in Dundle. *Hill's Fine Pork Products*! Some horseshit that was. Ya sit here scared of me, but let me tell ya kid, you dunno what real horror is. Real horror is transportin and slaughterin pigs. We'd take these beautiful creatures at only a few months old and cram 'em into the back of a tractor trailer, stickin electric prods against their assholes to get 'em movin. We'd punch their noses when they tried to wiggle free. I seen 'em packed into those trailers so they had no room to move, packed so tight sometimes a little balloon of guts popped out their anus while theys were still alive. Those that don't die from the stress of transport get taken to the factory, but that ain't what ya'd call lucky.

"At the slaughterhouse where I worked, we murdered a thousand pigs a day. No fancy tools to do it neither. And only so many stun guns to go around to sedate the poor things before we'd do it. I spent eight hours a day, six days a week, slitting their throats with a butcher knife as big as your arm. Folks think there's some special humane process, but there ain't. Ya cut their necks and let the pigs drain out, all squealin and cryin 'cause they've never gotten to run and play or enjoy their short lil' lives. They realize they're gonna die and they piss and shit and shake in your arms. They all die screamin."

The man looked away, tears in his eyes.

"Then ya toss 'em in a metal trough like they're nothin more than a bag of dog shit. Ya send 'em to the scalding tank, which shaves 'em down and sprays 'em clean, but lots of times they ain't even had time to bleed out yet, so they get boiled alive."

The tears rolled down the man's face, slicking the scabs at his chin. He sniffled and wiped his nose on the back of his hand.

"Still want yer bacon, kid?"

The boy vigorously shook his head *no*.

"Yeah. You're learnin, kid. You're learnin."

CHAPTER NINE

THEY'D BROUGHT TWO bags of food from Arby's back to Leslie's place. Two large curly fries, and two sodas they spiked, but just one beef and cheddar sandwich. Though she didn't jerk Chuck off onto the fries this time, she was still aroused by the fast food, undoing her blouse and running the grease across her nipples. She scooted to the edge of the couch, legs spread, sweatpants down around her ankles. She wore no panties and her bush was a wild briar, glistening in the one ray of sunlight that peeked through the living room curtains, highlighting the dust in the air. The room held them in gentle, beige shadows. Leslie pulled Chuck closer and he leaned in, taking one of her breasts in his hand. It was warm and plump, womanly, beautiful in spite of its sagging. The oscillating fan in the corner wafted the tang of her body odor, combining with the aroma of the sandwich's beef and melted cheese. The television mumbled softly, another news report about people going mad and screaming to their deaths.

Leslie had removed the sandwich bun and was rubbing her labia with the roast beef, warm flesh to warm flesh, one living and one dead. The cheese sluiced into her with a wet suction sound as she kissed Chuck's ear.

"You take it," she said. "Please, Chuck. I need it. I need you."

Chuck took hold of the sandwich and Leslie reached for more curly fries, moaning with her mouth full of them. Grazing the gray beef across her labia, Chuck massaged her breasts with his other hand, smearing grease and fry crumbs. He let the bun fall to the floor, working with just the meat now.

"Please, Chuck," Leslie whispered.

There was a tenderness to her voice he had never heard before— passionate, more romantic than lustful, like a girl losing her virginity to her first love. Chuck moved slowly, tenderly, feeling closer to Leslie than ever. He'd never known a woman could be like this. In this moment at least, they weren't two drunks screwing to pass the time. Today they were lovers.

There was a wet pop as he pushed half the wad of beef inside her. Leslie purred and took a fistful of fries, stuffing her mouth so full she could not close it, the fries twirling over her lips like mouse tails. Chuck wrapped the remaining beef around his index and middle finger. Cheese had slithered out of Leslie's opening, pooling in her anus, and Chuck slid two beef-covered fingers into her pulsing vagina and his pinkie into her ass. He pumped her softly, as all the while she gorged on curly fries, moaning through them.

She took Chuck's wrist. "The bun."

He raised it off the floor, wadded it up in his fist, and inched the first knuckle into her. He kept his hand balled, slowly pushing against the roast beef already inside her, Leslie breathing in short bursts as if she were giving birth. The lips of her sex closed around his wrist with a hiss of air, as if blowing him a kiss.

Her words were on a whisper. "I'm falling in love with you."

The doorbell rang.

Chuck said, "Goddamn it."

Leslie spoke with her mouth full. "Fugh em."

They were in Chuck's apartment today, Leslie having opened his door that morning to crawl into bed with him, saying she didn't want to sleep alone, that she was shook awake by nightmares. The doorbell rang again.

"Lemme get the door."

Leslie spit his dick out, the chocolate syrup dribbling. "Why? Fuck em."

"I think I know who it is."

"It better be a pizza," she muttered.

Chuck pulled up his slacks. Leslie was still clothed, but her sunflower dress was stained with brown drool. She was either oblivious or didn't care, probably both. She reached for her vodka as Chuck opened the door.

The teenage girl stood in the hallway, smiling and bright as a Christmas tree. She wore a tube top and those same cut-off shorts, her blonde locks constrained into pigtails that only made her look younger. Already hard, Chuck's dick pressed against his slacks, ready to shoot off at the sight of her.

"Hey," she said. "I didn't know how else to get a hold of you, so I thought I'd just drop by."

Chuck wondered how she knew which apartment was his but didn't bother asking. The girl looked over his shoulder at Leslie, who was eyeing her like an opponent in a boxing ring.

The girl looked back to Chuck. "I'm not interrupting, am I?"

"Nah, you're good. Come on in."

As the girl stepped past, Chuck sniffed without her noticing. She reeked of youth and he imagined her cunt must smell like flowers in spring and taste as creamy as buttermilk.

"Say," he said, "I don't even know your name."

"Brittany."

"Like Spears," Leslie said, smirking.

Brittany smiled but obviously didn't mean it. Chuck could sense her fear of Leslie just as strongly as he sensed Leslie's distain for the girl. He found her jealousy was a turn on. He'd oddly grown to appreciate her affection, so Chuck saw her possessiveness as an extension of that.

"I've got the stuff right here," he said, opening the drawer in the end table and handing Brittany the joints. She beamed, her teeth impossibly white and flawless.

Leslie said, "You had grass and didn't share it with me?"

Chuck looked at her. "Didn't know ya wanted any."

"That ain't the point."

Brittany shifted uncomfortably, glancing at Leslie's stained, wet dress. Leslie's eyes were hot iron, and Brittany looked back at the floor immediately.

"You hear that poor bastard die the other day?" Leslie asked her.

"Heard about it when I got home from school."

"School, huh? How old are you, little girl?"

"Seventeen."

Leslie turned to Chuck. "Old enough for you though, right Chucky?"

Chuck didn't reply.

Brittany grew red in the face. "I should go. I didn't mean to bother you guys."

"Yeah, ya should," Leslie said, "we adults have other shit to do than deal dope to kiddies."

Chuck groaned. Enough was enough. "Shut up, Les."

Brittany said, "Thanks again. I owe you one."

As she went out the door, Leslie called out. "You owe him one all right, and he's gonna take it too. Right outta yer tight lil' ass."

Chuck shut the door. "Gee, Les. Like her much?"

"You're gonna fuck that lil' bitch ain'tcha?"

"First chance I get."

"Fuckin men. All they care about is gettin their dicks wet."

"Not true. I also care about gettin drunk and smokin cigarettes."

"And what about me, Chuck? What about *me*?"

Leslie went to the counter and refilled her glass of vodka. She leaned over it, pulling her dress up around her hips, exposing her bare ass and its tiny scars. "You gonna fuck me now?"

"Yeah, sure."

"Get me somethin from the fridge first."

"Think I got a block of cheese."

"Anything. Just fill me up, ya bastard."

He went to the fridge, scanning past cans of soda he only used to mix drinks, a box of Arm & Hammer the landlord had put in there before Chuck had moved in, some expired eggs, and a half block of havarti.

"Why'd you bring up the dead guy?" he asked.

"One interesting thing happens and I ain't supposed to talk about it? Christ, Chuck, you saw it happen. You're the one who done told me."

"Thought ya should know. This Scream thing could be contagious, and someone right here in our building had it. Now he's deader than shit."

He turned around, holding out the cheese. Leslie's eyes had gone bleary with booze. Her hair was a tangled mop from him clutching it in both fists while she'd blown him. The woman was slovenly, downtrodden, perfect.

"I don't need no disease to make me jump outta windows," Leslie said.

"What?"

She held out her arms. "See these scars? See the ones on my face and back and everywhere else?"

"Sure."

Leslie smiled, but it was a sad smile, broken, its happiness a lie. "Tried to kill myself 'bout a year ago."

Chuck went still and silent.

"Jumped through the upstairs window of my house. Didn't open it, just jumped right the fuck through it. Didn't have this Scream disease people been talkin 'bout, but I sure as fuck was screamin."

Chuck thought he should take her hand but didn't. "Why'd ya do it?"

"Forget it." She looked into her empty glass. "Just fuck me, okay?"

"Come on, Les. Tell me what happened."

"What the fuck do you care? Ain't like you're my fuckin boyfriend or somethin."

Chuck poured another. "I still care."

She shot back the vodka in two gulps.

"Alright," she said. "Guess ya gotta know now. You'll just keep askin me every fuckin day until I tell ya." Leslie rolled her shoulders and hung her head, her hair covering half her face. She hid behind this curtain like a child hiding behind a door while listening to their parents fight. "Before I lived in this lovely fuckin place, I had me a nice house in a decent neighborhood. Real decent, Chucky. Outside of this bullshit city. Had a little lawn. My own tree. Two cars in the driveway . . . ." She took a deep breath. "Best of all, I had me a family. People to love. People who loved me. A girl and a boy, three and five years old. And I had a husband. Smart, funny, handsome guy. Sweet to me. Good job. I even had a decent job too. I used to work at a bank, see. Can you believe that shit? Just a teller but it sure beats retail. So we was doin pretty good, yeah?

"Anyways, Wayne, my husband. See, he had problems with depression. Had to stay in one of them special hospitals sometimes. Stressed me the fuck out havin to take care of the kids by myself while still workin. And every time he had to go back there, I got more pissed off, ya know? Here I was bustin my fuckin ass while he was laying around the funny farm just 'cause he's sad. At least that's the way I started lookin at it." She refilled her glass. "So this guy, Terry, down at the bank. He was always flirtin with me and sometimes I caught him lookin down my shirt. With Wayne being such a sad sack, never wantin to fuck or go out or do anything, I started liking Terry's attention. First we just went out for drinks while my Ma was babysittin, not that she knew anything about what I was doin. Soon enough I was goin back to his place. Yeah, I knew it was a rotten thing to do to my husband, especially while he was sick, but ya know what, I'm a flesh and blood woman and I got needs too. Wayne being the way he was got to be like havin a third kid instead of a man."

Leslie's hands had started shaking. Chuck lit them cigarettes.

"So I started fuckin Terry all the time, yeah? At his place on nights I could get away, but mostly on our lunch breaks. We'd do it in the bathroom down at this burger joint across from the bank. Even when Wayne came outta the hospital, I kept screwin Terry. I wasn't fallin in love with the guy or nothin. I just needed some laughs and some fun and some dick and he was always there to give it.

"One day we're goin at it in the bathroom and we forget to lock the door. A lady comes in with her kid and Wayne's got me bent over the sink fuckin the livin Christ outta me. The kid starts wailin and this soccer mom cunt has a straight-up *fit*. Before we can even get our pants up the manager comes over and I see one of the waitresses on the phone. The mom's yellin at the manager and he's gettin all pissed too. He knew us as regulars. Knew our names and that we worked at the bank. And I just knew who that fuckin waitress was callin. The pigs showed up right quick. There was no point in runnin. Terry tried to deny everything, but the crying kid and apeshit mom were a hell of a lot more convincing. So into the slammer we went. I was so naïve, Chucky. I figured two consenting adults—technically behind closed doors—wouldn't be no big deal, right? But sex crimes is a broader term than I . . . "

Leslie looked up to keep the tears from leaving her eyes. One long pull on her booze and she was able to go on.

"I had to make the hardest decision of my life. The pigs gave me one phone call. Should I call my mom to bail me out for indecent exposure and committing a lewd act in public, or do I call my husband? Either way he was gonna find out. I was a sex offender now. You can't hide somethin like that from your spouse, but I figured I could at least try and keep it a secret from my mom and the rest of the family." She hung her head and though only one eye showed from behind her hair, the tears were easy to spot. "So I called Wayne and came clean. About everything. I thought I was doin the right thing by confessing to him, Chucky. I knew it was gonna be hell on both of us but figured if he heard it all straight from me there might be a chance to save our marriage, ya know?"

She sniffed, loud and wet, and now Chuck did take her hand. She clenched him back.

"Turns out it was the worst thing I coulda done," Leslie said. "As bad as cheatin on my husband was, tellin him was worse. What a stupid fuckin move. I mean, the cheatin couldn't hurt him if he didn't know about it. But tellin him . . . that just broke him down completely. He wouldn't talk to me. Wouldn't talk to the kids. Wouldn't go to work or even get outta bed. The only time he spoke was whenever he refused to go back to the hospital. I told him he was right to be upset and begged him to take it out on me and not our children. Still he ignored them almost as bad as he ignored me. And I hated him for it. Hated him for bein a weakling and less of a man. Hated him for pushin me into the arms of another guy and then actin like it was all my fault. So one mornin I snapped and just started yellin at him. Told him just what I thought of him. Told him I was glad I'd fucked someone else, that he was a shit husband and a shittier father and a totally limp-dicked crybaby to boot. He just laid there and took it all, like I was talkin to a deaf mute. So I threw the clock at his head and stormed out and went to work."

She straightened and puffed her cigarette, collecting herself. She withdrew her hand from his to wipe her tears.

"That was the same day I jumped out the window. When I got home from work, Wayne had . . . he'd . . . ah, fuck." She paused. "Nobody answered when I said 'I'm home'. Kids didn't come runnin like usual. I thought maybe my yellin at Wayne had snapped him out of it and maybe he took 'em to the park or somethin. So I go upstairs to change outta my work clothes. I open the door to our bedroom and there they were . . . my family . . . all snuggled in the bed. They didn't move or open their eyes and here I am thinkin they're napping together and it made my heart swell up with love for them, all of 'em, even Wayne. Then I realize . . . their chests weren't movin from breathin. I put my finger under my daughter's nose and . . . nothin. I start sayin '*no no no*' over and over and I check my boy's pulse at his throat and his wrist. Nothin. I check all three of 'em over and fuckin over and shake 'em and fuckin scream and yell their names and smack their faces. Nothin. Nothin at all. They were fuckin dead. My whole family. *Dead.* So I just . . . *did* it. I jumped out the fuckin window. Through the glass and all."

Chuck closed his eyes, unable to look at Leslie, unable to comfort such a high degree of pain. He didn't smoke his cigarette or touch his drink. Didn't say a word for none of them would suffice. He just listened.

"I broke my leg," Leslie said, "got a concussion and all cut to shit but—of course—God didn't let me die. Found out later Wayne had fed them all rat poison for lunch. How's *that* for gettin back at your wife for cheatin, huh? How's *that* for depressed? Didn't leave no note or nothin. I knew he was fucked up, but I never woulda thought he could do somethin like that. Never to *the kids*. Guess no one ever could image such a thing. On their wedding day ain't nobody thinks they're marryin somebody who's gonna beat 'em up or murder 'em or fuckin kill their kids. It's only after years of marriage that ya realize you can never really know someone else."

She touched Chuck's arm and took a bite of the cheese, then slid the straps of her dress off her shoulders and pushed her breasts together with her arms, leaning into him.

"Now," she said, chewing. "Be a doll and fuck my memories away, would ya?"

That night, Chuck brought Leslie to the bar.

Though Eugene always badmouthed her behind her back, he spun on his stool to get a better look when she walked inside. Leslie had cleaned herself up into a tight, black mini-dress and heels. She'd even showered and put on some makeup, rare actions for her. She was bursting out the top of that too-tight dress, scars hardly noticeable in the dim glow of the bar. Chuck was actually proud to have her on his arm. Finally, something he could show off.

Two stools down from Eugene—likely to give him some germ space—sat Shitty. He was talking with two middle-aged Italians with inner city accents. Like most people, they were talking about the growing epidemic, The Scream. Chuck figured the men were tolerating Shitty's company to hear his story about the bag lady who'd gone mad. He was pretty sure these guys ran the deli down on the corner of Nickel and Main. Maybe they'd seen something too.

"Ay!" Shitty shouted when he spotted Chuck. His wrinkles cracked with alley dirt. "It's my buddy, Big Chuck."

Leslie smirked. "*Big* Chuck?"

"Ay," Shitty said, "everybody's big compared to Shitty."

The two men nodded to Shitty and went to the booths where other patrons were sitting around with their faces nosedived into their phones, even people who were there together. Chuck vaguely recognized two whores from down by the docks where he'd used to pick up fifty-dollar hookers before meeting Leslie and getting sex for free. He was fairly certain he'd banged one of them. The other patrons were just strangers, faces without souls, just more mouths sucking up booze to flush their deteriorating inner organs.

Shitty wiggled the turkey gizzards of his legs. Leslie gazed down at them without recoiling, without reacting at all. Her eyes didn't even stray until Barman approached. He was in his usual state of stoic indifference.

"What can I get you two?"

They ordered and Eugene got off his stool. Instead of throwing out the generically suave 'aren't you going to introduce me?', he muttered a watered-down, junior high "Hey".

Chuck introduced them anyway, and to his amazement Eugene shook her hand. He must have been willing to do anything to touch a woman.

"Well," Chuck said, "look at Germaphobe Gene here, actually makin skin contact with another human being."

Eugene's smile fell. Barman returned with their drinks, showing no interest in Leslie. He didn't even try to sneak a glance at her generous cleavage.

"Heard about your stair-diver," he said. "What a freakshow this city is. Goddamn human zoo if I've ever seen one."

"Ain't just this place," Shitty told him. "Welcome to America. I been all over this country and lemme tell ya it's *all* trash. People think I'm the one who lives in garbage, but guess what—we *all* do. I'm just smart enough to live free while I'm in it. That's what makes me a true American."

Barman crossed his arms. "You sleep in a gutter and shit in a storm drain."

"I'm a patriot."

"You're an alley cat. But you're right about one thing. This country is shit, all of it. Just like the rest of the world. One big bucket of shit. We've ruined this planet and soon enough it's going to return the favor."

Leslie turned to Chuck and whispered under the biker music coming from the jukebox. "These psychos are your friends?"

"Don't be anxious. You'll fit right in."

"Very funny." She sipped her vodka. "You sure know how to treat a lady, takin me to a fancy place like this. I thought we were gonna go out to eat, Chucky. Someplace nice for a change. Like a real date."

"Just thought we'd start with an eye-opener."

It was eight-thirty at night, but they'd been napping for hours, drained by alcohol and a fuck that had gone on too long. After passing out, they continued to sweat in bed and had woken up to soggy sheets they had to peel from their bodies.

"There've been more reports," Eugene said, scooting closer, particularly to Leslie. "Screamers are turning up everywhere. They say asylums across the country are over capacity. There's talk of stadiums and schools being used for the screamers, to quarantine."

Shitty leaned in too, his breath matching his namesake. "Lots of suicides, I hear."

"No big loss," Barman grumbled.

"Aw, come on, man. That's just mean."

"Too many people in this city for me to miss anybody who decides to bail out. They're doing the world a favor just by environmental reasons alone. Dead men leave no further carbon footprints. It's almost as good as never having children. I was watching the news earlier and there was a lot of talk about how the polar ice caps have been melting at an alarming pace. Australia and the Amazon burn away, thousands die in heat waves in the east, animals rapidly go extinct, and this summer's the hottest on record.

We're in a global crisis and ain't nobody doing anything to fix it. A good mass death is just what we need to cool the planet down."

Chuck sensed Leslie shifting uncomfortably beside him. Maybe it was best to head straight to the restaurant after all. He slammed back his whiskey and clacked the glass on the bar, a proclamation of his intention to leave.

"Easy," Barman said. "You break it you buy it, shitbird."

Leslie finished her drink and slid her arms into his as if they were walking down a carpet to the Academy Awards instead of the cracked floorboards of a dive bar.

"So where we gonna—"

Leslie didn't get to finish her question.

She was interrupted by a scream.

One of the Italians was climbing onto the table he'd been sitting at. He turned on his back, kicking his legs in the air like a child in mid-tantrum. His friend and the prostitutes who'd been sitting with him all recoiled. The man's hands were at his head, ripping his hair out at the roots, trickles of blood sliding down his temples. Leslie shrieked. The brunette hooker's face went pale as she scurried from the booth, tripping in her stiletto heels and falling to the floor, scrambling catlike. The friend grabbed at the screaming man's wrists, trying to get his hands away from his bloodied scalp, but the screaming man shook him off effortlessly, even though his buddy was nearly twice his size.

"Somebody help me!" the friend shouted.

Barman came around the bar. "Ah, for Christ's sakes."

Someone shouted to call 911. Phones came up, one person calling for paramedics while others took videos. Some of them came closer to the scene to get a better shot as Barman and the friend struggled to keep the screamer from kicking their faces. Chuck didn't want to help, but if he did Barman might employ him after all, or at least go gentle on him when he ran up his tab too high. He stepped forward.

Leslie pulled him back to her. "Don't!"

"Why not?"

"What're you, retarded? Don't get near him. The Scream is infectious."

"That hasn't been confirmed."

"That's how *everything* spreads. From patient zero to the last dead body in a burning pile." She nudged him. "Let's get outta here."

Eugene had the same idea. He'd jumped from his stool and was already out the door. With no one to help him down, Shitty was stuck at the bar just watching the chaos. Chuck wondered what the cripple would have done were he capable. The blonde hooker came to her fallen friend and helped her to her feet. They kicked off their heels in unison but only made it halfway to the door when the one who'd fallen began to shriek. She ran in circles, swatting the air as if a cloud of hornets was engulfing her. The change was so sudden it made Chuck's breath stop. Leslie buried her face into his shoulder, squeezing his arm hard enough to check his blood pressure. The blonde scurried backward, no longer brave enough to rescue her girlfriend, hoping now to just save herself. All the filming phones turned in their direction. Spinning around, the screaming brunette tore at the blonde's clothes, ripping the cheap vinyl as mascara tears ran rivers down her cheeks. The brunette gnashed her teeth, shrieking and biting the air at the same time.

The screaming man broke free of those who'd tried to hold him down, and like some deranged animal he leapt from the table, arms in the air, and crashed into the screaming whore, nearly knocking her over. The whore grabbed him back and the two of them began a violent dance, twirling and punching and kicking and snapping, a cyclone of raging flesh and bone. The man's friend tried to separate them. He was rewarded for his courage with a headbutt, the insane whore crushing his nose in a bloody spray. He fell hard on his back, unconscious, his nostrils gushing. Barman went to him, slid his hands beneath the man's armpits, and pulled him away from the psychotic duo as they ripped each other apart.

Everyone in the bar stood back and watched the carnage, some through the filter of phone screens, perhaps making the horror seem a little less real. Leslie pushed into Chuck like she wanted to sink beneath his skin. The screamers swung, connecting every blow for neither of them made any effort to block their opponent's attack or maneuver their bodies out of harm's way. Their only defense was a hysterical offense, a senseless thunderstorm of violence, of fists and knees, of pummeling and biting. And the brunette, a waif of a woman, held her own against the much larger man, hurting him just as intensely as he did her.

Chuck winced as her thumbnails went into the man's eyes with such force he could hear them pop. Another man in the crowd vomited at the sight of one of the eyeballs being pushed out of its socket and squeezed in the hooker's fist. She twirled her fingers around the connective tissue, getting a good enough grip to tug it free from the skull. The man had been screaming through the whole fight, so it was hard to tell if he felt any pain from it, particularly because he didn't stop fighting but instead reeled back and kicked the hooker in the groin, hiking up her skirt and buckling her legs. She was in mid-fall when he threw a chair that split her face down the center, releasing some of those gnashing teeth from their gums.

The sound of police sirens drew closer, but they weren't close enough. Barman made one last effort to intervene, for it seemed the screaming man was about to murder the hooker. Barman picked up a stool and sent it slamming into the screamer's back, but he just spun around and backhanded Barman hard enough to send him off his feet and onto a table that cracked beneath him. Chuck tried help but once again Leslie clutched him closer, harder.

And that's when the other Italian man started screaming.

CHAPTER TEN

SHE WAS TOO old to be veal.

The boy knew that. He'd been *taught* that. So what was the man doing with her? Sure, she was blonde and pale like so many others, but she was old enough to be the boy's mother. He tried not to think about that. Tried not to think about his parents at all. It was getting easier these days. That was his old life, a life that had begun to fade from his memory, like a dream does once you get out of bed. The past didn't matter anymore. Maybe it never had. Best not to let the thin remnants of a ghost world eclipse the reality of the farm. It would interfere with the work. The work was all that mattered, the only purpose in life, the only truth.

The man pushed the woman into the corner of the shed and she knocked her elbow against the base of the standing bone saw. A soft cry escaped her. Clearly the man had warned her about making noise. He hated the sounds these women made. He turned to the boy and shrugged, a self-deprecating smile on his face.

"Bitch done caught me," he said.

"Whadda ya mean?"

"There's a fresh piece of veal in pen number four. Looked like she was alone in the parkin lot, but, well, Mama Bear here was waitin in the car, watchin her go into the store. So when I made my move she pulled up behind my truck and started raisin hell, so I hadda gas her too."

That's what the man called it when he put the funny smelling rag to someone's face to knock them out, the same tactic he'd used on the boy all those years ago. How many was it now? The boy couldn't be sure. The man didn't keep a calendar on the wall. All the boy knew was he taller and stronger. He'd grown some hair on his genitals and in his armpits, and a tiny sliver on his chest. He had oily pimples

66

and had long ago grown out of the clothes he'd been wearing the day of his abduction. Now he wore hand-me-downs, mostly clothes from the girls the man kidnapped. Because the jeans were usually too tight, the boy had taken to wearing their dresses instead. It bothered him at first, dressing like a girl, but he'd grown to appreciate the soft material and the breeze that blew up from below on those hot summer days.

The woman looked at the boy, suddenly aware of his presence. Her eyes were like that of an animal in a trap. They pleaded with him just like all the others, even though she was the adult and he the child.

"Take off yer clothes," the man told her.

The woman's face pinched back tears.

"Ah, turn off them waterworks. I ain't no rapist, least of all to the likes of you. Now take off them clothes 'fore I bust open yer damn fool head."

The woman moved slowly at first, but then the man moved forward, just an inch but enough to startle her and speed things up. She pulled her shirt over her head, revealing breasts much larger than the boy had ever seen before. These weren't the budding breasts of teen girls. These were the full, plush breasts of a woman, and though her midsection was doughy the breasts made up for it. Even constrained in the plain, white bra they were big, the cleavage speckled by sunspots, nipples visible beneath the cloth. She slid out of her jeans, revealing thick thighs, the insides of which were raked by stretch marks. None of these traits diminished the boy's attraction to her. Maybe it was because he hadn't seen a grown woman since he'd been brought to the farm or maybe it was because the other females he only saw behind bars. It was too complex for a boy his age to process. He didn't even try. He simply stared at the woman, waiting for the underwear to come off and not feeling guilty about it. The nudity of the veal was one of the very few pleasures he got out of doing this. That and a job done well enough to make the man give him a proud pat on the back. When he worked hard and efficiently, the man gave him popcorn and let him read novels and watch TV. Now and then he even got a new book or a can of Schlitz. It sure beat getting a whoopin'.

Once the woman was nude, the man had her stand up. She tried to cover her privates and breasts with her hands, but the man smacked them both away, giving the boy a look at the protruding nipples and dark bush.

The man chuckled. "This one's carpet don't match the drapes."

The boy laughed even though he didn't get the joke. The man was in a good mood and it was rubbing off on him. The man flipped the power switch on the wall. Following his lead, the boy dipped the straight razor in the water bucket and placed it on the towel beside the can of shaving cream.

The man said, "Probably ain't gonna be enough to just trim the snatch. Gonna have to shave her legs too. These older broads get hairier than the veal."

"Okay."

The boy squirted a blob of shaving cream into his hand and came toward the woman. Her eyes were even more pleading now, flinching at his touch. His fingers tingled as he lathered up those full thighs, and when they reached her vagina, he had to resist the urge to explore this fleshy canal of wonders. The man instructed him to get her armpits too, and once she was shaved to the man's satisfaction the boy picked up the scissors and started chopping her hair off, something the man insisted on even though the only parts of the head they could use were the cheeks, ears and nose. The scalp was virtually useless. But the boy knew better than to ask questions while working.

The woman sobbed as her blonde locks fell about her, making it difficult for the boy to keep her head straight. He nicked her with the blades a few times, but it was her own damn fault. When he was finished, he gathered the barber tools and headed for the door. The man put his hand on the boy's shoulder. Had he forgotten something? No. He hadn't skipped any of the normal routine. Everything left to do now was the man's job. Always had been. Were there additional steps with a woman this old? What more was he supposed to do?

"Kid," the man said. "Sit down a spell."

The boy sat Indian style on the floor and the man sat on a crate. He patted the boy's back and gave him a small but genuine smile.

The man asked, "Ya know that card what was in yer pocket when we met?"

"Um, I think so."

"I held on to it. You don't remember it though, huh?"

He didn't. Another piece of the old life lost. "What kind of card was it?"

"T'was an I.D. card from your school. Had a little picture of ya on it. Said your name and address and phone number."

The boy still didn't remember. "Yeah. I think so."

"Know what else was on it?"

The boy hung his head and shook it, hoping the man wouldn't be mad at him for forgetting. They'd been having such a good day; he didn't want to see it spoiled. Luckily the man's good cheer remained. He was always happy after bringing home fresh veal, and it seemed the unexpected addition of the Mama Bear hadn't put a damper on things after all.

"Your date a birth," the man said. "July 31st."

"Yeah?"

The man snickered. "Can't ya see what I'm gettin at? That's today. July 31st. You turn thirteen today, kid."

A numbness crept across the boy's skin and then sunk into his bones. It was like nausea, only he didn't feel sick. Instead he felt suddenly hollowed, this information coring him out like a grave being dug.

Thirteen. A teenager.

He choked back a whimper.

Four years. I've been here for four years.

It seemed somehow impossible even though that day at the mall was his former life, one he'd lived then died and was reincarnated into this boy in this place, a complete overhaul of who he'd been before the farm. The child he'd left behind was a stranger at best, but more like a figment, a painful dream.

The man patted his back again, startling him out of thoughts that threatened to take him to the dark place he'd gone each night in his cage until the man trusted him enough to let him out of it, giving him a bed and making the basement more like the boy's own room.

"You're a man now, son. Least that's what the Jews say. I reckon I agree with 'em on that if nothin else."

The boy kept looking at the ceiling. *Four years.* At some point the naked woman had curled up in the corner, hugging herself, crying as quietly as possible. They ignored her.

69

The man said, "When I turned thirteen, my old man made sure I knew I wasn't a boy no more. Know how he did it?" The boy only shook his head. "He took me huntin. Sure, I'd been huntin before a'course. But bein just a squirt I was like a pack mule for bullets n' beers n' dead ducks n' such. My old man would lemme practice my shootin with the rifle, but never on prey, just on bottles we done lined atop the broke-down old Buick we had out back. Said I wasn't ready to shoot an animal yet. Said I had to learn the ways of the hunter first by watchin him do it all them goddamn years. Pissed me off somethin fierce at the time but ya know what?"

He waited for a reply. The boy conceded. "What?"

"He was right. Right as rain. All those years I thought I was just a stinkin mule, the old man was teachin me, waitin on me to be the right age and have the right set of mind. So, soon as I turned thirteen, he handed the rifle over to me when we stepped into them woods, and kid, it was the greatest feelin in the world, I tell ya. But later that day when I done shot me a big buck right through the neck . . . well, that was even better. I'll never forget that birthday."

The man held the boy's gaze. He stood up, the bones in his knees grinding like peppercorns, and put his hands to his lower back and stretched. He reached for the sheath on his belt, withdrawing his largest hunting knife, the one with the slit in the middle to make blood flow out faster. He flipped it once in the air, catching it by the blade, and held it out to the boy, handle first.

The boy took it. The man nodded toward the woman in the corner.

"Happy birthday, kid."

CHAPTER ELEVEN

THEY ESCAPED OUT the emergency exit. It was certainly appropriate. With three screamers raging inside the bar, Leslie had grabbed Chuck's hand and ran, pulling him with her. A few remaining patrons followed behind them with the sane hooker and Barman bringing up the rear. The bartender had taken Shitty from his stool and given him his cart so he could wheel out with the crowd. This kindness somewhat surprised Chuck, given Barman's seeming distain for all of humanity.

"Mother of all fucks," Shitty said as they tumbled into the alley like rats.

Three more patrons fled from the backdoor, horror bright on their faces. Barman held his back and his hand came away bloody. "I've been bartending two decades and that's the first fight I couldn't break up. Crazy prick threw me around like I was a teddy bear."

The hooker went to him. "Let me see. Maybe we can—"

"Take it easy, Fuckface Nightingale. It's just some scrapes from the wood."

Her face pinched. "Excuse me, my name is Angel."

"Nobody cares what your goddamn name is."

"I was just tryin to help. God, why are you always such an asshole?"

Leslie stepped between them, her voice hushed. "Shut the fuck up, both of ya. We need to get outta here before those fuckin maniacs come for us."

Shitty said, "Seems to me they were more interested in killin each other."

"Good," Barman said. "Let 'em."

"Didn't ya notice? I mean, yeah, they fought back when ya'll tried to break 'em up, but what they really went after was the other screamers."

"That's not a risk I'm willin to take," Leslie said.

"I ain't leaving Rudy's Place," Barman said. "I'm responsible for this bar, I could lose my job if I abandon it."

"You'll die if ya go back in there. These screamers have, like, superhuman strength."

"I'll just wait here until the cops show up."

"Fine, you do whatcha want. Chuck and I are goin home. Fuck this shit."

Chuck said, "Les, if we're gonna leave the bar we'll need to pick up some booze."

"You're awfully cavalier about all this."

"Whadda ya want me to do, stop drinkin?"

"Aren't ya the least bit freaked the fuck out?"

He shrugged. "It's messed up, but ain't nothin we can do about it."

A siren squealed. The group turned to the opening of the alley, watching as police cars raced by in a blur of flashing lights.

Barman stared. "They . . . they just kept driving."

A familiar voice came from behind them. "That's because it's happening everywhere." Eugene was crouched behind garbage cans, his eyes bugged out like a frog's.

"What're ya doin back there?" Chuck asked.

"Looking at social media." He held up his smart phone. "Everybody's posting videos of these screamers, all over the damn city."

"Jesus, Gene, come on—"

"Think I'm delusional, huh? Think paranoid ol' Gene is spouting off more conspiracy theories? Go ahead and look it up."

But they didn't have to. A scream tore through the night, sharp as a switchblade. Across the street, a woman was halfway out of the window of a third-floor apartment. She was topless and bloody, crying out to the stars as she tore out clumps of her hair. Further down the street came the sound of tires squealing against their brakes, followed by a shattering collision.

Barman paled. "This is really happening."

Angel crossed her arms to keep from shaking. She was a skinny, little thing. Girlishly petite, fragile as tissue paper.

"You guys smell that?" she asked.

Chuck inhaled. "Somethin's burnin."

Leslie took him by his shirt. "Let's get to my apartment. We'll be safe there."

"How do ya know?"

"Well, shit, it's safer than these fuckin streets. Safer than goin back in that fuckin bar."

Shitty chimed in. "Maybe them screamers in there all killed each other by now."

"Not possible," Barman said. "There's bound to be one winner, one left smashing the place apart."

"Heh heh. My money's on the whore."

Angel's eyes watered. "That's my friend your talkin 'bout, ya little freak!"

"No intents offended."

"Workin' girls are people too."

"So are bums. Heh heh."

Leslie walked, pulling at Chuck's arm again. "I can't believe we're fuckin standin 'round listenin to this shit."

"Alright, alright, we're goin."

As they started toward the alley's exit, Eugene stumbled through his barricade of overstuffed trashcans. "Wait up. I don't wanna head home alone."

"I don't wanna be alone either," Angel said.

Eugene smiled without making eye contact. "Well, you can come too."

Leslie groaned but was obviously tired of arguing. She kept walking but Chuck looked back at Barman and Shitty.

"What about you guys?"

"You live a lot closer than I do," Barman said, holding his back again. "I'm not jumping on a train when things are like this. Be like being in a submarine full of piranhas. I hate to leave my post, but your lady friend is right. The cops aren't coming."

Shitty said, "And I ain't got no home at all."

Chuck didn't have to look at Leslie; he could feel her eyes staring into the back of his head like power drills. He knew she wasn't interested in gathering every loser in the bar, but if hell were really breaking loose there'd be safety in numbers. Even if one of them was already infected and would turn into a screamer, it'd be worth it to have a few extra fists on their side. Hell, even Shitty could bite an ankle or reach up and twist a pair of testicles.

"Okay then," Chuck said. "Party at our place."

CHAPTER TWELVE

"WELL, WATCHA WAITIN FOR?"

But the boy had no words to answer. His mouth felt full of flour. The handle of the knife was slick with the sweat of his palm and the woman, naked in the corner, was pleading for her life in a tone so soft and high-pitched it was almost childlike. As much as the boy wanted to prove his value, he couldn't move a single step in the woman's direction.

The man put his hands on his hips. "Time to man up, kid. Ain't gotta be savage. Don't go all stab crazy. Just pull her head back by her hair and cut her throat. Go deep. Gotta hit the jugular."

The woman's sobs grew louder as she curled into herself like a fetus.

"That's how humans slaughter pigs," the man said. "Why should humans get any better treatment?"

The man nudged the boy, making him gasp. He was shaking now. This woman before him was going to die. Whether he killed her or the man did, she was destined for the same grim fate. If he failed to do it, the man would be disappointed in him, maybe even angry. The boy certainly didn't want that. He'd come so far. The chance to make the man proud was all the incentive he normally needed. Even aside from the payoff of junk food and control of the television, just having the man pat him on the back was a reward all of its own. His strong hand clasping the boy's shoulder was not only gratifying, it was the only physical touch the boy ever received from another human being, except for the occasional moment when one of the veal might reach through their cage, grab him and beg for help he could not provide. He'd never been kicked and scratched by them the way the man had, but then he'd never had to *prepare* them either.

"I know it's a big step," the man said. His tone was kind and understanding, the voice of a patient teacher. "But I believe in ya, kid."

Warmth rose up from the boy's stomach, wrapping around his heart. He looked back at the man to see he was smiling just as much as he was.

"Thank you, sir."

The boy returned his attention to the woman, his hand steadier, the knife suddenly weightless, a mere extension of his arm, his body, his soul. He understood now. Killing didn't have to be a bad thing. On a farm, slaughter was inevitable, a simple part of a wrangler's life. But this killing—his *first* killing—was more than just a chore like spraying the pens clean or slopping the hogs. It was an *initiation*, one into manhood itself. The woman's body was a doorway, and the hunting knife was the key that would unlock her, revealing a whole new world as her blood washed his childhood away. To slay her was not just to take her life but to also trade in his own. And from that moment on he would be a young adult, and the man would continue to guide him until he was less of a protégée and more of a peer.

The boy stepped closer. The woman sat up, her back against the cold steel of the shed, cornered like a mouse before a snake.

"Please," she said. "Please . . . I'm . . . I'm a mom . . . I just had a baby."

There was a time that would have mattered to the boy. But now he just grabbed a clump of what was left of her hair. His eyes fell on her breasts again. They were jiggling from her shivers. Feeling more masculine than ever before, he let go of her hair and cupped one. It was soft and meaty. He gave it a squeeze and her nipple began to seep. The boy recoiled, thinking it was pus.

"She's sick," he said. "Infected or somethin."

The man came closer and pinched her nipple. It dribbled more white goo.

"Shit," the man said, chuckling. "Guess she wasn't lyin 'bout havin a baby. This here's titty milk, kid."

The boy frowned in disgust. He knew sows breastfed their young, the litter scurrying beneath their mamas to attach to one of many extended teats, but he'd never known humans did the same thing. It seemed somehow perverted. The man did not share this revulsion.

He got down on his knees beside the woman and bent until his face was level with the woman's teat. This time he pinched her nipple with his mouth and slurped the creamy fluid down. When he came up for air, he smiled at the boy with off-white milk bubbling at the sides of his mouth.

"This here's what we all live on when we're born," he said. "Mother's milk is nature's perfect food. It's what humans are meant to eat all their lives, but instead they turn to defenseless cows for milk. My Mama breastfed me for years. Woulda probably run out by the time I was five, but then she had my brother. He died from what they call sudden infant death syndrome after just a month, so I got to go back on the tit 'til I was 'bout ten or eleven, 'til she just ran dry."

The man suckled at the woman again, squeezing her nipple to pump out the milk. She closed her eyes and bit her lip, face upturned in pale horror. With her throat exposed, the boy urged to cut it open while she was distracted.

The man said, "Gonna have to keep this one alive."

The boy's chest deflated. The testosterone that had boiled in his brain and loins fizzled with disappointment.

"Now don't go gettin buttsore," the man said. "Ya can't look a gift horse in the mouth, as the fella says. This bitch's titties will feed us up but good."

The boy didn't reply. He knew better than to be disrespectful with silence when he was being spoken to, but his unhappiness was getting the better of him. He put the knife on the table with the bone saw, making his point by pushing it away.

The man got to his feet. "Oh, alright. Don't need to gimmie them puppy-dog eyes. I said ya can't kill this one here while she's still givin milk, but that don't mean ya can't slaughter up another."

The boy looked at him, eyes alive again, bright as bullets catching sunshine.

"Go get us some veal," the man told him. "The new girl will do."

The woman screamed and the man kicked her in the stomach, taking away the wind she needed to beg for the life of her eldest child. The boy snatched the shackles from where they hung on the wall and darted out the door, frolicking through the mud beneath that ever-ashen sky, the hogs snorting in celebration.

THEY ALL DIED SCREAMING

He'd always wanted to help the veal before. It was strange not to feel that empathy now. For years the boy had felt a sort of kinship with them because they too were prisoners. But he didn't think of himself that way anymore, because the man certainly didn't treat him as one. Day by day the man had lowered the boy's guard through increasingly amicable expressions—making him a room, giving him free reign of the house, trusting him with important farm work. As the man became the boy's teacher, the fear had slowly ebbed. With a flash of the eyes the man could instill that fear right back into the boy's gut, but by being obedient and hardworking the boy had given him less reasons to be angry. A fondness had developed on both ends of their relationship, even a friendship. The man was his only companion. Without him, the boy would be alone, a thought that made him cold.

Early on, the boy had tried to make friends with the veal, despite knowing it would be short-lived, but they were always too terrified and tortured by their restraints to offer conversation. All they did was beg and cry and scream. He had pitied them. In a way he still did, but he'd also grown desensitized to young women chained to the floor in dog crates too small for them. More than that, he'd come to think of these females as livestock rather than fellow human beings because, in the end, that's all they were. The only real human beings in this world were himself and the man. All others were merely animals, and these girls were lowliest of all.

The pigs not only outnumbered the veal, they outranked them. The value of the swine was not monetary, as the veal's was. The pigs were not part of the farm, but part of the family, the one the man had made for he and the boy. Pigs were as smart and loyal as dogs, the man had told him, and the boy could see it in their very nature, and, like the man, he had his personal favorites among the drift. The man had even developed a romantic relationship with one of the parcel, a hefty, spotted sow named Polly. And while the pig brayed whenever he would consummate their union, she was as loyal and loving to him as any pet. The man was not just one of this group of pigs, he was their patriarch, lord of the swine. And most of all he was a *man*, the very thing the boy aspired to be.

Now was his chance.

Unlocking the cage, he took the new veal by the arms, connecting the shackles from her wrists to her ankles before undoing the leather straps that pinned her to the floor. He entered the combination on the lock and the chain clamored as it fell from her neck.

"Wha-what's happening," she whimpered, covering her privates with her hands. "Where . . . where's my m-mom?"

The boy nudged her to usher her out, but she recoiled.

"Who are you? Wha-what do you want?"

Her questions stirred something in him. Part pride, part arousal. It was as if this new chunk of veal understood the transformation he was going through at this very moment. Where the other veal had always pleaded with him as if he were the voice of reason between them and the man, calling him "little boy" when they asked him to set them free, this new one did not see him the way the others had. To her, he was no different than the man who had snatched her up. He was not a fellow prisoner, he was her *captor*.

The boy reached for the electric cattle prod and the zap filled the dark shack with a dreamy, blue light, and the sound that came out of the girl upon her first shock was almost pig-like.

But not enough.

CHAPTER THIRTEEN

DENTED TRASHCANS ON the sidewalks were overflowing with stuffed bags of rotting waste, cooking in the humid night. Screams echoed off the concrete heart of the city, howling through the alleyways like witch's wind. Sirens flickered in the distance. Tires screeched. Smoke billowed out of a third-floor window and twisted into the sky like a ruptured volcano. An ambulance sat in the middle of the street, immobilized by the abandoned cars ahead of it. The whole ambulance was shaking, someone inside thrashing and shrieking. People were running between the cars—some screamers, others normal people pleading with them, others fleeing from them. Friends and family tried in vain to save screamers from the fate of all the others. Clusters of fists and kicking legs, a wrench connecting with a skull, a woman's high heel thrust into an eye socket. As the six of them turned the corner, Angel cried out at the sight of a man hanging from an awning by a length of extension cord, his tongue out of his mouth, eyes wide and staring.

"Jumpin Jesus Jahoziphat!" Shitty said. "It's like a prison riot!"

"Where's the fuckin cops?" Leslie asked.

"They got their hands full," Chuck said. "It's a big city; who knows how far this has spread. Forget the cops, we need the National Guard."

They kept moving as the hot wind picked up, carrying the stink of ruin.

"The question is," Barman said, "why'd so many people turn into screamers at the same time? We went from there being a few here and there to all of a sudden they're transforming in droves."

Eugene kept his voice low. "The second phase. This didn't happen for no reason. It can't be random. It has to be part of their plan."

"Whose plan?"

"Our attackers. I'll bet it's a biological weapon, just like anthrax or depleted uranium ammo. They already gave us radiation poisoning, SARS, rice blasts. Someone's behind this new plague."

Angel's eyes went wide. "*Plague*?"

"What else can we call it when a deadly virus spirals out of control?"

"I don't like the sound of that."

"We're being poisoned. First, they did it with chemtrails and vaccinations that give us autism. Putting fluoride in public drinking fountains. Then they took it one step further, experimenting with the water supply in Flint, Michigan. Now they're going even bigger."

"You mean the water's causing this?"

"I don't know for sure yet. They could be using any sort of vehicle for it—the water, radio signals, even the very air we breathe. It's a full-blown assault on our central nervous systems, a way for them to—"

Leslie snapped at him. "Will you shut the fuck up? Stop tryin to scare everyone. We're already freaked the fuck out."

"Hey, I'm just putting the pieces together."

"No, you're pullin shit outta your ass. You don't know any more than the rest of us. Maybe this Scream thing just got stronger on its own. Shit, nobody knows what's goin on, not even the news."

"That's 'cause the media is controlled by—"

"I said *shut the fuck up*!" Leslie moved so quickly Eugene didn't have time to stop her from grabbing his shirt collar. "Don't make me kick your ass!"

Chuck laughed a little under his breath. Goddamn, Leslie was something else. That she would threaten to kick a man's ass was a level of bad bitch he rarely saw in a woman. It was just like when she told somebody to suck her dick. It made him like her all the more. He would have let her kick Eugene's ass too. There was no doubt she would be successful at it. She was thicker, for one thing. More importantly, she was *meaner*. Chuck didn't know if she could fight, but sometimes crazy was just as dangerous as skilled. But for the time being no fists were going to fly. Barman had gotten between them, gently prying Leslie off Eugene.

"Leslie, you calm down," he said. "And you, Gene, you really do need to shut the fuck up. Maybe we're all doomed and maybe we're not. But if we are, I don't wanna spend my final moments listening to your horseshit conspiracy theories."

Eugene opened his mouth as if to say something but quickly closed it. The group pressed on. Angel kept her eyes on the ground in an attempt not to see more death, but there would be no avoiding it. Anarchy was rising exponentially. Without a cure for this disease, no end to its horror was coming soon.

"Nishant's is just three blocks from here," Chuck said. "We'll be okay. Just hope he's still open."

"You're crazy," Angel said. "I can't believe ya wanna stop for booze at a time like this."

Barman said, "I've known him long enough to believe it."

"It won't take long," Chuck told them. "I ain't barricading myself without supplies."

"Something tells me you don't have flashlights and a first aid kit or anything useful in an emergency. Hell, you probably don't even have food."

"We'll be fine. Leslie always has food."

She shot Chuck a dirty look and he wasn't sure if she was mad because he'd exposed their reserves or if she thought he was alluding to her fetish. He hadn't meant to do either. He just wanted to get drunk again. Drinking, smoking and screwing were the only good things life had to offer. If shit was going down, he wanted to enjoy these simple pleasures while he still could.

Angel huffed. "I just think we need to get behind closed doors. We're too—"

A high-pitched scream pierced the night and Angel shrieked in reply, clutching Barman's arm. He nudged her off, so she pressed against Eugene, who didn't seem to mind. The group froze and the screaming grew louder, closer.

A child pounced from out of a doorway and tumbled into the street. He wore only a pair of Hulk Underoos, his knees scraped and bloody, his hair a briar speckled with litter. Running at full speed, he screeched and repeatedly punched himself in the face, his cheeks and forehead pink from the onslaught.

Shitty choked on his words. "Oh, no. Oh, fuckin shit, man."

"Whadda we do?" Chuck asked no one in particular.

Barman said, "There's nothing we can do."

"Unless we want to kill him," Eugene said. Angel pulled away from him and his face went red. "No, no, I just mean to put him out of his misery!"

"What are you gonna do, Gene?" Barman asked. "Beat him to death with a trash can?" He kicked the one closest to him and it rolled down the street, vomiting its stinking innards. "You can't just kill every screamer. What if there's a cure in the works? These people could get better."

"He's just a little boy!" Angel said.

Eugene's eyes darted. "I didn't mean to like, really do it or anything. I was just thinking out loud. Besides, Barman, when did you get so philanthropic? Thought you *wanted* a plague."

"Shit." Barman hung his head and sighed, guilty. "That was just . . . just bullshit talk . . . I don't know . . . "

Leslie was crying. Not sobbing, but silent in her flowing tears, her face stoic despite them. Chuck hadn't even thought about how the near certainty of this little boy's death would trigger her, pushing the blackest memories to the front of her mind.

"You okay, Les?"

At first she didn't speak, her wet eyes flashing against the glow of the streetlights. Then she started toward the boy, one sluggish step at a time, as if lulled into a trance. She was mumbling something Chuck couldn't make out. He didn't have to. He knew what she was doing, so Chuck grabbed her arm to keep her from approaching the child. He was about to tell her all the obvious things—that the kid was a screamer, that he'd only hurt her, that there was nothing she could do to help. But he didn't have to. Leslie didn't try to shake free from Chuck's grasp and didn't take another step. She was defeated before she'd begun, the weight of past horrors pulverizing her, disabling any confidence she'd dare to unearth.

"I think you're right, Chucky," she said.

"I am? 'Bout what?"

"About needin to stop at Nishant's. I'm not gonna face this sober."

The screaming boy dashed into the street, jumped onto the hood of a car, and used it as a trampoline. The man behind the wheel put his hands over his face, crying, then fled from the car, abandoning it as the child roared into the wind, no longer human.

The liquor store's windows were smashed out, but the bars had held up against whatever assault they'd endured. Witch's wind was howling down the avenues now, the signs and flyers on the storefront writhing and ripping free. Lights were on inside. Chuck's muscles twitched at all those beautiful, brown bottles glimmering within.

"I'll bet he's here," Chuck said, but when he tried the door it was locked. He cupped his hands to his mouth. "Hey, Nishant! You in there?"

Angel grimaced. "What kinda name's Nishant?"

"He's from India."

"Aw, great! A Muslim? It might be his people doin this to us, like some kinda terrorisim."

Barman groaned. "You dumb bitch. People from India aren't Muslim, they're Hindu if anything."

"Yeah, well, I ain't no racist, but I just don't trust no sand people."

Chuck ignored them. "Hey! Nishant! You in th—"

The sound of a pump-action shotgun filling its chamber caused Chuck to step away. The others retreated too, and Chuck suddenly found himself in the position of leader, something he'd never wanted to be in his life. Nishant's face appeared behind the iron bars, scowling, eyes tight. He was curt.

"What do you want?"

Chuck smiled in an effort to put the man at ease. "Just some booze, man. Come on, relax. You know me. I come in all the time."

Nishant scanned the others. "Who are these people?"

"Just some friends."

The barrel of the shotgun came up but did not point it in their direction. "No trouble."

Leslie eased forward. "No trouble, man. Ya know me too, right? I'm in here, like, every other day. Vodka."

"All women drink vodka."

"Right, right. We just need some to calm our nerves, ya know?"

Nishant paused, considering. "You have money?"

She nodded. Nishant scanned the others again as if an interrogation was about to come. His long, gray beard and thick eyebrows concealed any facial expression, making him unreadable.

"Alright," he said. "Tell me what you want and hand the money through the bars. Do it slowly."

Chuck and Leslie pooled together what cash they had and looked to the others. Shitty was the first to chip in, three dollars rolled into a ball housing some loose change. Barman drew his money clip and peeled away some twenties, grumbling. Angel was busted. She'd left behind her purse at the bar and her dress was far too tight to hold anything other than flesh and bones. Eugene, ever the germaphobe, only had his Mastercard and some sanitizing wipes in his wallet. Nishant took the cash, rejecting the credit card, and gave them two bottles of whisky and two vodkas, one gin, a case of club soda and a liter of RC Cola.

"We're headed to the apartments over there," Chuck said, pointing to the complex. "Join us if ya want."

"Appreciations, but I must protect what is mine. This is like L.A. '92."

"You were there for the riots?"

He nodded. "It was crazy but still made more sense than this."

"I know what ya mean."

A hot gust rushed by, the wind fierce. There was a loud pop as a transformer exploded across the street. Barman crouched while everyone else jumped. One of their bottles hit the ground and shattered. Chuck saw the power line hissing sparks as it came flailing to the ground. When he turned around, Nishant had the shotgun pointed at the group. He was shaking, startled by the bursting transformer.

"Get out of here!" he shouted. "I don't want to shoot you, but I will!"

Shitty got rolling, waving his arm to encourage the others to follow, even though he didn't know the way. Chuck lamented the bottle they'd lost, but he still had two whiskeys cradled in his arms and his companions had the others. Best not to haggle with a frightened, armed man for a replacement on the bottle that got destroyed. Everyone seemed to agree on that. But as the group left the storefront, one stayed behind. Not to argue, but to try and reason.

"Don't you see this is what they want?" Eugene asked the storeowner.

Nishant snarled. "I said move!"

"They want us to turn on each other, man. It's all part of their master plan."

Barman said, "Gene! Come on! This isn't the time—"

"But it is! We have to resist the negative energy they're feeding us!"

He turned back to Nishant a little too quickly, stepping too close. From what Chuck could tell, Eugene thought he was going to enlighten the man, but Nishant seemed to think the sudden movement was a threat, and he wasn't about to take any chances. The shotgun blast deafened Chuck, so he couldn't even hear Angel screaming beside him. Wet pieces of something hit his forehead and cheeks. Somehow everything seemed to slow even as it happened so fast. Eugene's face all but disintegrated from the peppering of pellets. It looked like his skin was melting at a rapid pace, defying gravity as it rose up and away from his skull in a red mist. These pieces of him had sprinkled Chuck. Had the shot been a direct hit, Eugene would have been decapitated by the blast, but the shotgun had bucked in Nishant's hands. Only some of the spray caught its target, but that was more than enough to tear Eugene's face off.

"Fuck!" Nishant panicked and fled deeper into the store. "Fuck! Fuck! Fuck!"

The old guy hadn't wanted to hurt anyone. Lots of help that did the bloody pulp of Chuck's neighbor, who was lying on the sidewalk, twitching and oozing. Barman was the first to respond, staying low as he went to Eugene's side.

"We're leaving!" he called out to Nishant. "Don't shoot! I'm just gonna help him up, and we'll get out of here! No trouble, just like you said!"

Barman lifted one of Eugene's arms over his neck and scowled up at Chuck.

"Help me, you moron!"

Still holding the bottles, Chuck looked to Leslie, who had buried her face in her hands. She was silent, frozen. Angel seemed to jog in place from nervous energy, her face streaked with mascara tears. Shitty was still rolling down the sidewalk, smart enough to flee.

Maneuvering one bottle into the crook of his arm, Chuck freed his other arm to help Barman with Eugene, who appeared to be unconscious at best. Chuck used the bottom of his shirt to wipe his own face of red bits of skin before reaching for Eugene. He certainly felt dead when Chuck had to support him. He was heavy, limp—a real pain in the ass, as always. As they dragged him away from the liquor store, Barman barked at the women.

"Move your asses! I can't carry all of you fuckers."

Chuck laughed. He simply couldn't help it. He felt Barman's eyes shooting fire at him but could not see the man's face because it was blocked by Eugene's lack of one. His head kept drooping to Chuck's side, the shredded flesh sticking to his shoulder. The smell of cordite and gunpowder rose off of Eugene's head, underlined by the coppery tang of blood. Heels clacked behind him. The women were moving again. Up ahead, Shitty was waiting on the corner. He'd already opened the gin and was drinking straight from the bottle.

Who could blame him? Chuck thought.

Leslie had a box of Band-Aids, but just the ones that go on your finger. Nothing useful in this situation. But who really is prepared to mend a near-complete removal of a face?

"Here," Chuck said, coming out of Leslie's bathroom with hand towels.

Unlike most of her things, these were clean. He took the bottle of vodka and splashed the towels with it to sterilize them, then came up beside Barman, who was tending to Eugene on the couch. Chuck put the booze-soaked rags upon the mush that had been a man's head less than an hour ago, half expecting Eugene to awaken from the alcohol sting on his wounds. But he didn't budge. If not for the slow rise and fall of his chest when he breathed, Chuck would have guessed Eugene for a corpse. As they'd struggled to get him up the stairs, avoiding the unreliable elevator, he'd wished Eugene *had* died so they wouldn't have to break their backs getting him to the apartment. Seeing as Eugene was almost certainly going to die anyway, Chuck didn't consider himself callous for wanting the reaper to get this over with already.

"We have to get him to a hospital," Barman said in a tone so soft and low it expressed the futility of the notion. "But with the city in this kind of chaos, hospitals are bound to be Bedlam."

"Overcrowded with screamers and their families," Chuck said. "Not to mention the victims of the violence this shit has caused."

"I'll tell ya, if I was a doctor or a nurse I sure as shit wouldn't be on the clock. I'd be at home protecting my own, oath or no oath."

Chuck didn't realize Leslie had come up behind him until he felt her hand on his shoulder. He looked up at her and she pointed away with her head, nudging him, so he followed her down the hallway, passing by Shitty and Angel. They were slamming back shots like a couple of college kids, only there was no joy in it. Leslie led Chuck into her bedroom and shut the door.

"What is it?" he asked.

She took a sip of her glass of Tito's. "I dunno. Just wanted to be alone with ya a minute."

Chuck furrowed his brow. "Ya mean ya wanna fuck?"

"Well, no, that's not what I called ya in here for, but yeah, may as well, right? I mean, if the world's comin to a fuckin end we might as well go out with a bang, literally."

She smiled, but it was a sad, hopeless smile, her nose still wet from sniffling.

"So why'd you call me in here, then?"

Leslie shrugged. "I just dunno what the fuck we're doin."

"Whadda ya mean?"

"What's the fuckin plan?"

He shrugged, surprised she would think he had one. It was just like a woman to expect a man to have everything planned out, no matter how batshit crazy things became. He looked down at his shoes and shook his head.

Leslie couldn't look at him either. "There ain't no, plan, is there, Chucky? We're just holed up in here waitin 'round to die, like that old song says."

"Don't be so dramatic."

"Fuck you, man. Ya gonna tell me I'm wrong? The fuckin world's collapsing out there. Even the ones who ain't screamers are goin nuts—like Nishant, shootin at us. Ya just know people are takin advantage of all this. All the cops are busy, so no cops means more than looting. It means rapes and beat downs—even murders; whatever cruel shit people wanna do to each other is free now. No charge."

"You make it sound kinda fun."

She scoffed. "That supposed to be funny? 'Cause I ain't laughin. That friend of yours don't have *a face*. Any one of us could turn into a screamer at any moment. It might be a virus and having us all packed in here makes it like a fuckin Petri dish. And I don't even *know* these people. I just met them tonight and now they're all in my fuckin home. Why? For how long?"

He put his hands on her shoulders, rubbing them gently, showing affection despite his natural declination to do so. Hopefully it would calm her down enough that he could drink in peace. The last thing he needed was Leslie or the others to become more hysterical than they already were. He knew their reaction to this was justified, but he was too emotionless to share their stress.

"Okay," he said. "Just settle down. As long as the madness is *outside* the apartment, we're safe, or at least as safe as we can hope to be. Have a few drinks. Let's get loose and screw."

Leslie took another sip. "Just fuckin ain't enough. If we're gonna die, I wanna go out big."

He kissed her ear the way she liked. "What'd ya have in mind?"

But he already knew.

"I wanna be full, Chucky. Fuller than I've ever been before. I wanna be completely fuckin *full* when I leave this earth."

CHAPTER FOURTEEN

BECAUSE THE GIRL hadn't been conditioned enough to be veal, the man told the boy just to carve out her shoulder clogs and thighs, remove her buttocks and budding breasts, and process the tougher meat in the grinder after stripping off the flesh, which would be dried and made into jerky. There was still a good amount of meat on her to be dressed, but it was a long process and it had already been a long day. The boy had permission to finish the butchering tomorrow.

Looking down at the steel tray, he grinded the meat for a third time, giving it the ideal leanness while leaving just enough fat for it to maintain flavor. He pushed the bar down into the shaft, making sure the meat wouldn't stick in the spout and cook from the heat. The spout dribbled as the chuck sluiced through the grate and plopped into the bucket, and when it was full he put the lid on and brought it to the coffin-sized freezer where the bulk of the veal chops and grinds were packaged for delivery. He wiped his forehead with the back of his arm. The remainder of the carcass would have to be condensed if it were going to fit in the freezer.

Handling the woman's corpse this way didn't faze him. He'd been grinding human remains so long now it was second nature, and the man had taught him to butcher a carcass years ago. What had perturbed him, at least initially, was doing the killing. Even when he'd decided he wanted to do it and had been excited by zapping the young girl, making her shriek, when it came down to actually slaughtering her, the hunting knife had shook in his hand. It felt suddenly too bulky and heavy for him, despite having used it hundreds of times.

"Maybe you'd rather just shoot her?" the man had said.

The boy was offended. "Nah, I can do it."

"It weren't no dig, kid. I shot my first, 'member?"

The boy didn't reply.

When he'd killed her, his eyes had stayed on the girl, willing himself to see through the tight fear on her face and into the valley of wonders beneath it, a blood-soaked path guiding him to maturity. He was realizing it was not the act of killing that would make him a man. He had to force himself to become a man if he were going to kill in the first place. It was the chicken or the egg (which came first?) an open-ended riddle. This girl's death by his hand was a gateway, there was no doubt about that, but it was not this knife that was the key, it was the boy himself.

"Please . . . " she'd whimpered.

That's when the boy had come at her. How dare she beg for her life? It was asking him to stay a child forever, to never be anything more than a minion, a troll. The audacity of this made his teeth grind. He lunged. Still in her constraints, there was nowhere for his victim to run, no way to fight as he grabbed her by the hair, tilting her head back with such force most of the hair was ripped from the roots, producing small bubbles of blood. The sight of them made his heart accelerate. His loins pulsed. He stopped breathing, his body becoming one flexed muscle, every inch of him rigid and roiling with the incredible epiphany that he was truly alive. The walls of the slaughter shack seemed to vibrate, the intense summer heat trapped inside, burning his lungs with every breath and pushing sweat out of his pores just as the beads of blood had pushed their way out of the girl's scalp. He stared down at the veins throbbing in her throat. Her face was pinched into a ball, eyes closed, lashes wet. The boy could not stand for her to be blind in this glorious moment. She had to share the magic him.

"Open your eyes," he'd said then, gently as her mother may have spoken long before she was bound and gagged in the corner, watching in abject horror. "Open . . . your . . . eyes."

The girl's eyelids fluttered open, the sclera bloodshot, pupils turned to pinpoints. But she wouldn't look at him. He told her more firmly to do so, and when she complied she urinated a bit, her entire body shaking as if she were being electrocuted. But the time for the prod had passed. It wasn't enough now. With their eyes locked, the boy moved so swiftly the girl didn't respond to what was happening.

THEY ALL DIED SCREAMING

The knife slid into her neck, steel teeth ripping the jugular, and the warmth of blood covered the boy's hands, washing him, freeing him. He pulled to the right, exposing the inside of her throat as her mother screamed behind her gag, kicking and writhing and slamming the back of her head into the wall. Now the boy's hands trembled not from adrenaline, but from sweet delight. He had opened the girl up for her life force to escape. He had taken all she had to offer the world in two simple flicks of a blade. With a mere twist of his hand a basic, everyday tool had snuffed out a life. Moments ago this was a living thing. Now she was only meat. It was exhilarating, empowering. And as if to emphasize his ascent into manhood, the boy spontaneously came in his pants.

The man had never been so proud. He didn't even have to say so. It was in the gleam in his eye and the way he looked at the boy just a little longer whenever he smiled. Nothing else could have bonded them the way his passage into adulthood had. The boy felt as if he finally understood something the man had been trying to teach him from the beginning, some unspoken wisdom handed down through generations of men.

That night they ate a celebratory dinner of eggplant parm and tomato sauce, with sides of carrots and peas from the garden. Being vegetarians, fresh produce was their mainstay, and one of the ways the farm brought in income. Local produce never failed to sell at the farmer's market. The boy had taken it upon himself to start growing new additions to the man's staple veggies and fruits. In anticipation of the boy's birthday, the man had brought home a cake from the supermarket. Having not eaten one since coming to the farm, the boy devoured two huge slices, smiling with frosting pooling in the corners of his mouth. Over the next four days, the boy ate a piece for dessert every night, surprised the man allowed it. As the week went on, he noticed he wasn't being told what to eat, he was being asked what he was in the mood for. He and the man actually had discussions about dinnertime. Having a say made being an adult sink in a little deeper, as did the additional benefits of being able to watch or read whatever he wanted, whenever he wanted, as long as the chores were done and the pigs were tended to. He and the man talked and joked and played board games. He taught the boy poker and blackjack and they bet using bottle caps. Their kinship deepened, strengthening the sense of family.

The man bought him boys' clothes from the Goodwill, clothes that actually fit his body instead of the tight jeans and blouses they pilfered from the veal. By the end of August, the boy was accompanying the man on his trips into town. They picked out chips and sodas at the drug store and the boy was allowed to check out books at the library, feeling too old for mere comics. He was given a small allowance he could spend at the arcade while the man made the meat deliveries to local butcher shops, diners and the family-owned grocery. The boy learned just how popular the veal was to these merchants, how customers insisted the taste could not be beat. Other cuts the man sold as duck, rabbit and other specialty meats not as commonly eaten as beef and chicken, which people could easier detect a taste difference. Though the man didn't eat meat now, he'd grown up on it, and had taste-tested their human veal and other products to compare their flavor and texture, deciding what they could be passed off as. At one time, the man had slaughtered pigs and chickens and had been inspected by the USDA, granting him a license allowing him to sell to retail outfits as long as he stayed in compliance. Once certified, the man started making his own illegal label marks to pass the human meat off as inspected. He had told the boy of custom exempt processing, which allowed individuals to consume whatever they hunt. He felt the government had no business telling people what they could and couldn't eat. And the town was a close-knit community with a small population. Everyone supported local farmers like him. The town was so small in fact that the man never picked up live veal there.

"Ya gotta go out to bigger, surrounding towns. Sometimes even into the city. Missin girl cases are less likely to be linked to one kidnapper if ya space 'em out."

The boy was gaining new wisdom, what the man called "street smarts". He was being taught social skills, which was tough given all the years talking with only the man, the veal and the pigs, the latter of which had little to say. Mostly he just observed how the man dealt with others in town and emulated that, smiling even when he felt no real desire to, saying hello and introducing himself as the man's nephew. The only thing he was not allowed to talk about was the source of the meat.

"Other people wouldn't understand what we do," the man explained. "They'd stop us—then *we'd* be the ones in cages. Besides, lots of people keep their recipes in the family."

The boy didn't understand why people would be against something as simple as raising and slaughtering veal, especially considering they all ate it. But the man had always warned him of the hypocrisy and low moral character of carnivores. So the boy let him explain the meat to his buyers. He just backed the man up, and folks seemed happy with that. Still, he was aware of his own awkwardness. He could see it reflected in the eyes of others, particularly other males, who were the strangest people for the boy to encounter, having not seen any other than the man for many years now.

"You'll get the hang of it," the man assured as they drove home one afternoon. "Shit, I don't like talkin to people none. Don't particularly like 'em. But ya gotta fake it till make it, young man. Gotta act like yer happy to see 'em and ya care what they gotta say. Makes yer time with 'em easier and keeps their noses outta your trash, if ya get my meanin."

He put his hand on the boy's shoulder and then slid his arm around him, scooting him closer across the seat. He was sweating from the summer heat, but the boy didn't mind that at all. The only person he loved was embracing him. His heart was bursting.

The man flashed his rotten teeth smile. "The only human being I enjoy talkin to anymore is you, buddy. You're my best friend, my family."

The boy put his head into the crook of the man's arm. The feeling was more than mutual.

CHAPTER FIFTEEN

THE OTHERS HAD turned on the television. Chuck joined Barman and Shitty in watching the footage of houses engulfed in smoke, people jumping out of high-rise windows, and bodies in the streets, all blurred for sensitivity. The legend on the bottom of the screen read: WORLD IN CHAOS. A scrolling legend below it fed information rapidly: *mandatory quarantine—president instates martial law—all travel banned—stay in your homes—do not attempt to evacuate—all emergency lines busy—millions without power—The Scream declared a fatal pandemic.*

The news pundit was uselessly describing the carnage on the screen. Barman changed the station. It was another news report. All regular programming had been switched to constant coverage, exactly like they had following the 9/11 terror attack. A newswoman rattled off places with the largest confirmed cases of infection. A white map of North America was on a window screen next to her, showing the pattern, the color red revealing the most dangerous zones. The majority of the northern United States were more red than white, Alaska and the entire country of Canada the color of blood.

When it went to commercial, Barman turned it to another network. On the program, two polished anchors were interviewing an older man in a suit with frazzled, white hair. Each of them were broadcasting from different locations, creating a split-screen conference. The legend read: TOP SCIENTISTS BLAME GLOBAL WARMING FOR SCREAM OUTBREAK.

The female anchor said, "So, your professional opinion is that greenhouse gases have caused The Scream?"

The older man nodded. "In a manner of speaking. The theory is extreme temperatures caused by the climate crisis have been melting

95

permafrost soils containing viruses that have lain dormant for several millennia. After thousands of years, these viruses have been released by the thawed ice."

The male newsperson jutted in, "But isn't permafrost supposed to be permanent? Isn't that the whole meaning of the term?"

"It *was* permanent when the term was coined. No one predicted weather patterns would change as drastically as they have over the last three decades."

"So," the female anchor said, "these ancient viruses can actually come back to life?"

"Some can, Tina. And it's already happened. Back in the summer of 2016, in a Siberian tundra in the Arctic Circle, a young boy died and some twenty people were hospitalized after an infection of anthrax. You see, anthrax forms spores, which can survive being frozen for more than a century, and the theory is that over seventy years ago a reindeer infected with anthrax died and its frozen carcass became buried under permafrost. Then, during the unprecedented heat wave of 2016, the deer thawed out, releasing the anthrax into the soil and water nearby. Thousands of reindeer became infected, leading to human contagion."

The male anchor leaned back, his face gone smug. "But modern medicine was able to kill the anthrax off and stop the spreading of it."

"Yes, but—"

"See, that's what I've been saying. In this day and age, America can heal itself. It's just a matter of time. Our great nation has developed antibiotics and medicines to fight every disease known to man."

"Well, *modern* viruses. And not even all of them. Humans have evolved and developed natural immunities to many of the viruses that killed our ancestors, but bacteria always finds new ways to adapt; new, more successful methods of infecting us."

The female anchor, Tina, said, "Professor Stanley, you stressed *modern* viruses. Why?"

"Because some of the bacteria under the permafrost might be kinds we've never encountered before. Scientists have already discovered RNA from the Spanish flu of 1918 in corpses buried in Alaska's frozen tundra. Bubonic plague, smallpox and other deadly viruses are likely buried in the Arctic Circle too, and natural antibiotic resistance is so consistent that many of these emerging bacteria already have it. In the past months, we've seen a disintegration of permafrost that surpassed our previous fears. And The Scream virus has been tracked moving from north to south in all parts of the world, not just North America."

"Come, on, professor," the male newsperson balked, "isn't this global warming hysteria a little too convenient for the extreme left? There's no evidence that The Scream is linked to a super virus that's come out of the ice like some sci-fi movie monster."

"But we believe it's probable. Many scientists have been warning of this exact danger for years now. This isn't the time for partisan politics about the climate crisis. And it's not just global warming causing this anyway. Being mined for gold and drilled for oil is hurting parts of the world under permafrost, exposing them. I'm a man of science and I'm giving you scientific fact—"

"Or is it liberal propa—"

"Excuse me, Shawn, but I'm talking. Scientists, not politicians, have been able to revive bacterium that is eight-million-years old. And anthrax isn't alone in staying potent after freezing. Even some fungi can last a long time frozen. We've already discovered giant viruses one hundred feet underground in coastal tundras."

Tina asked, "What is a *giant virus*?"

"One so large it can be seen under a regular microscope. They're extremely resilient, almost impossible to break. It's believed that The Scream is a giant virus. It's been speculated that what we're seeing is a direct result of this year's unprecedented polar ice catastrophe, that The Scream was a virus from a long extinct hominin species, possibly even Neanderthals or Denisovans. They both settled in Siberia and were positively loaded with viral diseases."

Shawn, the male pundit, crossed his arms. "Then why don't we have a record of The Scream virus?"

"Neanderthals didn't leave good records of anything, Shawn. They pre-date documented history; hence the term *pre-historic man*. If thousands or even millions of them died from The Scream or a similar variant, how would they have warned us?"

Shawn had no retort.

97

Tina said, "There are other concerns as well. Some biologists are saying The Scream may be spreading so quickly because it might be transmittable via parasites, namely mosquitoes. What are your thoughts on that?"

Stanley nodded. "This too comes back to the environmental crisis. Constant warm weather is a breeding ground for mosquitoes. Then there are ticks, birds, rats. We've already seen a drastic increase in reported cases of dengue fever, chikungunya, and The West Nile virus, all spread by mosquitoes and other such parasites. Diseases which were once restricted to tropical and jungle parts of the word are now turning up all across the globe."

Shawn said, "But The Scream is moving north to south."

"You're missing the point here. Once the virus reaches warmer and more densely populated areas, it spreads faster and more effectively. We must—"

Breaking news abruptly interrupted the show. A helicopter view of the nation's capital engulfed by flames, a newsman narrating, informing viewers that Washington D.C. had devolved into a full-scale riot. The White House had been evacuated after secret service men reportedly began screaming and firing upon the people inside, namely the top leaders of the country.

"Ain't that a kick in the balls?" Barman said. "They tell us not to evacuate, and then that's exactly what they do when the shit hits the fan in their backyard."

Shitty laughed at the images. "Fuck 'em. Hope every democrat and republican in D.C. gets set afire. Eat the rich, that's what I always says."

Chuck looked at Barman. "You believe that stuff about viruses in the ice?"

Barman put his face into his hands and then ran them over his scalp, hanging his head. "The Anthropocene apocalypse. I don't disbelieve it. But if it is some kind of super virus, like the man said, it's going to take time to develop a cure, and time is something the world is in short supply of."

Shitty turned toward him. "What 'n hell's Anthropocene?"

"The period we're in now, when human beings have the ultimate influence over Mother Nature, and all we've done is fuck her in the ass and shoot cum in her eye."

Chuck looked to Angel, the reason he'd come out of the bedroom in the first place. She was sitting in the far corner of the room, knees drawn up to her chest as she bit her nails to nubs. He approached her gingerly.

"Want some ketchup for them fingers?"

Embarrassed, she tucked the hand away. "Shut up."

Chuck ushered Angel into the kitchen so they could talk in private. Her eyes went low, suspicious. Barman watched them from the sofa, briefly curious, then returned to sorting the weapons they'd gathered.

Kitchen knives. A cigarette lighter and some cans of hairspray. A broom, a hammer and a big pair of scissors. Empty liquor bottles and lighter fluid. Some bug spray. A folding chair.

Chuck kept his voice low. "How much ya charge?"

Angel's eyebrows drew close together. "You fuckin serious? You're askin me that *now*?"

"Why not?"

"Um, *hello*? The whole world is goin to shit. Aint'cha seen the TV?"

"All the more reason to have a good time while we still can."

"You must be nuts."

"Arguably."

"Some caveman virus is killin everybody and you want a piece of ass? What about your girlfriend?"

"Actually, she's in on this too. It's more for her than me."

"Wait . . . she's a dyke?"

"Nah. She's never been with a chick before, but she's not opposed to it. We need more people for what we wanna do."

"A threesome."

"Not exactly."

Angel shook her head. "Look, I don't wanna be part of some—"

"Don't gimmie that. You're a dockside whore. You've done worse things than what we could come up with."

"Gee, way to get me to do it, asshole."

"Just tell me how much."

"It don't matter. I'm not doin no work right now. I'm too freaked out, alright?"

Chuck crossed his arms. "Okay, then, but what about this—

you're in Leslie's place, honey. We're givin you shelter, food, protection. What the fuck ya givin us?"

Angels' face paled. "So, you sayin I *owe* you a fuck?"

"Like the old sayin goes, put out or get out."

Though tears were brewing in Angel's eyes, she blinked them away before they could fall. Chuck saw in her a familiar defeat, a failure of wills she'd experienced before, probably multiple times. This shell of a woman was constructed from the pieces of a broken girl, a wilting rose having grown out of a life of pure fertilizer. It was not hard to imagine the sort of things she'd been through to lead her to turning tricks, but it was difficult for Chuck to sympathize. He hadn't had a normal upbringing either and the years had not been kind. Chuck was a firm believer in taking what you need when you can get it, no matter whose feelings got hurt. Angel was a prostitute he barely knew. Her happiness was not as important to him as Leslie's was. He hated to admit he'd developed feelings toward someone, but he wanted Leslie to achieve the sense of fullness she'd long been searching for, or at least go out trying if this was humanity's final days.

"Alright," Angel said. "Whatcha want me to—?"

Frantic knocking at the door startled them.

"Fuck!" Angel said, tucking her body into his.

Leslie came out of the bedroom and joined Chuck on his way to the door with the others. Barman was on his feet, a butcher knife clutched in his hand. Shitty hopped down from the love seat and onto his rolling cart. Chuck also sprung into defensive action, raising the folding chair like a pro wrestler after handing Leslie the broom. Angel remained in the kitchen, cowering, watching from behind the counter. Eugene remained lifeless. No one spoke as another knock came, then another, each coming faster than the last.

"Chuck, you in there?" a young voice cried. "It's me, Brittany! Please, let us in! Chuck? Miss Leslie?"

Recognizing the voice, Chuck approached the door. "Us? Who's out there with you?"

Another female spoke. "Keisha."

"Who?"

"Keisha. You were there when my husband . . . when he jumped down the stairs."

Chuck ran his hand from his forehead to his mouth. Could they afford two more people, two more mouths to eat their food and smoke their cigarettes and drink their liquor? It seemed like a dog turd of an idea. He looked to Leslie. She was glowering, clearly having the same thoughts.

Barman whispered. "Friends of yours?"

"No," Leslie answered for Chuck. "Just neighbors."

"Whadda we do?" Shitty asked.

Leslie looked away. "Nothin."

"Nothing?" Barman asked her. "They sound terrified."

"Of course they do. Who here isn't?"

Shitty gazed up at her. "Maybe we should consider—"

The knocking grew more feverish. There were screams, but they didn't belong to the women behind the door. The hall reverberated with the sound of fast, stomping feet and Chuck felt Leslie's hand tense around his arm.

He put down the chair and opened the door. The others stepped back as the newcomers tumbled into the room, tears in their eyes and blood spattered across their clothes. Keisha was holding a dripping box cutter. Brittany was limping. Chuck was slamming the door just as the pursuing screamers crashed into the sliver of space between the door jam. A scrawny arm pushed through, grabbing at Chuck's wrist, and when he took his hands off the door to fight his attacker, another screamer forced it open. That's when Chuck recognized them as the two little fuckers who were always running up and down the halls making noise. Two jaundiced boys, both about thirteen years old.

But for all the noise they'd made before, now they were absolutely deafening. Their mouths were unhinged, tongues black, teeth glistening in banshee shrieks. The blonde boy who'd grabbed at Chuck was wearing a Superman t-shirt so badly ripped it was halfway off one shoulder, revealing the welts and bruises on his skinny frame. The boy who'd forced the door open was taller with dark hair. One of the lenses of his glasses was shattered, the eye behind it bloody and swelled shut.

As Chuck threw Superman into the wall, Barman came at Glasses with the knife, slicing the kid's forehead open. The flesh separated easily, blood dribbling into the kid's one good eye. Superman bounced back at Chuck, but by then he'd picked up the folding chair. He smashed it across the kid's face. When he drew it back, a string of bloody tissue ran from Superman's head to the back of the chair, but the boy didn't seem fazed even as his nose gushed red. Glasses came at Shitty instead of Barman, arms flailing, landing a few blows to the top of his head. Shitty grunted as he punched the kid's thighs and Barman returned with the butcher knife, grabbed the kid by the hair, and sent the blade deep into his stomach. The kid collapsed, slamming his face into the end table. As he rolled to the floor, blood and teeth spilled out of his mouth. Still, he tried to scream.

"Kill the prick!" Shitty shouted.

Barman sat on the kid and stabbed him repeatedly, the blade sliding in and out of the screamer's back, sometimes failing to enter when it was bounced off ribs. The folding chair rose above Chuck's head and, in a downward swoop, connected with the top of Superman's head. There was a sound like a firecracker hitting a brick wall. As the kid fell forward, he grabbed at Chuck's shirt, throwing him off balance. Leslie shouted his name and ran up and punted Superman in the balls. The kid curled inward, eyes bulging out of his skull, veins standing out at his scrawny neck. But he kept on screaming.

"Fuck you too!" Leslie screamed back.

She snatched the chair, opened it, and slung it over the boy so the horizontal bar across the back legs came down upon his throat. She sat on it backwards, choking him with her body weight. His scream became a wheeze. He was pinioned, and though he pawed at Leslie's feet he couldn't do any damage. Leslie leaned forward, applying more pressure.

Shitty roared. "Crush that little fucker!"

The others watched on as Leslie descended upon the boy's throat, shifting his Adam's apple. Her face pinched, the lines always showing her age when she was angry. In those wrinkles Chuck saw a tight knot of grief, a wounded heart that couldn't possibly heal. That grief often came out in drunken tantrums. Today it was white-hot rage. But she was interrupted just as she was about to crush the boy's trachea completely.

"Wait!" Eugene said, holding out his hands.

In the chaos, no one had noticed him rising from the couch.

When he spoke, the holes in his cheeks stretched and Chuck could see the molars behind them, but his face was only dribbling now, not gushing as it had been before. The flesh was singed, mangled, a crusting ruin.

"Jesus," Barman said, staring at him.

"Don't kill the kid," Eugene said. "Not yet."

"The fuck for?" Leslie asked.

"Maybe we can, like, study him. Find out what's really causing all this."

Chuck's brow furrowed. "I thought you'd be the first one to wanna get 'em outta here, them bein infected and all."

"Well . . . after what you all said about that other kid we saw . . . "

Barman said, "I know I said we can't just kill every screamer, but what else can we do in this situation?"

Chuck stared at Eugene. "Ain't ya worried we'll catch it from them?"

"Look, man," Eugene said. "I just woke up with my face burning. It's all sticky! I mean . . . *fuck*! What's left to be scared of once your face's been blown off? Things are just gonna keep getting worse out there if somebody doesn't figure out this thing."

"The fuck we know 'bout diseases?" Leslie asked. "We wouldn't know the first thing 'bout studyin these lunatics and besides, I don't want 'em in my apartment."

"I know it's dangerous, but maybe it could give us some answers."

"Bull-fuckin-shit."

Leslie leaned forward and jerked her body, bouncing in the chair. Superman's face purpled, chest heaving, little clicking sounds coming out of his mouth.

"Wait . . . " Eugene said.

With one final bounce, Leslie landed hard in the seat. There was a loud snap as Superman's neck broke. The pressure caused one of his bulging eyes to pop from its socket, and it hung from the connective tissue upon his upper cheek like a dead snail. Yellow tears of pus spewed from it, making his peach fuzz glisten. And as the group looked down at this deceased teen, they breathed a little easier, but Chuck felt something thick and black spread through them all, a sense that somehow, they were even worse off than they'd been before.

CHAPTER SIXTEEN

HE FIRST NOTICED the wound when the man was changing out of his muddy slacks into the sweatpants he wore around the house. Catching a glimpse of the man's bare legs, the boy spotted the ring of holes punched in his calf, the swelling flesh already purple and scaly.

"What happened?"

"Ah, nothin. One of the hogs done bit me."

"Mr. Buster?"

The man chuckled. "Yep, you know it. He's an ornery sum-bitch, ain't he?"

At the time the boy laughed, but by the end of the day it wasn't so funny. The man had wrapped the bite up in an old t-shirt but had to remove it because it was irritating the wound. Soon he couldn't even wear pants because the pain of the material grazing his leg was too excruciating, and despite the cool, autumn weather, he wore shorts while working outside and just underpants around the house. He didn't even bathe because the water stung his bad leg no matter the temperature. And it looked horrible, having inflamed from purple to a vicious, scarlet red. The teeth marks had deepened and were much more frightening holes than they'd been initially. Blisters seemed to orbit around them, fizzing and hissing when the man picked at them.

"Ain't there nothin we can do for it?" the boy asked.

"Fixin too."

The man retrieved his chosen remedy from the cupboard, a bottle of Wild Turkey. He'd been sipping on the bourbon between spells of nausea and vomiting, touching it up with Pepto Bismol. The boy didn't know much about medicine but figured there had to be something better than just propping up the leg and getting drunk to kill the pain. But whenever he suggested going to see someone, the man adamantly refused.

"Can't trust doctors, kid. They don't make money fixin ya, they make it by keepin ya sick, keepin ya comin to 'em over and over."

Soon the boy's workload on the farm nearly doubled, the man unable to take care of his share of the chores. Mostly he handled the business end of things by going into town, but this became difficult too, it being his right leg that was injured, making it difficult for him to use the gas and brake pedals. The man had already been teaching the boy to drive the truck, but now the lessons became a high priority. At fourteen he was still too young to get his learner's permit, but he looked old enough to drive so the man let him take the truck into town, making deliveries alone because the man was too sick and in pain. Now the boy *had* to start talking about the meat to the locals. As for details, he only repeated lines he and the man rehearsed. When he was asked anything that could only be answered by going off script, he just played dumb and told the buyers they'd have to ask his uncle.

"Don't go tellin 'em the truth," the man advised. "First of all, they ain't earned it from us. Second of all, I don't want people thinkin ill of our livestock. Folks already think pigs ain't nothin but dumb animals. We can't give 'em any fool reason to think they're dangerous. So if'n they wanna know what's goin on with me ya just tell 'em I done broke my leg fallin off a ladder. Let 'em think I'm a klutz. Don't matter. Won't hurt business none."

"Okay then. That's what I'll do."

The tears in the man's eyes shocked the boy. "Never let 'em think ill of our pigs; especially not my sweet Polly girl."

"Polly ain't done nothin. T'was Mr. Buster that done bit ya."

"Well, I don't want nobody thinkin bad of Buster neither! He's a good ol' boy. He's just cranky 'cause he's eighteen now. We all get cranky like that when we get old and gray. Even my Mama—an *angel* who done fed me from her own teat long as she could give milk— even she turned into a big ol' witch when she got old. Ain't nothin wrong with Mr. Buster. And my leg's gonna heal up just fine. Just takes time."

But time only made it worse.

Three days later the entire leg was discolored, and the bite holes had opened wider until they joined and became a single, concave lesion. At least two pounds of flesh and sinew festered off. It was as if invisible maggots were feasting upon him every day, but despite this deterioration, despite his rising fever and chronic fatigue, the man still refused treatment.

"Ya need to go to the hospital," the boy said, nearly choking on the words.

"I keep tellin ya not to worry. I'll be fine."

"Well, I am worried! You oughta be too! When I's up at the library I looked at pictures of skin conditions in one of them medical books, and I saw folks whose bodies looked just like yours."

The man turned away, drinking his whiskey straight from the bottle, his feet up in the reclining chair. He said nothing.

"I think ya got the same thing as them. It's an infection called *necrotizing fasciitis.*"

The man scoffed. "Well, ain't them some fancy words. All that readin's makin ya a little genius there, huh?"

He ignored the jab. "It eats your body away. Your tissue is basically dyin. Ya got bit by Buster and his mouth was all dirty, right? And ya kept workin out there in the shit and piss and mud. And ya was gettin blood and other stuff on ya from preppin the veal. Who knows what all's in that wound. And ya ain't been washin it or puttin on ointments—"

"Hurts too much!"

"—so it's just gettin worse. It's *spreadin*! The other effects are dizziness, pukin, fever. Ya got all of 'em. That book says if ya don't get a doctor to fix it . . . " The boy sniffled, a lump filling his throat. " . . . you're gonna die."

The man took a deep breath, still staring at the TV though the set was turned off, his shadowy reflection gazing back at him from the dead screen. The only sound in the house was the choked tears of the boy. The footrest lowered. The man took a heavy swig off the bourbon and stood up, leaning on his good leg.

"I ain't gonna die, son."

But the boy knew the man was wrong, and that was scary in and of itself. He'd grown up believing the man had all the answers. That first year, it had been drilled into his head to never question him. The man had long been the boy's only source for new information, his only guide. Nearly everything the boy knew he credited to the man. But now, looking at the man's strained stance and mutilated calf, the boy realized he knew something the man didn't. He was right and the man was wrong. It left him feeling lost and godless, somehow abandoned.

"Anything," the veal said again.

The boy stared into her eyes, detecting no trickery there, only wild desperation. The eyes were powder blue and emphasized by her long, blonde hair and pale skin, flesh made all the more pale by the merciless pressure that comes with unbridled fear. She was chained to the floor just like all the ones who'd come before her, but not with the same brutal restrictions. Now that the man was incapacitated, the boy decided how to handle the veal, and while he knew the extra length of her chains wasn't ideal for keeping the meat soft and tender, he'd given her the slack in an effort to make her like him.

"Anything you want," she whimpered.

She'd told him she was seventeen. It had come out during one of the many conversations they'd had over the past two weeks. She was the last veal the man had brought home before being crippled by his infection, making it impossible for him to go hunting. Being in such agony, the man was always drunk now, making him poor company and no help around the farm. The boy had grown bored and restless without his companionship. This was one of the reasons he'd given in to the veal's efforts to talk to him, but not the only one.

She was pretty.

As he'd hit puberty, he'd begun to look at the veals' bodies in a different way. They were not just steaks and chops to him anymore, but objects of a more mysterious desire, something tantalizing and confounding at once. And they were always nude and pinned to the ground, their helplessness an attractive lure, underscoring that he was in charge and could do with these fragile creatures whatever he wished. But so far, he hadn't approached them the way the man approached Polly, even when his penis stiffened as he wiped the veal with a rag after they'd peed. He dreamed about the veal, and woke with his underpants sticky, but he simply didn't know how to go

107

about sex. He had a sense of where he was supposed to put his penis, but not how it went in or what to do once it was there. Library books only explained so much about mating. The only thing he knew for sure was he wanted it, badly.

"Please," the veal said. "I'll do anything you want if you'll just let me go."

The boy looked down at her from his stool. She was so earnest, further beautified by integrity. Those pleading eyes, so alluring in their creamy azure, so pure and bright with the very life she was bargaining for. The boy ogled her. The curve where her hips began, the plush of her small breasts, her face like a cherub's, lips like bubblegum.

He stood. "Do ya know how to mate?"

He thought he saw a twitch in the veal's face, but it was gone the moment he detected it. She smiled, obviously forced, but all that mattered to the boy was he wanted to believe it.

"You mean sex?" she asked, more statement than question

The boy nodded. "Ya said anythin I want."

"I know. It's okay. We can do that. Whatever you want, okay. Just don't hurt me."

If he wanted to do that, he would be going at her with the electric prod. But it wasn't this veal's pain he was enticed by, though inflicting it on others had given he and the man many moments of joy and laughter.

"What exactly do you want me to do?" the veal asked, no longer looking him in the eye.

"Teach me sex."

She fell silent, then said, "You have to open the cage."

"I know that." He took the keys from the clip at his belt and popped the latch on the crate. The veal gave him a sad little smile, but he didn't give one back. "I'll release ya from the floor, but your cuffs have to stay on."

He helped her scoot across the cage and onto the molding planks of the pen. She gazed at the ceiling as if she were seeing the world for the first time and the boy put his hands into her armpits, sliding her the rest of the way. With her stretched out like this, the boy could better take in the sight of the veal's body. Warmth filled his loins as he ran his fingertips up the inside of her thigh, both he and the veal breaking out in goose bumps, but for different reasons. He journeyed further, stroking her belly and cupping her breasts with both hands. When he brought his fingers to the pink opening between her legs she shivered with a barely audible gasp. He wasn't sure if it had felt good or bad to her, but his curiosity kept him pressing, prodding. Soon his thumb was inside the moist meat of her hole. He plunged it in and out, like popping a cheek.

"Okay," the veal said. "You need to take off your pants."

The boy grinned. He could feel his heart accelerating. He undid his belt and dropped his jeans and underwear to the floor, then got to his knees beside her. When she reached to his groin with chains and cuffs jangling, the boy instinctively moved back.

"It's alright," she assured him.

The veal reached out again. This time he let her take him in her hands. The boy shuddered as she started stroking, making him grow bigger. His entire body went rigid in unison, pleasure tightening every muscle. When she withdrew her hand, he opened his eyes, having not even realized he'd closed them.

"The chains at my feet," she said.

"Huh?"

"You have to take the cuffs off my ankles. That way I can . . . you know . . . spread my legs. You won't be able to . . . to get in me if I can't open them."

The boy bit his bottom lip. The man had always warned him about the dangers of giving veal even the slightest bit of freedom, and this one had already been given far too much. But his dick was twitching, testicles drawn high and tight, hormones assuring him everything would be alright, that he was the one in charge here. The boy was a man now. And in this world, men had all the control. He undid the cuff of just one of her ankles, watching her, waiting for her to make a frenzied dash. But she remained on the floor, looking up at him with the eyes of a ghost. He touched the inside of her thigh and her legs spread open, warm and inviting. She stank so good. The veal took his erection in her hands again, caressing him, guiding him forward, inching him closer, and just as the tip of his penis touched her fleshy opening, her palm went under his crotch and she squeezed tight, her fingernails piercing his scrotum as she crushed his testicles.

The boy inhaled in a backwards scream. Pain beyond comprehension ached through every inch of him. Stars clouded his vision. Bile pooled in the back of his throat and his body was instantly useless, too weak to counterattack. He curled inward but the veal kept twisting his scrotum, nails drawing blood as they sank deeper. As the boy grew faint the veal shoved him off of her, rolling him to one side where he quivered like a newborn. He heard her feet, dragging the chain behind her. Her breathing was panicked and the sound carried out and away as she swung the door wide and tumbled out into the dirt. The sudden fall made her scream, but as the boy rolled over she got back up, running naked in the night without any sense of where she was. She started toward the house but quickly retreated, obviously remembering. The boy struggled to get to his knees. His pants were around his ankles, confining him the way the veal had been before he'd stupidly undone her shackles. If he could just let the man know what had happened, if he could just make enough noise.

But he didn't have to. The girl's scream was all it took.

There was a sudden crack like a tree snapping in half. The sound echoed through the black stillness. When the boy looked up at the house, he saw a second muzzle flash from the window, another *crack*, then heard the veal hit the ground with the same impact of a slab of meat hitting the chopping block.

The man had dropped her. She lay in the weeds by the side of the path, quaking, sobbing. Her hands, still cuffed, were high at her chest in an attempt to hold in the blood pouring where the breast met the shoulder. The hole was gorged, revealing itself as an exit wound. The man had shot her in the back and the bullet passed through her petite torso.

"Kid!" the man yelled from inside the house. "Chain that lil' bitch!"

Still woozy but fearing the consequences if he didn't comply, the boy leaned on the wall and dragged himself up along with his pants. His legs felt numb, so he rolled his hips to move them, then reached for the broom in the corner and used it as a walking stick as he exited the pen.

"Get that cunt!" the man said. "Get her 'fore she runs again."

But the girl wasn't going anywhere. She shook in the dirt like an ant being fried by a beam of sunlight. The boy wondered if it was the pain that really paralyzed her or the fear of being shot again. He hoped it was a little bit of both. He'd never wanted anyone to suffer the way he wished it upon this veal right now. She'd hurt his body and his sense of manhood. Worst of all, she'd embarrassed him. How was he going to explain this? He could lie and say the cuff broke on its own, but he *never* lied to the man. It would be a breach of their bond, tainting what they had together. The man hadn't punished him physically in a very long time, but the boy would rather own up to his mistake and face the belt on his ass than risk fabricating a bullshit story and jeopardizing the love and acceptance he felt with the man now.

When he reached the girl, the boy lifted the broom above him then swung it wide, cracking her in the side of her face. The movement of her body caused her hands to drop, and he shoved the top end of the broomstick into the gaping wound her chest, digging it in as forcefully as she'd pulverized his testicles. She squealed as she got exactly what she deserved. He twisted the broom deeper, widening the new flesh cavity, amused by how she'd denied him entrance to one hole and now he was penetrating another. He imagined sticking his penis in the exit wound to mate with her bloodied tit instead of her lying brat's body. She batted at the broom and it exited her, so he kicked her in the stomach repeatedly, his crotch aching with each blow, then eased his way down and cuffed her ankles together again, leaving the chain with just enough slack so she could take baby steps toward the house. The man was waiting for them, the hunting rifle parting the curtains just enough to see the rotting hell of his face.

"Guess it's my fault too," the man said.

He sat across from the boy, who was on the couch with his head down, an ice pack on his naked crotch.

"I shoulda explained the birds n' the bees to ya," he continued. "After all, you're a man now. You're bound to get urges. But that still don't excuse lettin a piece of veal go free."

"I didn't let her go fr—"

"Ya let her free 'nuff to run. That's all the free she'd need to get outta here and maybe make it into town. Ya want that?"

"No, sir."

"That'd be the end of everythin for us, ya know."

"I know. I'm sorry. T'was just a mistake."

The man leaned forward to scratch at his scales. He found one blackened crater in his thigh and dug into it with his thumbnail, flaking away the dead skin.

"Well," he said, "what's done is done. And like I say, this is partly my fault. I just didn't think ya looked at the veal that way. But ya work hard—even harder now that I'm all laid up like this. I saddled ya with too much work and not enough fun, kid. I reckon ya deserve to have things your way from time to time. So if'n ya wanna poke one of these girlies now and then, well, I suppose it's okay by me."

The boy was able to breathe again.

The man pointed at him. "But there's a right way and a wrong way to go 'bout it."

"Yes, sir." The boy looked up and their eyes met. "Will ya teach me how to do it to 'em?"

The smile on the man's face was coy, even bashful, but the deterioration of his left cheek made the warm gesture grotesque.

"Bring that bitch into the room," he said. "Get, 'fore she dies on us."

CHAPTER SEVENTEEN

"WHAT DO WE do with them?"

Barman's question chilled the room. There was no regret in his voice. No emotion at all. It was a simple question, but one the group had no answer to. The fresh corpses of the preteens lay across the floor like sacrifices. They were still bleeding and Superman had pissed himself at the point of dying.

Chuck looked to Eugene. "Still wanna study 'em?"

He shook his head *no* and turned away from the bodies.

Barman said, "That professor on the TV mentioned rats. This damn city has been swarming with them lately. Maybe they're exacerbating the problem like they did with the black plague."

"That was cats," Brittany said from the corner. "People thought it was carried by rats, so everybody got themselves a cat, right? Only it was really the cats that carried the disease, which just made the whole thing spread faster."

Chuck said, "These two screamers were different from the others. They were coming for us, not each other."

"The disease is changing," Eugene said. "It's getting more advanced."

"Or maybe it affects each screamer differently."

Barman sighed. "Maybe lots of things."

"Is there a bathroom I can use?" Eugene asked. "I need to tend to my face. See how it is."

Barman said, "You don't want that. Trust me."

"Is it that bad?"

"Worse."

Leslie sat at the table, smoking as she poured herself a tumbler of vodka. Her cheeks were flushed and her brow was sweaty as if she'd been fucking.

"Can I get some of that?" Shitty asked.

She took one of the used glasses off the nearby kitchen counter and filled it. Shitty accepted with his usual dirty smile and the two of them drank, saying nothing, looking at nothing, eyes blank and lifeless. Angel was crying somewhere, heard but unseen. Keisha and Brittany, new to the group, stayed close to each other while giving the others distance. Keisha particularly looked distressed, sitting on the floor with her head hung.

"We gotta toss these dead bodies out," Chuck said.

Barman nodded. "We should be careful about contagion. Maybe wrap them in garbage bags. You guys have any gloves?"

Chuck looked to Leslie. Her voice was like broken chalk. "Got dishwashin gloves under the sink. And my winter gloves are somewhere. Dunno if they'll fit ya."

"Them dishwashin ones'll do," Chuck said.

He went to the kitchen, passing Angel who was staring off into space with her knees drawn up to her chest in a self-hug. It had made her too-snug dress hike up around her waist but she either didn't notice or didn't care. He retrieved the items and Chuck and Barman wrapped the corpses in the plastic bags, Barman moving the limbs because he wore the gloves. The others watched but offered no assistance. Clearly they were afraid.

"Now what?" Barman asked.

"Outside, I figure. As far away as possible."

"You want to drag these two through the hall and down the stairs? Fuck that."

"I was thinkin out the window. They're small. They oughta fit."

Barman smirked. "So they could fall down onto the sidewalk and splatter like water balloons?"

"So what if they do?"

Barman looked to the others to back him up. No one did.

"Chuck, we can't just turn into barbarians here. Just because things are chaotic out there doesn't mean we start tossing dead kids out of fourth story windows. We have to maintain some basic human decency."

Chuck waved his arms. "Seriously, where's this comin from all of a sudden? Ever since I've known ya it's been nothin but nihilism. Fuck people, fuck everything, let it all burn. Now all of a sudden human life has value?"

"Never said I was a nihilist, and sure as shit didn't say human life has value. I've never had much faith in the human race and, if anything, this whole screamer crisis has proven me right in that regard. But that doesn't mean I can't object to us losing our collective scruples."

Leslie laughed. "Scruples? You really usin that word to talk about *this* buncha lowlifes?" She gestured to the group. "Ya gotta *have* scruples in order to lose 'em."

"Shut up, you drunk bitch. You don't speak for us all."

"Don't call me a bitch!"

Keisha raised her head. "Maybe we oughta all calm down a little. I mean, we gots ta figure out hows we gonna deal with them screamin people."

Barman ignored her, still speaking to Leslie. "Just drink your booze and let me think."

Chuck noticed Leslie staring at him, as if she expected him to defend her honor and make Barman take back his words. When he didn't, she turned away and poured herself a refill. She belched in defiance.

"Look," Chuck told Barman, "it's either out the window or we gotta drag 'em all the way to the parkin lot. Who knows what other screamers are runnin 'round this place. Ya gotta stop thinkin of these two as kids. They're dead, man."

Barman nodded. "And we killed them."

"Had to."

"Oh, please. I'm not saying I regret it. I'm saying it because it could incriminate us. You may not see them as kids but the law sure will."

"The law? *What* law? Take a look out that window, pal. That'll convince ya there ain't no reason not to drop these bodies outta it. There ain't no laws in hell."

Leslie slurred. "Then why don't ya go there, Chucky?"

"We're here already, damnit."

The group fell silent.

A shadow moved into the room. "Do it," Angel said. "Throw 'em out the window."

Chuck said, "There ya go. She's talkin sense."

"She sells her snatch to sailors," Barman said.

"That don't mean she don't get a say."

"You're only saying that 'cause she's siding with you."

Keisha stood. "Maybe Chuck's right."

"He *is* right," Angel said. "Draggin 'em downstairs is too dangerous and we don't know what might happen if we keep their bodies here. I mean, shit, what if they're not dead?"

Barman pointed at the corpses in their bags. "Believe me, honey, these two are as dead as Lincoln."

"That don't mean nothin."

"Sweet Christ, woman. What the hell does it mean then?"

"I'm just sayin . . . we dunno how this sickness or whatever works, do we? What if they can't be killed. What if they're, like, *zombies*?"

Barman shook his head before mocking Angel with a grin. "I don't know, they seem more like Dracula or The Wolfman to me."

Eugene spoke up. "Be serious. We don't know yet what's true."

"Don't *you* start. I don't need any of your conspira—"

"It's not a conspiracy, Barman, it's a possibility. Yesterday would you have believed normal people would be doing what they're doing now? Screaming and ripping each other to pieces?"

"They're nuts, not immortal. One is real, the other isn't."

"We don't know that."

"Christ, Gene, if your face wasn't Silly Putty I'd bash it in right now. I told you I don't want any of your cockamamie theories."

Eugene cowered away.

"Listen, ya'll," Keisha said. "I dunno what to call 'em, but them boys came at us just like zombies, ain't they? If we dunno what this sickness is than hows we gonna know what it ain't?"

There was stillness then, filled only by the sound of ice floating in glasses and smoke leaving lungs. Finally, Shitty wheeled forward, breaking the stalemate.

"We can vote on it."

No one spoke or looked at each other.

"Alright then," Shitty said. "Who wants 'em out the winder? Show a hands."

Barman was the only one not to raise his. He showed his begrudging acceptance by taking one of the dead boys by the ankles and dragging him toward the lowest windowsill that faced the street.

Chuck hoisted the other end, cradling the corpse beneath the back. He was no longer sure which kid it was. He supposed it didn't really matter. With the window all the way open, Barman popped out the screen and tossed it inside, and the stench of a flaming dumpster rose up to greet them. There were distant screams that spoke of terror and anguish, of mothers losing sons and husbands killing their wives. The infected cut the night with the harmonious roar of shared insanity. There were no sirens now, only shattering, detonating noises, gunshots and battle cries and the crackle of flames being fed. No police. No firemen. No paramedics. Those whom society relied upon for help had either been overwhelmed, killed, or were now protecting themselves and their families. The citizens were alone and no one—*nothing*—was coming to save them.

They shoved the body out.

Barman looked away but Chuck watched it tumble through the air like an autumn leaf until it slammed into the concrete, the white plastic of the garbage bag swelling red in a flash before busting open from the force of the splintering limbs. There was a cry of horror as someone down below saw the body hit the pavement. But Chuck felt witnesses didn't matter. Like the corpse, all rules and decency had gone out the window. This was plague times. Chuck recalled reading that during the Black Death, bodies were merely piled in wagons to be taken out of the villages. This was hardly any different.

The second body turned upside down during its descent.

The head exploded upon impact.

"What's your problem anyway?" Chuck asked. "Why ya actin like such a cunt?"

He'd taken Leslie back to the bedroom. Her eyes were bleary with intoxication and there was a foul odor when her breath hit his face. She clutched her drink in one hand and his arm in the other for balance.

"Fuck you," she muttered.

"Really, what is it, Les?"

But she wouldn't give him any kind of answer, wouldn't even look him in the eye.

"Is it about killin that kid?" he asked.

"No."

"Good. 'Cause ya had to."

"Yeah, yeah, yeah."

"Get yourself together."

"The fuck for, Chucky? This is it—*the end*, of *everything*. The Scream's infectin the whole fuckin world. It's only a matter of time before we fuckin die, man. Either we turn into screamers too or screamers will get in here and fuckin murder us."

"I thought we were gonna try and make the best of this apocalypse. A few drinks, a few laughs—"

"Where's my fill? There's not a lot of time left. How many times I gotta tell ya? *I just wanna be full*! For once in my life I don't wanna feel this fuckin nothingness, this fuckin *hole* in me."

Chuck raised his eyebrows. "That's what this attitude of yours is about? You're pissed 'cause we ain't worked out *the big fuck* yet? Christ, I was talkin to the whore but then shit hit the fan and—"

"Excuses, excuses. Typical fuckin *man*. Can't be counted on for a fuckin thing. All y'all are good for is a dick to ride and half the time ya ain't even halfway decent usin it. You don't care 'bout fuckin me no more, Chuck! You've only got eyes for that lil' blonde bitch out there. That's the only reason ya opened that fuckin door to save them two. You're pathetic . . . a man your age lustin after a teenager—"

Chuck slapped her in the face and she tumbled backward, falling on her ass and spilling what was left of her drink into her lap. She stared into the empty glass and started crying.

Chuck sighed. "Jesus fuckin Christ."

He tried to get her up on the bed, but she slouched over the mattress and lied there face down, bent at the waist so her feet still touched the ground. She was still wearing the black mini-dress and it rode up one butt cheek, revealing pink panties and matching pink scars. Chuck had the sudden urge to pull those panties down and just spit in his hand and sodomize her, but he knew that wouldn't be enough. It seemed like nothing ever was when it came to her search for fullness. So he let her rest there, lighting a cigarette on his way out to fetch Angel. Without a word he took her by the arm and led her into the bedroom. The hooker didn't argue or resist; she simply followed, still a professional, even though her makeup had run with tears and her eyes had gone bloodshot, even though she was still trembling after the attack of the screamers and their brutal elimination. They entered the room in silence. Leslie was just as Chuck had left her, ass in the air as if waiting for them, calling to them. Chuck wondered if she was still awake.

"Ya still ain't told me what ya want me to do," Angel said.

"Does it matter?"

Angel sniffed. "Guess not."

Though Angel wouldn't look at him he could see her eyes were as dark and empty as a fresh grave. He went to Leslie and smacked her exposed butt cheek. She stirred and groaned.

"Whaaa?"

"Angel's here, let's do this."

Leslie rolled over, hair matted to her face. The dress had fallen a little further and one of her mighty tits had popped out and lay drooped over the side of the material. If she felt any gratitude or arousal, she didn't show it. The only thing Chuck saw in her was determination. For Leslie this was a mission, a bucket list desire to be checked off at this final hour.

"One more thing 'fore we start," she said.

Chuck blew smoke from his nostrils, waiting for the next request, wondering why all of this was important to him. Sure, not as important as it was to Leslie, but important nonetheless. She curled her finger to get him to come closer, then whispered in his ear. He had to ask her to repeat it, sure he'd heard her wrong the first time.

But he hadn't.

Chuck lifted Shitty onto the bed.

Convincing him to join them in the bedroom had taken little effort. Shitty's face turned tomato red at the implication, even after Chuck told him not to get his hopes too high. Chuck wondered how long it must have been since this homeless cripple had been with a woman. It was hard to imagine even a bag lady wanting to get it on with a man so physically mutated and filthy. Why would Leslie want to bring this dirty bastard into the mix? Why not the strapping Barman or one of the other women? Why not get everyone involved in some capacity, even the faceless Eugene; that way the others wouldn't wonder what this exclusive bedroom rendezvous was all about. Would they think Chuck and Leslie were conspiring against them by making some sort of pact? It was ludicrous to imagine Chuck choosing the whore and the bum for their inner circle over the stronger, sharper others in the apartment, but everyone was on edge and that poured gas on paranoia.

"This sure is interestin," Shitty said, gazing back and forth at the women. "What a night this turned out to be."

Angel recoiled. "I'm *not* fuckin him!"

"Ya won't have to," Leslie said.

"Yeah? Then what the hell am I doin here?"

Shitty frowned. "And what am I doin here?"

Leslie crept across the mattress to Shitty, seeming more cognizant now, sobered by these prospects. Chuck thought for a human mess she still looked pretty damn good. Not twenty-year-old sexpot good, but your high-school-friend's-slutty-mom good. He liked the idea of fucking Angel and Leslie at the same time. Shitty, however, was a less exciting addition to this orgy, but clearly Leslie felt differently. She took off Shitty's wool hat and ran her fingers through his matted hair. The poor man's lower lip trembled at her touch and he reached out and squeezed her tits with both hands in an impulsive fumble.

"Oh, Mama, look at 'em. Holy tap-dancin Jesus on a pinwheel."

"Take off your pants," Leslie said. Shitty went at the twine that served as his belt while Leslie turned to the others. "Angel, get naked and slide into bed with me. Chucky, take your dick out, babe."

Even he was hesitant. "Where's it gonna go?"

"In my mouth."

"Okay, then."

And so they gathered there in a circle of flesh, not the silken flesh of youth but the seasoned flesh of the downtrodden and the used, scarred and tattooed and wrinkled, flesh that had been sucked, fucked and fondled into a harrowing oblivion. Leslie removed her panties and stretched out with Shitty and Angel sitting on either side of her. Chuck stepped up to the edge of the mattress and Leslie turned her head to his groin. She told Angel to go down on her and the whore did as she asked, leaving Shitty the only one not engaged in some sort of fornication. His dick was like a small plumb in an old gym sock and he began jacking it while feeling Leslie's tits and thighs. Leslie turned on her side, pushing Angel's tongue away. The whore wiped her mouth with the back of her arm and awaited further instruction. Saying nothing, Leslie took Angel by the wrist and guided her hand to Leslie's anus. The women briefly locked eyes, a wordless exchange Chuck couldn't decipher. Angel began prodding the sphincter with one finger, then two. Leslie reached for Shitty.

She ran her fingertips along his shrunken, scraggily leg and scooched closer. The glistening lips of her sex grazed Shitty's toddler foot, inching it into her body one toe at a time while he watched with staring eyes. Angel turned away so not to look, but continued probing Leslie's colon, now four fingers in. Chuck couldn't look away. Leslie closed her eyes and gulped his cock all the way into her throat, then took hold of Angel's wrist and Shitty's leg and simultaneously pushed them in deeper. Angel's small fist disappeared into Leslie's ass. The ten inches of Shitty's gnarled flesh went further into her than any man could have gone before, the paralyzed leg fully immersed and wiggling from the motion of his feverish masturbation. Leslie writhed back and forth as her every orifice was vigorously pumped. Her eyelids fluttered, and it was that subtle glimpse of serenity that made Chuck ejaculate down her gullet. He grabbed her hair in both fists and she swallowed hungrily, moaning in her orgasms.

She was joyous. Content. Full.

Chuck smiled seeing her smile around the head of his cock.

It was like the love they'd made with the Arby's sandwich, only deeper.

That's when Angel started screaming.

When Shitty ejaculated, he'd purposely leaned forward so to get his jizz on Angel's face, so at first Chuck assumed her screams were of disgust. But as her cries rose in pitch and intensity Chuck went cold, knowing it was more than revulsion that had set the whore to screaming. Shitty's milky semen dribbled into Angel's eye, mixing with a rising custard pus, but she did not close them against the sting. She roared. Shitty tried to bounce away but his leg was still inside Leslie. The contraction of her vagina combined with his disabilities locked him in place. Leslie tried to back away, but Angel still had her whole fist in her ass, and in her newfound rage she was shoving harder, deeper, half the forearm raging up to pummel Leslie's guts. Chuck charged at Angel, grabbing her by the hair and punching her in her face. It was rapidly turning yellow. He yanked her head back, put his other palm beneath her chin, and twisted her neck as hard and fast as he could, over and over. She was scrawny enough that on the third twist the neck snapped, killing her instantly. Her body collapsed, the arm still submerged in Leslie's bloodied anal canal. Shitty was wiggling his way out of her just as Barman opened the door, a kitchen knife held high in his hand.

His face pinched at the sight. "What in the fuck?"

"It's okay now," Chuck told him.

He moved to Shitty and helped slide his foot out of Leslie as painlessly as possible, speaking to her softly in an effort to get her to relax her muscles. She was holding herself, sobbing and shaking, horror flooding her very core. Looking at the arm buried in her colon, Chuck winced at the magnitude of pain she must be in. Though he'd never been the empathetic type, he certainly hurt for this woman he'd come to know more deeply than any other. Wrapping his hand around the nook of Angel's elbow, he put his other hand on Leslie's butt and started prying them apart, hissing through his teeth at the dribbles of blood that came from her torn and gaping anus. Leslie groaned, choking on her agony. She had new scars now; internal ones to match the many exterior wounds life had branded her with.

Misery, they read.

"You know," Barman said, "any other day, barging in on a doubly penetrated woman and a dead prostitute might rattle me."

He ran his hand over his head. He looked so much older than he had yesterday, the stress lining his face.

"She turned into a screamer, Barman."

"I know."

They stood in the kitchen, having left Leslie to shower on her own, per her request. Chuck had helped her as best he could until she'd turned against him, shouting at him to get the fuck out. She didn't want sympathy or help patching herself up, so he let her be. Sometimes you just need to sit in the tub and cry it out. Chuck only wondered if she'd ever leave the bathroom again. Perhaps a long, hot shower was exactly where she wanted to be ensconced if this were her last day on earth. There was a hell of a lot worse places to die.

When he'd walked her out of the bedroom, Leslie had been bleeding profusely from her gaping anus and couldn't stand up straight, shaking and clutching her stomach. He wondered just how bad the internal damage was, all the rips and bruising they couldn't see.

"After today," Barman continued, "I don't think anything will ever surprise me again. I'm curious as to what the fuck was going on in there, but ultimately it's not my business, and there isn't enough time left to care."

A pale light was growing between the cracks in the curtains.

"Sun's comin up soon," Chuck said.

"Won't help much and won't last neither."

"Any updates on the news?"

"Not any *real* news. Just talking heads speculating on TV, politicians broadcasting from the safety of their homes, both parties already blaming the other for not preparing the public for this, even though shit went haywire almost overnight. People are posting all over social media, all contradicting each other. Some say it's an airborne virus, others a neurological anomaly, others an attack on America, even though this is happening all over. Then you got people like Eugene, the nuts blaming everything from aliens to God's vengeance. It's amazing. People are still arguing online even as the world crumbles on top of their empty fucking heads."

"So . . . you think this is really it?"

"You mean the end of the world?" Barman crossed his arms with a long exhale. "You know what this reminds me of, Chuck? *Evolution.* When nature sees a species is no longer viable, that it has nothing to offer, it finds a way to terminate it. Usually it's slower and more graceful than this, but that's not nature's fault, that's *our* fault.

THEY ALL DIED SCREAMING

We're the ones tearing each other to ribbons. It's our brains that are wired to turn us into screamers when this virus hits us. I think that says a lot about what we are. Other species fade away while we go out in a blaze of blood and violence. And you want to know why? Because society had its chance and we all blew it. Humankind is about as noble as a septic tank full of maggots. The wars, the rapes and murders, the police brutality, the racism, the animal cruelty, the glorification of greed. Humans trample each other at stores for fucking Black Friday deals and hoard toilet paper at the first sign of trouble. Only makes sense that we don't die off as one, holding hands, but rather as a civil war of the species. Our minds go right to rage when we get nature's goodbye kiss."

"I don't think it's a conscious decision." Chuck lit a cigarette, saddened by how low his pack was getting. "This Scream just makes people crazy. Must have some sorta effect on the brain's aggression button."

Barman smiled, but it was bitter. "Decades ago, this guy named Charles Whitman climbed to the top of some tower in Texas and shot as many motherfuckers as he could. His autopsy revealed a brain tumor they say might have been pressing that 'aggression button', as you call it."

"Well, shit, there ya go. Maybe this thing makes a tumor in your head, I dunno."

A shadowy figure loomed at the end of the hall. "That's horseshit."

Eugene stepped forward. Before Leslie had gone into the bathroom, he'd patched himself up, his face a hodgepodge of small bandages and bloody toilet paper, a mummy dipped in marinara.

Chuck groaned. "Is this where ya tell us Elvis and Marilyn made this virus in a test tube down at Area 51?"

"All your skepticism has grown tiresome," Eugene said. "As has your cynicism. With all of the madness you two have witnessed today, can't you open your eyes, or at least your mind a little?"

Chuck shared a glance with Barman.

"Okay," Barman said. "What've you got?"

Eugene glanced over his shoulder into the living room. Keisha and Brittany sat together on the sofa, neither of them speaking, just staring at the TV news, looking so very tired but too frightened to sleep. Eugene leaned into the other men to whisper.

"It's an STD," he said. "The virus is transmitted *sexually*."

The men stood there in a stunned silence.

Chuck scoffed. "Bullshit. You gonna tell me those two screamer kids who done barged in here caught this thing after getting laid? Get the fuck outta here."

"No, man, listen. The virus can manifest itself naturally, but if you fuck someone you can pass it off to them, like crabs. But in this case *they* get it and you walk away clean. It jumps from host to host."

"So these screamers are tryin to fuck us?"

"No, no. By the time you start screaming it's already too late."

Barman frowned. "You're retarded, Gene. Totally fucking retarded."

"Yeah," Chuck agreed. "I just saw somethin that might make ya think otherwise of your theory . . . " He was about to tell Eugene about the orgy, how Angel had turned into a screamer *during sex*, but Eugene spoke first.

"I have it on good authority. One of the podcasts I follow, who has been right about *everything* leading up to this, just announced this information. They say this whole melting ice bacteria bullshit is fake news. They say it's a transmittable disease and the way to get clean is to dump it on somebody else, preemptively, before you show symptoms."

Barman stepped closer. "Oh, yeah? Well, that's sort of like what some people in Africa believed about AIDS, that fucking a virgin would cure them. But that just spread more AIDS at the added expense of—" here his voice trembled "—raping a teenage girl."

Eugene pointed at Brittany with his eyes. The young girl seemed to sense his gaze and she glanced at the men huddled in the hallway, then averted her eyes just as quickly. She twirled a strand of hair in her hand, a subconscious tick, the blonde lock wrapping around her fingers again and again.

Eugene's voice fell even quieter. "A *virgin* is exactly what they said work best."

Barman grabbed Eugene by the collar and pressed him into the wall so hard a framed photo fell to the floor.

"Listen to me," he said. "If you think I'm gonna let you force yourself on that girl, you're sorely mistaken."

Eugene smiled. "I'm reasonable, Barman. I don't want her all to myself."

Barman shoved him again, causing some homemade gauze to fall from Eugene's face, and took the kitchen knife from his belt.

"I will shove this through what's left of your head and pluck every one of your teeth out with it. This isn't a goddamn cure, you fucking imbecile. It's just some far-fetched excuse for men to sexually assault women, even *girls*. There are no cops holding up law and order, only a basic moral code, so this podcast shitbird is trying to validate cruelty and incite violence upon women for his own twisted reasons. I'll be damned if I'm going to let you or anyone else take part in it."

Eugene seethed but couldn't wiggle free from Barman's grasp. He looked to Chuck but found no loyalty there, only indifference to his potential ass-kicking.

"Alright," Eugene said. "It was just an idea."

Keisha was approaching now. "What's goin on? Everythin okay here?"

"It's fine," Barman said, releasing Eugene. "Just getting a few things straight, right, Gene?"

But Eugene didn't reply. He simply walked around Keisha and sat down at the table, pouring himself a glass of whisky, his back turned to Brittany, for now.

CHAPTER EIGHTEEN

THE MAN DIDN'T teach by showing. He had the boy mount the girl and coached him, rather than demonstrating by mounting her himself. He always taught the boy things this way, be it chores or handling veal. Besides, he couldn't have mated with her if he tried.

"My dick's all but rotted off," he explained.

The man took hold of the boy's erection and guided it into the veal's vagina for him, spitting on the tip to make entry easier. As the girl's private parts enveloped the boy's, the man sat on the arm of the sofa where they lay fornicating, watching and giving advice. After a few thrusts the boy began to shudder. He pumped faster. The veal whimpering behind the sock they'd used to gag her only got the boy more excited.

"Get in there real deep," the man said. "Then go on ahead and pop off inside 'er. I gots me an idea."

The boy did as he was told.

The veal didn't die in the coming days. It seemed the bullet had passed through her without puncturing anything vital. This surprised the boy, but not as much as what the man added to his chore list.

"Keep on doin her," he said. "You're young, so you're gonna want it every day anyhow."

And so the boy mated on the regular, gladly. He even concocted a new way of restraining her in the pen, so she was chained to the floor facedown with her hips elevated by a stack of two-by-fours beneath her. This way he could penetrate her without undoing the restraints, so there was no fear of her escaping and no way for her to hurt him the way she had when he'd been foolish enough to trust her. He'd learned the hard way that the man was right about veal. They were all liars, all cruel. They weren't human the way he and the man were, not even the way the townspeople were. The veal were some sort of horrible mutation. Their aberrant behavior was such that they couldn't be trusted or even remotely understood. Unless to give them orders, the boy would never speak with them again.

He was thrilled when the man asked him to drive him into town, particularly to go to the pharmacy. The man wasn't going to see a doctor yet, but if the pharmacist gave him the same medical advice as the boy had, he might finally listen and make an appointment, maybe even head straight to the hospital.

The truck rumbled down the street, belching in its need for an oil change. The man pulled his coat around him tighter, then reached into his pocket and retrieved a wool cap.

"You stay in the truck," he said.

"But I wanted to look at some—"

"Don't argue with me, young man. This ain't some happy-go-lucky trip to the store. This here's serious business."

His tone made the boy tense. He hadn't heard such harshness since his earliest days on the farm.

"Yes, sir."

"Now when we get there, I want ya to park 'round back of the buildin. Keep the motor runnin. Any cops show up you bolt the hell outta here even if I ain't with ya, got it?"

The boy gulped. "What's goin on?"

"Just do like I tells ya. Antibiotics is somethin ya need a 'scription for and I ain't got one. And with me not able to hunt, our meat production's dropped off somethin fierce. We need money if we're gonna keep gettin by. I inherited the farm. It's paid for, no mortgage. But we still need cash to live on and keep the pigs full and healthy. I'm just gonna go in there and get what we need."

"But ya can barely get around!"

"I'll be fine."

"Lemme do it instead."

"No way."

"I'll be faster."

"I said no, damnit. I appreciate whatcha tryin to do, kid, but ya ain't never pulled no robbery before. I have. Ya just don't know what to look for to keep from gettin caught and there ain't no time now to teach ya."

"Well, how am I gonna learn nothin less'n ya let me try?"

The man unrolled the wool cap down his face, revealing it was a ski mask. He ran his chaffed digits over the material.

"I just don't wanna see ya get hurt, son." He reached over and patted the boy on the thigh, making his eyes mist. "I gots to do it on my own."

As they rounded the corner, the boy gripped the wheel tight enough for his knuckles to run white. This was another one of the man's bad ideas. They seemed to be coming more frequently as of late. Was the man's brain sizzling and festering just as his flesh did, the necrotizing fasciitis working its way inside his cranium, deteriorating cognizance? But he'd argued with the man about it enough. Any further opposition would be insubordinate and disrespectful. He couldn't have that, especially not now. The boy's guts were already twisting with concern for the man without fearing things would go sour between them, particularly if the necrotizing fasciitis might soon kill him.

So the boy acquiesced. After pulling around the back of the store, he reached for the rifle on the rack behind them. The man struggled to hold it with one hand and open the passenger door at the same time, but he managed. It was walking the boy was the most concerned about, and watching the man limp his way toward the building didn't give him any encouragement. The boy wished he'd had the courage to say goodbye, just in case this would be the last time he'd ever see him. It was a black and poisonous thought he failed to shake from his head.

He sat there with the truck idling for what felt like a long time, the back lot as empty as that one he vaguely remembered from so long ago. Sweat boiled in his every fold. He chewed the inside of his cheek. He kept waiting for something to go wrong, for an alarm to go off or, worse yet, a gun. But the only sound was of the running engine and the soft whispers of disc jockeys on the radio turned down low. And there was nothing to see but the drab, gray concrete of the back of the building, a wall that refused to tell him what was going on behind it. So, he watched the corner intently, ready to put the truck in drive the very instant he saw the man come around.

When at last he did, he moved faster than the boy thought possible, shuffling in a strained gait more quickly than he'd been able to in some time. He held the rifle low, leaning on it with the butt hitting the ground like a walking stick. In his other hand was a plastic shopping bag with a smiley face on it. *Thank you and come again.* The boy popped into gear so quickly the brakes screeched. Smiling wide, he opened the passenger door for the man and he climbed in with assistance, and then they were out into the street, swerving down side roads in a frantic escape.

"Went well," the man said, lifting his mask. His rictus grin added much needed life to his zombified face. He opened the bag and the boy caught a glimpse. Pill bottles and a small white box. There were also bandages and skin creams alongside a pile of cash wrapped up in bands. "Got lucky. Safe had some deposits that hadn't gone to the bank yet. Not a fortune but enough to last a couple months. And I gots them medicines."

"Alright!" The boy almost said he was glad the man was okay but didn't want to risk insinuating he couldn't handle pulling this off. "That's great."

"Got something for ya too."

The man took the white box out of the bag and tossed it in the boy's lap. He kept his eyes on the road as he blew through a stop sign, then glanced at the printing on the package.

Home pregnancy test.

The boy looked at the applicator, then away, then back again, as if the color would change. It didn't. It glowed up at him like a middle finger.

"No," he whispered. "No, no."

But he wasn't really sure what he was so worried about. The man seemed to think it would be a good thing if the boy impregnated the girl. Her teets would give milk, the boy knew that much, but was that worth the hassle? Whenever one of the pigs was pregnant, extra care had to been given to her and when the litter spewed out, they became even more exhausting to care for than the mother sow. How many babies would the veal deliver?

The boy certainly didn't want to be a father. Having extra hands around the farm would have its advantages now that the man was incapacitated, but he would have to raise the kid up and teach it the right ways to do the chores. The thought was overwhelming. Could he really be as good of a teacher as the man? Could he tolerate the aggravation of it all?

He gazed down at the veal. She was still bent over the stack of wood, the puddle of piss pooling around her feet. He'd made her pee because he needed urine for the test. That seemed weird, but even weirder was the reality that she was carrying his seed. They would have to be parents together. Would he have to *love* her? No, that would be impossible. She was veal, filth, nothing. The bitch was just meat. Certainly the man wouldn't expect him to *marry* such a thing.

Grumbling, he left the veal and returned to the house. The man was stretched out on the couch, the pill bottles on the end table beside his glass of bourbon.

"She's knocked up," the boy said.

The man smiled. "Hot diggity dog. Ya done good, son. Humped 'er like a real man."

He was almost afraid to ask, but had to. "What's all this about?"

"Somethin' I'd thought about before, but never done went through with. Dunno why. Guess'n I just thought it'd be impractical."

"What?"

"Knockin' up the veal. I coulda done it myself 'fore my dick turned to mincemeat, but I just ain't interested in humpin 'em. They don't give me no itches the way they do you. I prefer the gilts, 'specially Polly. She's been my bride a long time now. Ain't made love to any others since. Nothin could ever compare to my Polly, 'specially not some goddamn piece of veal."

The boy squirmed in his skin. He hated when the man talked romantically about the pigs. The boy understood the importance of them, and loved them in his own way, the way any boy would love a pet. But there was something unsettling about the man mating with swine. He'd never shaken the sight of seeing the man fucking Polly in the mud, back when he'd only recently arrived on the farm. It was a memory he wished he could drill out of his head, so of course it stuck like Crazy Glue.

"Anyways," the man said, "even if I did have the sex with them veal, and managed to get 'em impregnated, I didn't think keepin 'em alive for the nine months it takes to get the baby'd be worth it. Ya gots to keep 'em fed and all that, and meanwhile it's one less grind and shipment. Pounds of meat ya can't process."

"So why do it now, then? Just for the milk?"

"That's a bonus, yeah, but it ain't the thought I had. The payoff would be the baby."

The boy threw up his arms in a huff. "I don't wanna be no daddy!"

The man's brow lowered. At first the boy thought he'd angered him, but the expression was of confusion, followed by a smile.

"A daddy?" the man chuckled, then bent into laughter. "Shit, I wouldn't put that on ya! A *daddy*, Jesus, that's rich. Ya sure do crack me up sometimes."

"So whadda we want with 'em then?"

"Son, this lil' lady ya been dumpin your dick snot into is veal, nothin more. So any baby that comes outta her is just another veal. But see, babies don't have to be tenderized like grown veal do. Ya don't have to make 'em anemic. Their tissue is already super soft. *Baby soft*, as folks say."

The boy nodded. "Okay. So, they're special?"

"I was thinkin' . . . *gourmet*."

The boy's face went slack.

"We can charge much more," the man said. "Call it organic, prime veal. Top of the line, best of the best. We'll just have to figure out the timing of the slaughter. The longer we let the baby live, the tougher the meat will get, but the more meat we'll end up with. We'll have to find that middle ground. I'm thinkin a year and half, maybe two years old. Get 'em to be thirty pounds or so."

The boy didn't respond. It was as if he'd forgotten how to communicate at all.

"Plus, we get the milk, like ya said. And the mama veal gets fat, at least for a while. With her swoll up, we can get extra meat outta her long as we grind her up 'fore she shrinks down again." He stared at the boy who couldn't look him in the eye. "So whatcha think, kid?"

There was a long pause before the boy spoke. "They'll be my sons n' daughters. At least half mine, half veal."

"*Half* veal is *all* veal, son. Ya just planted a seed, like ya plant seeds in the vegetable garden. Ya ain't raisin kinfolk, you're *manufacturin* a product."

"Even at thirty pounds, ya know a lot of that's gonna be scraps—bone and guts. How much we'd get for one baby's meat? A couple hundred bucks? After all the food we'll have to give it to keep it alive—"

"The mama will feed it with her teets."

"But they need diapers and stuff . . . "

"Nah, they don't. They'll stay in the pens like the veal they are. If they shit or teethe or whatever else, ain't our problem."

"It'll die."

"If it does, we'll just cut n' grind it up and sell what we got."

Something went tight within the boy's chest. It formed into a lump that rose in his throat like phlegm. The man noticed and eased his way off the couch. He shuffled over to the boy and put a festering hand on his shoulder.

"Alright. If it bothers ya this much—"

"It ain't that. I'm just worried is all."

"Worried? 'Bout what?"

"*You.* I don't mean no disrespect, but I think your brain ain't workin right. I know you're smart—ya done taught me everythin in life—but I'm really scared your brain is sick just like your body. Ya keep havin these ideas that just don't make no good sense. We can't be no baby factory. That ain't no way to keep the meat comin. Nine months is way too long. And it'll be too much work for too little payoff." The boy gazed up at him now. "Just teach me to hunt. I'm old enough now to catch veal on my own. Lemme hunt! Shit, we won't be missin no deliveries then. They'll be plenty of meat."

He waited for the whoopin he may have earned for questioning the man. He hadn't been belted in almost two years, but telling the man he was sick in the head was asking for a smack upside his own. But he'd had to do it. His concern for the man's mental state was eating at the boy just as the necrotizing fasciitis was eating at the man.

Finally, the man said, "Maybe you're right at that."

The boy could breathe again.

The man grabbed his shoulders in both hands. "Maybe I've been pullin at strings, but I've just been stressin 'bout this here situation." He gestured to his disintegrated flesh. "I ain't afraid a dyin so much as I's afraid to leave ya all alone in this shitty, rotten world."

"Don't say that. Ya ain't gonna die! Them pills gonna fix ya right up."

"Well, I don't want us goin broke waitin or for folks to forget all 'bout our farm 'cause we ain't deliverin as much meat as we done used to. Now I dunno if this bein sick has warped my brain—I don't feel like it has, but who knows—but I realize now I ain't been treatin ya like the man you've become. You've proven yourself and then some, kid, ya oughta be allowed to go out on the hunt."

The proud tears in the man's eye made the boy's heart skip, and he struggled not to cry himself.

"Ya mean it?" he asked. "You're gonna let me take in my first veal?"

"Reckon it's time. But on the first run I ride shotgun, so I can teach ya how to do it right n' good. All goes well—and I reckon it will—ya can start huntin and baggin 'em on your own."

The boy sniffled. "I won't let ya down."

"Ya never have. We'll head out tomorrow night. We've had enough excitement for one day. Best to lay low while the coppers are lookin into the robbery. And one other thing. Long as that bitch is knocked up, might as well see how things go with the baby idea. We ain't got nothin to lose. Not sayin we'll turn into no baby farm. Just wanna see what happens."

The boy knew how to pick his battles. One objection was reasonable; two was insubordinate. He certainly didn't want to anger the man into changing his mind about tomorrow's hunt.

"Okay," he said. "Reckon I better chain her so she ain't on her belly no more."

"Good idea."

Though there was no more to say, the man still clutched the boy's shoulders, his smile wide, warm despite being skeletal. He pulled the boy into an embrace and the boy kissed him on the cheek, unbothered by the decomposition.

The man breathed deep. "I love ya, son."

"I love you too . . . Pa."

It was a daring word. He'd never called the man that before. He'd never called him anything but *sir*. While that level of respect was right, it just seemed too formal now. Maybe he'd crossed a line, but he felt it was one the man wouldn't mind being crossed, one he himself had been hoping the boy would step over. He'd come to think of the man as his father long ago, but had doubted himself until this tender moment. He'd taken a lot of risks today, but they'd all been worth it. He hoped this one would be too.

When the man hugged him tighter, the boy knew he'd been right.

CHAPTER NINETEEN

"**I** **JUST WANTS** to talk to ya," Keisha whispered. At her insistence, they'd gone into the kitchen for privacy. "What happened up in that other room?"

"The hooker," Chuck said. "She turned into one of 'em. We had to kill her."

Keisha's mouth curled. Chuck knew why. She wanted to know what they'd been doing in there in the first place. But she didn't ask.

"That other woman—your wife? She okay?"

"Not my wife, and no, not really."

Keisha didn't seem to know what to say to that. Her gaze was distant, her soul lost somewhere beyond reach. There was desperation there, a sour mixture of fear and hopelessness.

"I know we don't really know each other," she said, "but ya did try 'n help me when my husband . . . well, ya know. I 'preciate that. I knows yous gotta good heart."

Chuck looked away. Women had been wrong about him before, but this was the most delusional one yet. He was no Samaritan, no hero. He was two hundred pounds of drunken, pointless shit. He needed a damn cigarette and a blowjob to finish what Leslie started. Maybe this black chick would be in for a fuck. Given the state of things, this was possibly the last time she'd be able to. The lingering presence of death was a natural aphrodisiac.

Keisha went on. "See, I need y'alls help."

"We let ya in here. Ain't that enough?"

Her face pinched, but she composed herself quickly. "And I 'preciate that too. Ya gots ta know I do. But see, I can't be stayin. I gots ta leave."

"Nobody's really stoppin ya, but if that door gets opened one of them fuckin screamers could rush on in here. Best it stays closed." Her eyes grew damp and Chuck crossed his arms as if to armor himself against this showing of emotion. "Why'n the hell ya wanna leave anyway? Ya begged me to let ya in and now ya wanna go back out?"

"Listen . . . I was just gettin home from work when them crazy kids came after me. That girl Brittany was in the hall when I came up the stairs. I . . . I didn't get to my apartment."

"So? What's so important 'bout goin there?"

Tears rolled down both cheeks. "My babies."

"I hope you're just referrin to cats."

"Naw. Twins, a boy n' girl both. Nine months old. They're at home with Mama. I gots to get to 'em, to be with my family and make sure theys be okay. I was hopin that, maybe . . . "

"Ah, Christ."

"I hate to ask but—"

"Yeah, yeah. I know. You're a small lady. Ya go out there on your own and some screamer could snap your skinny ass in half."

"It's just down the hall. Won't take but a minute."

"And a minute is all it takes to get killed."

She took a deep breath. "Okay. I understand. Well, can I at least take one of them knives?"

"I didn't say no to helpin ya yet. What all ya got in your place?"

"Whatta ya mean?"

"Any cigarettes, booze, food? Stuff ya can give me? If I'm gonna risk my neck I get to cherry pick what all ya got."

Keisha's frown deepened. She sniffed it all back. She had to.

"Okay then," she said. "I gots food and some wine. Maybe a bit of party liquor. Don't smoke none but Mama probly gots some. She say she quittin but sometimes I smell them Newports on 'er. Take what alls ya want. Just leave the stuff for my babies."

Chuck smirked. "Don't want your baby food, but I'll take that wine. And menthols are better than no cigs at all."

Suddenly Barman said, "I'll go."

He was standing at the end of the hall, looking in.

Keisha beamed. "Oh, mista! I'd be so grateful for your help."

"Thought you were too beat up from earlier," Chuck said to Barman. "From when ya got hurt at the bar."

"I'm not one hundred percent, but I'm better now that I've rested. I can do this. I'll take her."

"Wait a second. *I* get to cherry pick. I need those cigarettes."

Stepping into the kitchen, Barman appeared grayed by exhaustion. Though a big man, he looked somehow smaller now, more fragile if not exactly meek. But the hardness of his eyes remained, black and empty like a shark's.

"I'll get you your damned cigarettes, Chuck. You just stay here and take care of your woman."

"Ain't nothin I can do for Leslie."

Barman stepped uncomfortably close. "You can goddamn be here for her. Don't let her suffer alone. Depending on how bad her injuries are she could be dying in that bathroom while you're worrying about smokes and booze. Shame on you. She's your woman whether you want to call her that or not. Wife, girlfriend, or friends with benefits—the semantics don't matter. Now treat her right, you miserable, dumb fuck. Do some good for once in your life."

Chuck grit his teeth but kept his lips pressed to hide it. Accuracy made Barman's insults sting. Chuck had done nothing with his life, always blaming his failure as a human being on the terrible circumstances of his existence, the shit hand he'd been dealt, the pain he'd been bad lucked into by sheer chance. He'd been given the fuzzy end of life's lollipop and had used that to excuse himself from all ambition and dignity. If it wasn't booze, drugs, or pussy, he never gave a damn about it. All he wanted was numbness; moments that would make the pain of being alive go away for a little while. In this way, he wasn't much different than Leslie. He understood her need to be full, a need that had brought her to where she was right now, suffering on the threshold of a screaming armageddon. But at least she'd had a goal, one she'd achieved at that, despite the end result.

"Suddenly you're the caring person, huh, Barman?" Chuck said. "Long as I've known you, you've come off as a misanthrope. It still don't make sense."

"I don't owe you an explanation for the things I do." Barman turned to Keisha. "You should be with your family right now, not with scumbags like us. Get the blonde girl too. She'll be safer with you and your Mama than she'll be here."

Keisha went to hug him, but Barman gently nudged her away. She left the kitchen and went to Brittany who was resting in fetal position on the floor, her face turned to the wall. Keisha made gentle circles on the girl's back with one hand, the calming touch only mothers can give. On the other side of the room, Shitty was sloppy drunk and still in a daze from all that had happened. His head hung low, eyes closed, mumbling. Eugene was stretched out on the sofa again, possibly asleep. Some of his face had scabbed over now, leaving him looking like old pizza.

Barman told Chuck, "I want to get these two away from Gene . . . and away from you."

"Wait just a damn minute, I didn't say nothin 'bout rapin them like he did."

"I know. I'm not concerned about you being a threat, but you sure are a bad influence. That whole mess in the bedroom could've been avoided if you'd been thinking with the right head. You'd follow your dick into an active volcano, you know that? I don't want these ladies here to be led into the lava."

"And what about you, Barman? I guess you've decided you're gonna stay with 'em? Be their big protector? You don't wanna protect them from us, you just want 'em all to yourself."

Barman shook his head. "No I don't."

"Yeah, right. You expect me to believe—"

"I'm asexual, idiot."

"You're what?"

"I'm not attracted to anyone, man or woman. I have no interest in sex. I've been this way a long time."

Chuck smirked. "You tellin me you're a virgin?"

"Said I *don't* have sex, not that I *never have*. I became asexual in my twenties."

"Bullshit. That can't be a real thing."

"I don't know why I'm explaining this to you. I don't owe you that. But I've been given food and shelter here. I couldn't have made it on my own. So I owe you whatever help I can give you. I'm coming back here once I get those ladies into Keisha's apartment. I'll bring the smokes but not any food."

"What about the wine?"

Barman chuckled. "You'll never change."

"Why bother?" Chuck leaned on the counter, suddenly tired. "There's only one type of people in this world: people who die."

Leslie didn't answer when Chuck knocked. Trying the handle, he was surprised to find she hadn't locked it. He stepped into the bathroom, practically a closet of cracked, yellow tile with a toilet that faced the sink cabinet so closely your knees hit it when you sat down. The soap-stained sink was littered with lipsticks and hairy brushes, bobby pins and used Q-Tips. The shower was running, curtain closed, distorting the image of Leslie behind it. She was lying in the tub with her head back, silent and still in a way that made Chuck's shoulders go tight.

"Les?"

A murmur. "Go away."

His tension eased. She wasn't dead; at least not yet.

"Come on, Les. I brought ya a drink."

Chuck opened the curtain just enough to hand the glass to her. He expected to be hit by steam, but she'd been in the shower so long the water was coming out cold. Wet hair was matted to her face, her lower lip trembling, her essence as gray as old snow grown filthy in the streets.

"How ya doin?" he asked like a moron.

"How do ya think?"

"Not good. How bad is it?"

She gulped down half the vodka. "The bitch ripped my asshole out, Chucky. It won't stop bleedin." She pulled the curtain back to give him a better look at the russet stream running from her butt down the drain. She smirked, winced. "Women bleed for seven days without dyin. But this here's different." Her smirk gave way under tight pain. "I think she put holes in my fuckin colon."

She downed the rest of her drink and shook the glass for another. Chuck retrieved it, taking notice of Barman, Keisha, and Brittany talking in the living room in preparation of their escape. When he returned to the bathroom, Leslie had turned off the water and was struggling to get up. He put the drink on the toilet tank lid and reached for her, but her legs were failing and she was just wet, dead weight in his arms. He changed his grip just in time to not drop her. Leslie helped by locking her arms around the back of his neck.

"Where ya wanna go?" he asked.

"Bedroom."

"I'll have to put ya on the toilet a sec so I can get some clothes on ya." He looked around the bathroom, noticing there were no clothes. "Guess I'll have to get 'em."

"Nah," she said. "Just take me to bed."

Chuck remembered the disturbing state they'd left the room in. Blood on the sheets, the hooker's dead body on the floor. "It's still a mess in there."

"I don't give a fuck. Everything hurts, Chucky. It hurts so fuckin bad. I wanna be in my bed."

"Okay, lemme wrap ya in a towel."

He reached with one hand for the towel on the rack, but it slipped and fell to floor.

"Shit!"

"Just carry me out. I don't care if anybody sees me naked." Her words came out in gentle sobs. "That kinda stuff doesn't matter anymore. Nothin matters when we're all dead."

Chuck maneuvered, getting the door open. He almost lifted Leslie's legs up to wrap her around him but didn't want to risk any further damage to her anus, so he carried her with her feet dragging across the floor, toenails clicking on the tile, flecks of their chipped paint falling away just like the drops that fell from Leslie, some shower water, some tears, some blood. In the hall, Chuck made it a point not to look and see if anyone was watching them. He didn't want the others to see Leslie like this and didn't want to know if they had. Once in the bedroom he closed the door with his foot and placed Leslie on the plush chair while he went to the closet for a new set of sheets. She rolled on her side so not to put any pressure on her butt. The sheets changed, Chuck deftly laid her out upon the mattress.

Angel was spread out on the floor as if she were being quartered by horses, her limbs and twisted head forming a macabre star. The shattered vertebra in her neck had made large lumps beneath the flesh and turned her face at an awkward angle. One of her hands was still slippery with brownish blood. Chuck dragged the whore's body to the window, which was almost too small to throw her out of. But he just didn't want Leslie's assailant in the room with them, even if she was dead. Lifting the body, he nudged Angel's head out first to make sure the shoulders could pass through it. He had to tilt the carcass at an angle and the rusty frame of the window scraped away some of her skin as he shoved her through. He managed to drape her over the sill on her belly, the upper half of her body out and dangling. Next came the hips. Angel was a scrawny woman, but this was a tight passage. Her hips jutted out, so Chuck had to put his back into her butt and shove against her, thrusting, pounding. The frame tore through the fabric of her dress, metal peeling away the flesh like a carrot. He lifted her legs and pointed her in a downward slant, and finally gravity did him a favor, sending this Angel back to earth, the window frame coming with her, stuck around her waist like a belt of daggers.

The dead whore sailed in the same star shape she'd been in upon the carpet, arms and legs outstretched, cutting the summer air on her way down to the car on the sidewalk. It was wrapped around a telephone pole. She seemed to float for a moment, light and ethereal, and then she hit the car's roof, indenting it, her limbs snapping and contorting. Her body bounced off and she was briefly in flight again before smacking the pavement. There was no splatter of blood, but a pool of it quickly formed beneath her. Now her corpse was so twisted up it looked not like a star but a swastika made of broken bones.

Chuck looked away, up at the city skyline and the luster of the rising summer sun. The sky was clear and baby blue. The only clouds were of black fog coming from burning buildings and automobiles. Homes in flames, random piles of trash in the streets, all ablaze and reeking of decay. The cruel heat of day had not yet arrived and the air was warm and dry, reminding him of long lost summers that lasted forever instead of racing by in a flash, growing shorter with every passing year. Over all the noise in the distance, he heard the rustle of the leaves on the bushes that lined the windowsills of the complex across the way. They were lush and green, alive with the blessing of the season. And instead of a pigeon, a cardinal landed upon the branches, fluttering in colorful indifference to the grievous horrors that had fallen upon human beings.

It was a beautiful fucking day in the neighborhood.

Chuck returned to Leslie and sat beside her on the bed. He ran his hand over her head and wiped the sweat on her brow. She gazed at him with half-closed eyes.

"I feel sick," she said.

"Ain't there any medicine ya can take?"

"What the hell do ya take for a mangled asshole?"

"I dunno."

She raised a hand and patted his shoulder. Her palm went to his face, cradling one cheek like a loving mother. "It's okay, Chucky. Ya done good by me."

He didn't know what to say to that.

"Got a smoke?" Leslie asked.

"Nah. We're all out and I'm nic-fittin like a fiend. But we're gonna get some."

"How's that?"

"Barman's takin Keisha back to her apartment down the hall."

"Just for fuckin cigarettes?"

"Nah. Turns out she's got babies."

Leslie's eyes opened all the way and she sat up. "Babies? That woman has fuckin *babies*? We gotta go and help her—"

Chuck gently pushed her back on to the mattress. "Take it easy."

"Where are they?"

"In the apartment with their nana."

"How's some old bitch gonna protect 'em from the screamers?"

"That's why they're goin. So Keisha can be with 'em. Brittany's goin too."

She soured. "What about you, Chucky?"

"Don't worry. I ain't leavin ya."

"Fuck that! Them babies are more important."

"Barman can handle it. He's bigger and stronger than I am."

"Just promise me you'll make sure them babies are taken good care of, Chucky." She poked him in the chest. "Promise me with your whole fuckin heart."

He took her hand in both of his. "Alright. I promise."

"Swear on your mama."

"I'll do you one better. I swear on my father."

"All dads are bastards."

"Not mine."

"Fine. But don't fuckin go back on that swear now. A promise is a promise. Your word may be all ya have left in this shit-ass life."

Chuck lowered his chin to his chest. "I know, Les. I know."

He savored her touch as she ran her fingers through his hair and he bent down, down, down into her chest, resting himself in the plush of her bare breasts like a suckling. She cradled him then, two lost souls just breathing in a crappy apartment on the shattered edge of the world.

"She's in bad shape," Chuck said.

Barman rubbed his chin. "But is she going to make it?"

"I dunno. She's all torn up on the inside." He explained what had happened before Barman walked in on the chaos, where Angel's hand had been when she'd gone berserk. "Leslie thinks her colon's been punctured."

"Let's hope not. That would be very bad."

"She can't even stand up."

"If she has a perforated bowel, she could get an infection. That can lead to sepsis."

Chuck rubbed his neck and sighed. "What'n the hell's that?"

"The body's bad reaction to infection. Sepsis can kill her."

"So then, whatta we do?"

Barman looked away. "There's nothing we can do."

A weight fell through Chuck's stomach and he had to put his back against the wall. The thought of Leslie dying—especially in such a terrible way—sent a nasty tingle through him. His emotional response to the situation would have surprised him at any other point in his life, but he had to admit he'd grown to care about Leslie a good deal. She was just as fucked up and ruined as he was and there was a pathetic magic to that, two puzzles connected by their broken pieces. Her friendship meant more to him than he'd ever fully been aware of until now, and the very real potential for her death made him realize what he felt for her was love, or at least the closest thing he could come to it. This tingle going through him was the first struck chord of grief, a premature mourning.

"The girls are ready," Barman said. "I'll be back fast as I can. Then we'll come up with some plan of action."

"Meaning?"

"Maybe we can get your woman to a hospital after all, or at least find her some medication."

Chuck nodded. "Rob a pharmacy."

"It's not exactly a robbery if you just take what you need in a time of crisis. Hopefully antibiotics can fight off the infection long enough to find a doctor or nurse. I still think it's a long shot that a hospital won't be a war zone, but . . . " Here Barman could only shrug. "Let's get this other woman to her babies first. Now, we want that door to open and close as quickly as possible just in case there's a screamer or two out there."

"We'd hear 'em if they were. They're loud as shit."

"Yeah, well, who knows how this virus has affected them. They've gone from killing each other to killing us. Maybe the next phase is silence, so they hunt better. Or they might scream until they're too hoarse and lose their voice. Let's just play it safe."

They stepped to the door where the women waited. Brittany gazed up at Chuck with wet, bloodshot eyes, clutching the broom with both hands. Keisha had the lighter and hairspray. Barman held the butcher knife in one hand and took up the folding chair with the other, raising it in front of him as a makeshift shield. Chuck picked up the hammer and as he positioned himself behind the door Shitty wiggled his way on to his wheeler.

"I wanna go too," Shitty said.

Barman said, "You'll slow us down. We're all safer if you stay here."

"Don't wanna go with ya on this here mission, I just wanna *go*. I don't wanna be here no more." He hung his head. "I don't like what all's happened in this here place. Don't like the things I done here. Hell, I don't wanna go out doin nasties, bein the piece a shit I been all these years. I don't wanna be *Shitty* at the point of dyin. I wanna be Paulie again, Paul Bartholomew Shuck, just like Ma and Pop named me. I wanna go out with peace in my heart."

Chuck and Barman shared a glance but said nothing.

"Just lemme go," Shitty said. "I done looked out the window and saw how pretty this day is. It's dangerous out there, but at least I'll get to feel the sun on my face and the wind in my hair one more time. Get to enjoy all of creation. Better than dyin in this dark apartment with y'all. No offense."

145

Barman said, "Alright. It's your choice."

"And I made it."

The others stepped out of the way, falling hush as Chuck turned the doorknob, slowly, every little click sounding like shotgun blasts in the tense silence. Chuck's skin went slick with dread. With the hammer held high, he cracked the door open and Barman peaked outside.

"Looks clear," he whispered.

Shitty glanced up. "Thanks for all the drinks."

Shitty rolled forward and Chuck opened the door just enough to let him through. There were no goodbyes. A farewell would have seemed inappropriate, given that Shitty would almost certainly die today. At least he was serving a purpose. By wheeling his way through the hall, he would draw the attention of any screamers who might be lying in wait for a fresh victim. The others would learn what they were up against. Chuck wondered if Shitty had this in mind when he'd chosen to leave, if he'd wanted to sacrifice himself for them out of some sense of nobility. He doubted it. Once Shitty was in the hallway, Chuck and Barman watched through the crack with bated breath.

Chuck figured Shitty would never make it outside, or even to the elevator for that matter. It may or may not be working and was all the way at the other end of the hall. The stairs were closer, but it would take an hour for the cripple to scoot down them on his butt, step by grueling step. The hall was empty, at least from what Chuck could see. Shitty was moving cautiously, creeping along, and Chuck wondered if he wouldn't be better off just rolling as fast as he could before a screamer heard his wheels clacking.

Barman whispered, "I should go out there with him."

"Nah," Chuck said, thinking of his promise. "Ya need to take care of this woman and her babies. Shitty knows what he's doin."

"Horseshit. He's even dumber than Eugene."

"Gene ain't dumb, he's crazy."

"That probably applies to all of us now."

"He's the one we should toss out there."

Barman winced. "I thought Gene was your friend."

"So did he."

"You're a special kind of scumbag, Chuck."

"And then some. But that don't mean Gene ain't a threat."

They fell silent when Shitty suddenly turned around. It was one swift move, the man lifting himself by planting his fists on the floor and spinning his torso to face the way he'd just come. He paddled faster, panting.

Chuck stared. "What the fuck?"

Barman straightened. "Shit."

"Here he comes. Whatta we do?"

"Get him inside. A screamer must be after him."

"I don't hear any screams."

The only sounds were of Shitty's strained wheezing and the cart's wheels clicking on the floorboards like tap shoes.

"We close the door," Chuck said, "and whatever's chasin him won't get us."

"He must've seen it from afar if it hasn't caught up to him yet. Get him inside. We can't let him die out there."

"Fuck him. He made his choice."

Barman shoved Chuck aside and positioned himself in front of the door jam. "You cocksucker. You'd let your own mother get eaten alive by alligators if it meant saving your own ass."

"He's one person. We're *six*."

Barman's face went slack as he took that in, as if his mind was changing, but by then Shitty was just a few feet away from the door.

"I just can't," Barman said. "I can't let someone die because of me."

Then they heard the scream.

Shitty had waited until he was upon them before releasing a hellish battle cry. His mouth went impossibly wide, his jaw unhinging from the force of his scream. The bones in his face cracked audibly. He roared and brayed, a rabid animal come home to annihilate those who'd cared for it. One arm darted through the cracked door before Barman could close it. He stepped back to raise his butcher knife and Chuck ran at the door, putting his shoulder into it with all his strength. There was a loud snap. He hoped it was Shitty's arm and not the doorframe. He lunged again but Shitty wheeled forward even as Barman sunk the knife into his shoulder. The little bastard was almost in the apartment now. His rotted teeth gleamed as he continued to scream, his one good eye rolling back, seeping. As Barman tugged his knife free, Shitty reeled back his head and then shot forward, stabbing his upper teeth into Barman's shin. Because he still screamed, Shitty couldn't fully bite down. Barman twisted away, spilling across the end table. Chuck shoved once more but it only served to pop Shitty into the room.

The women had been shrieking in the living room. Keisha, seeming to summon her courage for the sake of her children, came charging forward with her meager weapons. When Shitty rolled toward her, she shot him in the face with hairspray, then lit the mist on fire with the pocket lighter. The makeshift flamethrower set Shitty's scalp ablaze, balding him instantly and blackening his forehead. She kept spraying, singeing away his eyelashes, blistering his nose. His lips bubbled and oozed, but he never stopped screaming. He reached for her blindly, but she dodged his hands. She sprayed more fire. His cheeks melted. His eyes burst. The skin sizzled and ebbed. Still he did not fall over. Still he screamed.

Chuck swung down with the hammer, missing with the first blow and cracking Shitty on the shoulder. He drew his hand back to avoid the flames and came down again, smacking the head of the hammer upon Shitty's cranium. Keisha stopped spraying, letting Chuck cave in the cripple's blackened skullcap. A stew of hot brains and bone fragments showered Chuck's jeans and Shitty fell forward. Barman came to their aid now, stomping out the flames. In doing so, he separated some of the dead man's flesh from the bone. Having not crusted over yet, the tissue oozed off as if Shitty had been in a slow cooker for days.

"Fuck!" Chuck said. "Holy fuck!"

"The door!" Barman shouted.

Keisha shut it in place, but the knob wouldn't set into the lock. Something had broken when Chuck tried to shove Shitty out.

"Fuck it," Barman said to Keisha. "Let's get to your apartment. Now."

Keisha turned. "Brittany. Let's go, honey."

"You nuts?" Chuck asked. "After all that noise? Screamers must be comin for blocks."

Barman said, "That's why we gotta move. Once they fill that hall we'll never get out."

Brittany came out of her hiding spot in the kitchen. She still had the broom, but from the looks of her it wouldn't do much good. Her whole body was shaking. Her eyes were wet and couldn't settle on what to look at.

Barman said, "You okay, kid?"

"Y-ye-yeah."

For the first time, Chuck wondered what had happened to the girl's family during all of this. Who had she said she was living with? Her aunt? Her cousin? Did she want to get back to her own apartment or had she already seen her loved ones ripped apart by screamers?

Barman took a deep breath. "Okay. Let's—"

"Your leg," Chuck said.

"What?"

"Shitty bit your leg."

"So what?"

"So if a zombie bites you, ya become one, right?"

Barman groaned. "For Christ's sakes, man; zombies again? This ain't *Dawn of the Dead*. We have no reason to think a bite will transform me into a screamer."

"Bullshit!" Eugene said, rising from the couch. It was hard to tell if he was smiling or if it was just the damage to his face giving him a rictus grin. "Chuck is right. If Shitty's saliva got into Barman's blood, he'll be infected."

"And where'd you get that?" Barman said. "Twitter or some shit?"

"It's just common sense."

"Something you've always been in short supply of, asswipe. I'm getting these women to safety. We don't have time for this nonsense."

Eugene stepped closer, his dark eyes on Brittany. "Get the mother to her babies. But leave the girl here."

Barman extended the knife. It still dripped with traces of Shitty and the window's touch of sunlight fell upon the blade, making it gleam through slivers of blood.

"Gene," Barman said. "You have five seconds to get away from her before I stab you to death. Man, I mean it."

"What about all that humanitarian talk about not letting someone die because of you? I heard you say that."

"I don't want to kill you, but I will if it means protecting her."

Brittany's jaw fell, realizing Eugene wasn't trying to keep her in the apartment to protect her, but for his own lurid purposes, whatever they may be.

"Why are you so damn passionate about her, anyway, Barman?" Eugene asked.

Barman sneered but didn't give an answer. He looked to the women instead. "You two ready?"

Keisha went to him, but Brittany hesitated. Perhaps she feared Barman's potential for infection, but one quick glance at Eugene got her moving. Chuck swallowed hard. The women had a much better chance of getting to Keisha's apartment with Barman's help, but if he turned into a screamer, they'd be dead before Chuck could assist them. But wasn't that a risk either way? So far everyone who'd turned into one of those insane monsters had done so spontaneously and randomly. No one had been bitten before transforming; it had just happened, like some internal switch had been flicked. Any one of them could turn at any moment, but they'd all chosen to stay together. And the women decided to go with Barman knowing he'd been bitten. Who was Chuck to change their minds if he hadn't even made up his own?

Barman opened the door.

CHAPTER TWENTY

THEY FOUND HER at the mall.

It seemed so appropriate, even poetic. It was the very place where the boy had first met the man. It was a foggy memory, like some sentimental dream, but clear enough for the boy to recognize the place, even if some of the stores had changed.

"It all comes full circle," the man said when they entered the parking lot. "Ya can't escape fate, son. It's like death that way."

Even if the man were physically capable, he wouldn't have gone inside with him. This wasn't his catch; it was the boy's and the boy's alone. It was his time, his journey. He'd observed and listened and learned. Now it was open season.

The mall was a veritable buffet of veal. The girls flocked around shops like ducks to breadcrumbs, all smiles and laughter and joy, eyes bright with youth, energized by an ignorant enthusiasm for life. Blondes, brunettes, and redheads shot adrenaline into his heart like a hundred EpiPens. But there was no lust for the game in this moment. He stalked them with a nobler purpose than mere carnality. His very manhood lied in the balance. He could not disappoint the man. Perhaps more importantly, he could not disappoint *himself*. He had to separate this desire for victory from the one that tried to worm into his penis at the sight of the veal's nubile bodies. Young, small and lean. Tight asses packed into tight jeans. Budding breasts indenting their blouses. Black ones, white ones, brown ones. All were worthy of the hunt. Thoughts of mating had to wait until after capture. He couldn't let their fledgling beauty muddy his thoughts. The boy's mind had been molded into a strategic database, an organic encyclopedia of all the man had taught him. The approach, the bait and the snatch. The precautions and baby steps. How to choose the right calf from the herd. How to confuse, dominate, and possess her. Electrons of information burst through his anxious brain. Sweat pooled in the pits of his work shirt. The ring of useless keys on his belt jangled as he walked, each movement causing the badge on his chest to graze his skin with its pin backing.

The boy was just old enough to pull off the look now, or at least to the veal he would choose from. Hard farm work had developed lean muscle and he was tall for his age. The man said in the right light the boy could pass for twenty. It seemed like a stretch, but the boy didn't question it. Besides, the man insisted it was more about attitude than age when it came to such appearances. Veal were young, simple creatures—easily fooled. They feared authority, but also trusted it. They had yet to wean off their parents and still obeyed their schoolteachers. They were respectful to policemen (at least to their faces). Even a mall security guard could benefit from that deeply ingrained, automatic respect.

The perfect veal had just finished her slice of Sbarro pizza and was on her way out of the food court, accompanied by two female friends. Though they'd been browsing the clothing outlets, none were carrying shopping bags, only small purses. They'd purchased nothing but snacks. The boy noted this useful information. He loped along at a careful distance, the girls loitering another forty minutes before parting ways. It was a school night. There would be homework and dinners with their families. Dogs had to be walked and curfews had to be kept. Love letters to boyfriends had to be written in multicolored pen. The boy licked his lips as he trailed the selected veal, the brim of his guard hat low upon his brow, the black plaster of the visor reflecting the neon sign of the toy store. He touched the badge patch upon this hat for reassurance.

This was really happening.

He picked up the pace.

The veal was a lithe brunette with fair skin and a smile that reeked of innocence, of a life that had seen no personal tragedy. In that bright face, true pain had never existed. It made the boy want to crush her. Though he guessed her to be fourteen, there was already a slight sway to her gait, the hips moving with the first touches of female sexuality as she moved toward the fountain. The sound of running water added ambience to the scene, drowning out the laughter of children who ran around the fountain, flicking pennies with their thumbs. The boy's air stopped in his chest. A sudden coldness seeped into him, rippling his skin as his stomach went hollow. His collar felt too tight.

It wasn't the thrill of the chase making him nervous. It was the fountain. He dragged his footsteps, almost afraid to get any closer. It didn't make sense to him. Why was there this sudden sense of dread? He'd certainly never feared water before. It wasn't like he could drown in such shallow water, if he'd somehow fallen in. An inexplicable feeling a *déjà vu* threatened to paralyze him. He looked back, half expecting a shadow to put its hand on his shoulder.

But he'd already made his selection. He had to press on.

The veal brushed her long hair from her neck as she rounded the edge of the fountain. One of the kids tapped the other's shoulder—*you're it*—and ran off. The other child pursued, leaving predator alone with prey. He clenched his fists against the taunt of the fountain's ghosts and came upon the teen just before she turned toward the exit doors.

He dropped his voice an octave. "Excuse me, young lady."

The veal turned around. Her eyes were the color of earth and they grew wide at the sight of his uniform. "Um, yeah?"

"I'm with mall security. Spotted you shopliftin. You'll have to come with me."

"But I didn't—"

"Better to not embarrass yourself by causin a scene. Just come along and we can straighten all this out."

She clutched the strap of her purse with both hands, making him wonder if she really had shoplifted. Not that it mattered. The rise of her brow had already assured him she'd bought into his charade. She looked at the floor, shoulders curling her in on herself, a sheepish manner reflecting her age. The boy took her by the arm. It was a bold step, but she complied. The soft flesh of her stirred something in him as they walked.

"Are you gonna tell my parents?" she asked.

"Just come with me, kid."

They approached the exit doors and she asked where they were going. The boy just opened the door and ushered her through. A couple entering the mall glanced at them but were too busy wrangling their rowdy children to get a good look at the boy or question his role as mall cop. A small group of teenagers were by the curb several yards away from the exit, otherwise the lot was empty. Night had fallen in full. Dodging the lot's streetlamps would be easy enough. He led the veal around the side of the building.

She slowed. "Wait . . . "

"The office is in another part of the mall. That's where we're goin."

"Why're we outside?"

"It's the fastest route."

"This doesn't seem right."

She tried to move away from him and he gripped her arm harder. They were almost to the cover of the bushes separating the mall from the rear lot where the man had kept the truck running. But the veal was getting squirmy. She might scream at any second. She tried to pull away just as they came under the shadow of the overhang.

"Let me g—"

The boy punched her in the stomach. The veal crumpled over, wind snatched from her, stunning her into silence. The boy looked around. Hedges and shadows concealed them, but he still couldn't keep his hands from shaking as he dragged her into a row of bushes. He fumbled with the vial in his pocket, the vapors rising. There was no time for the cloth; he just poured the chloroform directly onto her face and pressed his palm over her mouth and nostrils. The veal writhed like a beached fish. She bit his hand, but he kept it in place in spite of the pain, muffling her cries, and in her panic, she took in as much air as she could, causing her to spiral into unconsciousness all the quicker.

The hardest part was dragging the veal around the side of the building to the truck. Every nerve in the boy's body had spiked, fearing a car would drive past at any second, that he'd be seen, that he'd be caught. He put her in a fireman's carry and flung her limp body onto the bed of the pickup, then folded down the bed's rolling cover over her and locked it, entombing the girl. As the boy climbed into the driver's seat, he saw proud tears in the man's eyes.

"Quite a catch, son. And a ballsy one at that."

The veal lay in the truck bed. He'd taken off the cover and lit her with his flashlight.

"Can't believe I finally done it," he said.

"Done it and done it gooder n' hell. From now on, I'm gonna be livin through you, boy. Gonna do my huntin, processin, sellin and even my fuckin all through you."

The boy chuckled. "Come on, now, Pa. Ya just keep takin yer meds. You're gonna pull through this. Then we can do all those things together. Like men?"

"Like men."

The veal was stirring now, slowly coming to. They were safe on the farm again. She could scream all she wanted.

"So what're we gonna do with her?" the boy asked. "We only got that pregnant one up in the pen. Guess we could use this one here for steaks and chops. She's young, so we ain't gotta keep 'er chained up long. She's probably already tender as it is."

The man put his hand on the boy's shoulder. "She's your catch, son. Do what'cha want with 'er." He winked and nudged him. "She is a young'n, though. You're right about that. Almost *too* young for matin but, like my Uncle Merle always said, if she's old 'nough to bleed she's old 'nough to breed." He chuckled. "He was a real character, ol' Merle. Use to tell me, if there's grass on the field, play ball, and hell, if there ain't, roll her over and play in the mud!"

The man's laughter was raucous, loud enough to cause the veal to rise in a sudden jolt. She spun her head, lost in darkness, the only light in the woods coming from the flashlight shining right at her.

"Where am I? What's going o—"

Her face soured as the memory came back to her. Instead of screaming, she began to cry with closed-tight eyes. Her small hands closed over her heart.

"Please," she whimpered. "Please . . . "

But she didn't specify what she was pleading for. It was a vague, desperate utterance, one that left the boy wondering who she was asking, he or God. In this moment, perhaps they were the same.

"Hush now," he said. "Ain't nobody wanna listen to your blubberin."

Her words transformed into a stifled whine that sounded more like a squeak—a cornered animal, a dying infant. It was this sort of pathetic hopelessness that had tricked the boy in the past, the veal having preyed upon his emotions, gathering sympathy they did not deserve. These low bitches manipulated and betrayed at every opportunity. Though he might have seen a hint of himself in this girl, reflected by the very same fear that had paralyzed him during his first days upon the farm, he knew better than to empathize with mere meat. He'd been educated the hard way about the pitfalls of doing so. Veal were all liars, all venomous snakes and sewer rats. They might appear human, but they were the furthest things from it.

He handed the flashlight to the man and unwound the leash and choke chain. The girl recoiled when he tried to put it over her head, so he backhanded her and lassoed the chain around her neck. He drew it tight, far tighter than he would on any other living thing, and the veal tried in vain to put her fingers beneath the chain to pull it loose. Her tongue hung out and her eyes bulged.

"Careful now," the man said. "She's just a lil' thing. She'll break easy."

The boy eased the tension, but kept her locked in the loop. He was not so much enraged as he was excited. This was his catch; it would be his slaughter. He would process the meat and deliver it himself. He'd contributed to the farm in every other way, but now he'd be bringing in cash from scratch. This made him bloom with pride. He rubbed his crotch without thinking about it.

"Well," the man said, "I'm bushed. I'm gonna lay down for a spell. You lovebirds have a good time now, ya hear?"

The veal gasped when he said 'lovebirds'. She gazed up at the boy, her pale cheeks trembling from chattering teeth. The boy tapped the choke chain, silencing her preemptively. And as the man shuffled into the house, the boy admired his prize.

Fresh meat was only one use for her.

There were so many options.

The veal was being impossible. No matter how hard he yanked that chain she wouldn't follow him into the meat shed. She just curled into a ball to become dead weight. He wasn't even going to kill her yet; he just wanted her in the meat shed so he'd have privacy to mate with her, the man being in the house and the pregnant veal in the pen. If this new girl saw the other one chained to the floor and bloated in the belly, she'd go into even worse hysterics. He had to get this veal alone, teach her the new rules. Compliance came easier when they weren't insane with fear.

He tugged the choke chain once more. The veal gagged but didn't budge. The boy clenched his jaw, then reared back and kicked her in the ass, hard. She rolled over with a yelp and he kicked her in the ribs.

He leaned down. "Had enough?"

The veal crossed her arms in a protective huddle. Sobbing, her speech was unintelligible.

"Get in that shed," the boy told her, "or I'll stomp the life outta ya, right here in the goddamn dirt."

She got on all fours like the livestock she was, then slowly stood, shoulders hunched, head hung, hair covering her face like a funeral veil. She stepped into the metallic glow of the shack and the boy pulled the door closed behind her. Its clang was musical to him. Once the lock was in place, he removed her leash and hung it on one of the meat hooks he'd suspended from the ceiling with old bicycle chains.

"Take off yer clothes."

The girl didn't move or even make a sound. She wasn't even crying anymore. It was as if she'd been struck by sudden catatonia, her mind disconnecting so her body would not feel all that was to be done to it. But when the boy made a sudden move toward her, she flinched and took a step back, bumping into the meat grinder.

"I know ya can hear me," he said. "Now take off your clothes."

Her face turned the color of strawberries as she slid out of her sweater, then pulled her shirt over her head. She hesitated, continuing only when he stepped closer. The pink sneakers were kicked away, the tight jeans peeled off like a second skin.

"Come on, now. Bra and undies."

She hugged herself and stared at the wall. This brought heat to the boy's neck and he came at her, grabbing one of her bra cups. He pulled her closer and she shoved him back, causing the bra to rip and fall halfway off, exposing one budding breast. Screeching now, the girl made a pinwheel of her arms, battering him with fists that failed to cause any real damage. Having had enough, the boy grabbed her around the waist and tried to bend her over the grinder, but she scratched his face and kicked her legs. In her thrashing, she by chance hit the red button on the side of the grinder. It came alive with a hum, sending soft vibrations through their bodies as they battled against its base.

The veal stabbed her thumb into one of the boy's eyes and he lost his grip on her. When he opened his eyes again, the girl was reaching for the slab on the wall that held the butcher knives and meat cleaver. The boy's eyes protruded. As she reached for the closest knife, he pulled her arm behind her back, twisting it high, and when she shoved back he clenched her forearm and forced her hand into the spout of the whirring meat grinder. He pushed down with all his weight, feeding her into the drill's turning blades. Her scream was so sharp it made his ears pop. The blades clanked against her bones as they skinned them, but her fingers weren't big enough to halt the grind and soon red noodles of flesh were oozing through the grate.

The boy grabbed the veal's elbow, pushing down harder, obliterating her delicate hand. Because the blade was spinning against bone, the meat came out so slowly the heat of the machine began to cook it, the girl's tissue browning as it sluiced through the grate. Her face waned with horror. The boy kept feeding the grinder until the veal's bones jammed up the works and the machine came to an abrupt stop. The girl passed out and he let her fall to the floor, her mutilated arm draped over her torn bra. Only her thumb and half her index finger remained. They were without flesh, the bones stubbed. Splinters of shaved cartilage glistened in the remaining morsels of sinew. More than half of her hand was gone, the rest decimated into an unwoven mitten of gore.

The excitement left the boy breathing heavy. He knelt in the red puddle forming around the girl's stump. A stray vein dangled out of her wrist, the blood running out like a garden hose. He tried not to look at it as he removed her panties, then reached for the rubber apron hanging on the wall and draped it over her mangled limb so its grotesqueness wouldn't put him off. He knew it wouldn't be long before she'd bleed to death. There would be no time to deplete her iron and make her softer. Best to slaughter this one tonight.

Spreading her legs, the boy unzipped his pants so to put his first catch to more than one use.

No sense in being wasteful.

CHAPTER TWENTY-ONE

LIKE SOME DISCOUNT Captain America, Barman led the way with his folding chair-shield held out in front of him, the women to the rear and on either side of him, Keisha with her cheap flamethrower, Brittany with her broomstick staff.

The blonde girl looked infinitely younger to Chuck than she had when he'd first seen her, back when he'd touched himself while watching her get off the bus, the summer wind and her pleated skirt playing peek-a-boo with his dirty-old-man eyes. He didn't regret objectifying her—even now he was admiring her nubile body—but her present fear amplified her youth, dread stripping all hints of maturity from her face like makeup remover.

Keisha, on the other hand, looked older now. Though she was close to two decades younger than he was, Chuck thought she seemed worn out, the stress of being a mother during this crisis having busted the poor woman. Maybe it was the violence she'd been forced to inflict upon Shitty, a man she likely would have ignored if she'd walked by him begging in the streets just two days ago. Maybe it was the humbling realization she and her babies were extremely vulnerable, that bad things didn't just happen to other people, they happen to us all.

Chuck watched the trio from the door jam. He wanted to get back to Leslie, to check on her at the very least, but was compelled to keep the door open a crack, not just in case the group needed to retreat but out of his own curiosity. Would everyone who left the apartment turn into a screamer the way Shitty had? Was there something in the air out there, some pathogen Leslie's apartment sealed them off from? He doubted it was so simple. Shitty's transformation was likely just another spontaneous fluke. But anything was possible in a world that made no fucking sense.

He also wanted to see if screamers pounced upon them. If so, he would get a sense of what he and Leslie would be up against when they left the apartment. They definitely had to leave if she were going to live. Chuck had to get her medical assistance, whether or not Barman was coming back to help.

He watched as Barman led the women in at a steady pace. He held the bloody knife out as if he were in a fencing competition, his gait altered by his minor injuries. The bartender was large and headstrong, but not without jitters. He was too intelligent to be fearless. They'd already made it further than Shitty had, but the end of the hall was still a long ways off, longer than it had ever seemed before. Many doors were open. Anything could be lurking within those apartments.

"They're gonna die out there," Eugene said.

Chuck glanced back. The faceless man was sitting at the table where Chuck and Leslie had first shared drinks together. It seemed a lifetime ago. The cat Chuck had forgotten about was purring in Eugene's lap as he poured two glasses of bourbon, sipped from one with shredded lips, and leaned back in his chair like an old man watching the sun go down.

"Here I am petting this cat," he said. "And it might be the most infected out of all of us. Who knows what he's been in contact with."

"He's an indoor cat."

"You might as well have a drink with me, Chuck. It's not like you'll be able to do anything for them."

"Why's that?"

"Well, you could run out there and get yourself killed too, but that won't save them, now will it?"

"And how do ya know they ain't gonna make it?"

"*How do I know*? 'Cause it's the fate they chose. Barman chose failure the moment he stopped listening to reason. All we had to do was fuck little blondie and we'd be in the clear, but no."

Chuck almost argued with him, but decided it was pointless. Eugene had lost what few marbles he'd had to begin with.

"Come on, Chuck. Have a drink with me while we still can. You cherish each bite of every sandwich once you really understand you're going to die. So I think it's safe to say this is the best bourbon we'll ever taste."

He had a point.

"One sec," Chuck said, watching the others. "They're about two thirds of the way down the hall now."

"Maybe they can say hi to my mother for me."

"Shit." Much like the cat, Chuck had forgotten all about her. "You probably wanna go to her, huh? Make sure she's okay?"

Eugene snickered. "The way that old battleaxe keeps the apartment locked up, she's safer than anybody else. She's so out of touch with the outside world she probably doesn't even know it's coming to an end."

Chuck was surprised by Eugene's apathy regarding his mom, but it wasn't about to become his problem. The only people he felt remotely responsible for the safety of were Leslie and the babies he'd sworn he'd look out for. It was their mother he was concerned about, not Eugene's. He watched intently as she drew closer to those babies with every step, for the nervousness he felt for Keisha was actually for himself. If she failed to get to her children, he would have to go instead. The last thing he wanted was to care for infants during this inexorable odyssey toward death.

"Kids and their mothers," Eugene said. "We never *truly* get away from them, do we? If I hadn't been forced to fill my dad's shoes at such a young age, I wouldn't have had to take care of Ma and could've been more popular. I could've had girls; got me some of that young stuff. Teenage girls have to be the best lay, otherwise society wouldn't have fetishized them, right?"

Though he agreed, Chuck didn't answer.

"I never got to find out," Eugene continued. "I've never had the luxury of fucking a teen, not even when I was one. Course that could've changed today, but that stupid bastard had to ruin it for us both. You can't tell me you didn't want a piece of that girl."

Chuck couldn't, so he didn't. The trio was nearing the end of the hallway.

Eugene poured himself another. "I've never been able to talk to girls all that well, let alone ones that pretty. I suppose I could've paid for one, but hookers and strippers are so ripe with disease. That's why I didn't try and fuck Angel. I should have, but it's too late for that now, huh? Even if she was alive no amount of money would get her to spread her legs for a man without a face."

"Gene, will you shut the fuck up?"

But Eugene was too lost in his own reverie, this dreamy, sentimental mourning for untapped pussy. He had the crushing despair of a man who hadn't fucked enough (*if at all*, Chuck thought bitterly), a remorse that weighed twice as much now that the clock of all humankind was nearing hour zero.

"No way that blondie has diseases," Eugene said, eyes glazing. "She's so young and clean-looking. I'll bet her cunt's as pure as the Virgin Mary's and tastes like water from a natural spring."

Chuck flinched when the trio's stride suddenly broke. They scrambled at the doorway of an apartment as a stout, chubby black woman came charging out, her screams breaking the silence. Even from this distance, Chuck could make out her white Afro and cotton nightgown as she came at the group with raging arms.

Keisha cried out. "Mama! No!"

The older woman was in full screamer mode, clawing at Barman with her fingernails as he battering-rammed her with the folding chair and pinned her to the wall.

"Don't hurt her!" Keisha said.

But Barman had already raised the knife. "She's got The Scream! Look at her!"

The old mother howled, trying to shove him off.

Keisha sobbed. "Mama!"

The screamer managed to grab hold of Barman's hair, and in the split second he pulled his head away she squeezed out from behind the chair and was free, arms flailing as she ran at Brittany. She stood there helplessly, shell-shocked. Barman stabbed Keisha's mother in the chest just as she got her hands around the young girl's neck, rescuing Brittany but causing Keisha to drop her weapons and put her hands over her face, shrieking loud enough to drown out her mother's roar. Chuck could tell Keisha hadn't transformed into a screamer. Her cries were from emotion, not contagion. Barman was taking away any hope Keisha had that her mother might survive this nightmare, that she could be cured. As the older woman crumbled inward, Barman withdrew the blade and stabbed it down into her back. A jet of blood rose into the air, champagne popped from a bottle.

"Mama!"

THEY ALL DIED SCREAMING

When Barman wielded the knife for a third stabbing, Keisha snatched the broom from Brittany and swung it at his face. Not expecting the attack, Barman caught the blow right on the nose. The bridge of it shattered, blood and mucus cascading from both nostrils. He wobbled, losing the chair as he bounced against the wall. Keisha gasped in instant remorse. The mother, perhaps sensing Barman's weakened state, lunged.

"Oh fuck," Chuck said, opening the door.

Chuck moved forward with the hammer. The rabid woman pounced on Barman, wrapping her legs around his waist, digging her nails into his shoulders and latching on. Her teeth disappeared into his neck.

Keisha cried out, "Mama, no! Don't! He's a friend!"

Chuck was running now, surprised by his own action and not entirely sure what he was going to do when he reached the others. He wanted to protect Barman so he could help him get Leslie to a doctor or pharmacy, but he also wanted to protect Keisha so she could be with her babies again. Killing the crazy old lady would be a given if Keisha wasn't so mixed up about the reality of the situation. If Chuck bashed in her mother's skull, wouldn't Keisha come at him the way she had Barman? And then there was Brittany—an afterthought but a thought nonetheless. Eugene's comment about the girl's vagina echoed in his head confusingly.

Barman started spinning in circles, slamming the clinging screamer into the walls. Brittany darted into Keisha's apartment to escape the violence. Keisha was holding her head in her hands, still screaming, her eyes shut tight against the horror of it all. See no evil, hear no evil.

Out of shape, Chuck breathed heavily with exertion. He was nearly to the group when a massive form stomped into the hallway. It came from another apartment, its huge, jaundiced body snapping the doorframe on its way out. In life, the obese man must have gone in and out of the apartment sideways; as a screamer, he just barged his way out, crumbling drywall and scraping his skin. He wore only a pair of gym shorts, and acne and bedsores spattered the rolls of his undulating lard. His sweat-glazed tits wobbled, the areola encircled by red hairs, the only ones on his chest. Bloodshot eyes stared the men down. He charged with his head down, a human rhino making thunder upon the floorboards. His roar was deep and guttural and manic.

Chuck gasped. "Jesus!"

The hammer suddenly felt so tiny and useless in his hand. He continued toward the group, retreating from the huge man at the same time. Chuck had made his decision. He had to rescue Barman from that screaming mad bitch. It was the only chance Chuck had of getting out of this hallway alive, because he couldn't take on the fat monstrosity alone. And there were bound to be other screamers. Lots of them. Getting Leslie medical assistance would be nearly impossible without Barman's help. This chaos had convinced Chuck of that.

"Hold still, Barman!"

The bartender stopped spinning and Chuck grabbed the Mama screamer's afro, tilting her head back. Her teeth brought a chunk of Barman's neck with them, but Chuck was able to hit her with the hammer. Three mean blows fractured the top of her skull and she crumpled to floor like a discarded marionette. She was still twitching, so Chuck got down and hammered her madly until the top of her head started caving in. Keisha opened her eyes just long enough to see her mother's face sink inward. She fell to her knees, shaking.

By now the rhino man was just ten feet away. His bulk made him a slow runner, but the determination was tireless. He wouldn't stop until either he or everyone else on earth was dead. Barman clutched his neck wound. His pained face gave way to a pale dread as the monster lumbered forward.

"What the fuck?" he murmured as he snatched up the chair-shield, gripping the butcher knife.

Chuck glanced at the discarded broom but felt better about the hammer after killing the old lady with it.

"What's the plan?" he asked.

"I dunno," Barman said. "Go berserk?"

It wasn't much of a strategy, but it was all they had time for. As the rhino came upon them, he bowed his head forward, his bald spot shining as the light of a new day poured through the window at the end of the hall. At the last second, Barman tucked the knife under his belt and swung the chair with both hands. It bent in half upon connecting with the rhino's head and flew from Barman's grip, but the rhino didn't stop charging, didn't even slow down. The men jumped aside like matadors as the beast passed by.

"Keisha!" Brittany called from the doorway of the apartment, her arms outstretched. "Keisha, come on! Think of your babies!"

This opened Keisha's eyes. She blinked away her tears and got to her feet just as the rhino spun around, the walls shaking in response to his every movement. Keisha was faster than the fat man. She would have made it had she not slipped on her dead mother's blood. Her left foot slid out behind her and she spilled to the floor. Trying to catch herself, one elbow bent in the wrong direction and it snapped against the hardwood. Bone protruded from the flesh in a red spray. Chuck rushed to get her out of the rhino's path, but he just wasn't close enough to make it in time. When the rhino pounced, Chuck had no choice but to get out of his way. The giant came down on the frail woman with two football-sized knees. Three hundred and fifty pounds of corpulence, cellulite and elephant bones pulverized her. Keisha popped and crackled, her spine breaking, shoulders dislocating. Her eyes bulged and blood dribbled from the sockets. She vomited a crimson jet. The stench of voided bowels filled the hallway.

Now the rhino was between the men and the doorway of the apartment.

In one swift move Barman planted one hand on the rhino's head and jabbed the knife through his left eye with the other, then twisted the blade and withdrew it, expunging the split eye completely. Half blind, the rhino swung a wild backhand that just barely missed Barman. He started slicing at the rhino's face and neck in another attempt to land a good stab. Chuck went for the head too, for a hammer attack on the body would be futile. There were too many protective layers. He bashed the screamer's skull, using the bald spot as a target, but the rhino got to his feet anyway. The two men backed away and the rhino grabbed Keisha around the waist. Her broken, contorted body wiggled grotesquely as he picked her up. Barman gasped as the beast started swinging Keisha's carcass, wielding it as a weapon.

Chuck stepped back. "Run!"

He turned around. Barman turned too, accidently walking right into the twisted chair on the floor. He regained his footing just before Keisha's head collided with his own.

The crack was like a baseball bat on a fastball.

Barman went down.

The screaming rhino raised Keisha's corpse over his shoulder, holding her by the ankles, then slammed her down upon Barman as if he were hammering in railroad spikes. Barman made an agonized cry and Chuck ran back to him, to the rhino, to his own doom. The butcher knife had spun away from Barman and Chuck snatched it up as he came forward, staying close to one wall, deliberately taking the path parallel to the rhino's blind eye. It wouldn't make him invisible, but he'd be harder to see.

The rhino behaved like all the other screamers, continuing to attack his target instead of protecting himself from oncoming threats. Keisha's rag doll body was his sledgehammer. Ribs were now pushed out through her breasts. Barman took more punishment. Every time he came close to getting up, the dead body bashed him back into the floor. He coughed blood.

Chuck jumped at the rhino while he was bent over, catching him from his blind side, and used both hands to bayonet the jugular. The rhino froze, dropping the corpse on top of Barman, and Chuck pulled the blade out. Blood shot from the screamer's open throat, effectively silencing him. He shoved the knife into the rhino's neck once more, and when the big man started to fold, Chuck withdrew the knife and plunged it up and down, punching a tapestry of wounds into the screamer's neck.

"Die! Die, you fat fuck!"

The rhino bent forward as if doing as he was told. The floor shook as he fell still. The screams having stopped, the hallways went eerily silent, the only sound being the gentle dribbling of blood and Barman's moans. He rolled onto his side as he struggled to breathe. Chuck got on his knees beside him.

"Aww, fuck," Chuck said. Barman was in terrible shape, his nose and neck wound gushing, arms covered in cuts, bite marks and welts. "Christ, Barman. You okay?"

Barman wheezed. "What . . . the fuck . . . do you think? No! Of course I'm not okay." He coughed a mist of blood. "I think . . . think that fat bastard . . . broke my back."

"I can carry you into Keisha's apartment—"

"Don't move me. I'm fucked, man. I think my . . . ribs are broken. Can't breathe. My insides hurt like a . . . son of a . . . b-b-bitch."

"Okay. Ummm. Fuck. What—"

Barman looked into his eyes. "I . . . I want to tell you something." He surprised Chuck by taking his hand. "Something I've never told anyone. I need to get it off my chest while . . . while I still can."

Chuck gripped his hand back. "Alright."

Barman's every breath came out with a whistle. Blood sluiced through the gaps in his teeth. There was sharp pain in his face, both from his injuries and the effort to reveal what was troubling him.

"I'm a terrible man," he said.

"Bullshit."

"Shut up and let me talk. I'm not looking for compliments . . . or reassurance." He coughed and his breathing steadied. "I need to confess this to someone . . . before I die. I need to repent. Not to god or any of that shit . . . I just need to admit to what I've done. Own up to it. I can't keep it bottled up anymore. I tried to make up for it today . . . at least. Tried to do what was right. I was hoping to pay back the world for making it just a little more evil of a place to live."

"You were a bigger help to all of us than anyone else was."

Barman ignored the praise. "I have a dark past, Chuck. It all goes back to when I was young and I . . . I did horrible things to people, to women."

Chuck felt a sudden chill. He shifted uncomfortably, not wanting to hear any more but unable to abandon his friend.

"Chuck . . . I hurt young women. I'm . . . I'm a *rapist*." He spit out the word like spoiled milk. "I was young . . . stupid. I didn't attack them or anything like that . . . but I still raped them . . . three before I couldn't take the guilt of it anymore. I . . . I date raped them, you know? A friend of mine taught me how to do it. Putting stuff in their drinks so I could have my way with them after they passed out. Roofies . . . sedatives and sleeping pills." He winced, face tight with pain. "Never got busted. The girls knew what had happened to them . . . but they never reported the rapes. Most never do. Only this one girl confided in her parents. And you know what they did? They told her to keep it a secret and gave *me* a warning to never tell anyone. See . . . they didn't want to hurt the family's good name by *her* being a rape victim . . . as if it was *her* fault. Poor thing stayed silent for months before killing herself.

"If any other girls ever told friends or family they'd been . . . been . . . sexually assaulted, it never came back to bite me in the ass. I wish it had. I wish I'd paid for what I did to them. The guilt . . . made me hate myself . . . hate the world. And I couldn't *stand* having sex anymore. I stopped caring . . . about everything. It's why I am the way I am. Why I've lived with so much hate inside. It's why I don't deserve a life . . . or even a name." A series of harsh coughs and he turned and spat blood. "That poor girl killed herself . . . because of what I did to her. My orgasm was worth more than her life. Shit, Chuck. What kind of God would let me live and her die?"

Chuck bit his upper lip. He struggled with what to say. "It's okay, man. It sounds like you didn't really know what you were doing at the time."

"Like hell . . . I knew *exactly* what I was doing."

"But you didn't realize what you were doing was *wrong*, not at first. You were led astray by *somebody else*, by that friend who taught you. In your mind, those girls weren't like people. They were . . . objects."

"I treated them like pieces of *meat*," Barman said. "I was . . . a *pig*."

Chuck swallowed hard, his chest tightening. He needed a drink. He needed darkness now. Darkness and Leslie and some semblance of peace, no matter how artificial or temporary.

Barman said, "Maybe that's what The Scream is all about, Chuck—God is making up for his past mistakes."

Barman smiled, the first time Chuck had ever seen the man really do so.

Then he died.

CHAPTER TWENTY-TWO

OVER SIX MONTHS PREGNANT, the veal's belly had ballooned, grotesquely hanging from her frail body. Initially the boy was torn between causing her malnourishment to keep her tender and feeding her enough for two. It hadn't mattered either way these past few weeks, for the girl rarely had an appetite, which he found strange considering her condition.

He groaned at the thought of having to deal with this shit for three more months. She had so many more needs now. It was constant maintenance, adding chores to his already stacked list. The past few weeks she'd been vomiting several times a day. She peed all the time, soiling her cage, insisting she couldn't help it. She bitched about being sick and was always sneezing and coughing. Recently she'd been running a high fever. The boy began to wonder if she had health problems beyond just being pregnant. He fed her noodle soup and pig milk warmed on the stove. It was similar to cow's milk in composition, though more watery and with a higher fat content. The man absolutely loved it and claimed it had better healing properties than any meds they could give the veal, if she really did have a cold or the flu as she so often insisted.

Though this veal seemed ill, the man had undergone a slight recovery from his necrotizing fasciitis. The boy had bathed him and tended to his sores, keeping him on a healthy vegetarian diet and making sure he took his antibiotics with each meal. Still the man was heavily scarred by the ordeal, his flesh patchy, boil-ridden and covered in small holes. Pink, burn-like spots covered his face and neck. Discoloration ran up his legs like shingles. But he wasn't rotting anymore. With the help of his cane he moved around almost as easily as he had before the ailment, though he was still rebuilding his upper body strength.

"Ya done saved my life, son," he'd said over last night's dinner. "And ya done saved this here farm to boot."

"T'weren't nothin, Pa. Just did what all was right."

"You're a man of the highest water, I tell ya."

The man was able to work again, but mostly tended to the house and other light duties, slopping the hogs and handling shipment orders over the phone. The boy tended to the livestock and veal, handled all the hunting and the majority of the slaughtering and processing. He'd brought home five additional young women after his first capture. That first girl had given him some trouble, so he was extra hard on the ones that followed right from the get-go, making them too afraid to strike back by driving into their puny brains who was in charge. There was a pasture between home and town where he took the veal for initiation, adjusting their attitudes and asserting his dominance over them before even bringing them to the farm. He subjected the girls to indignities and flurries of pain that were sexual in nature. Instead of forcing himself on them, he forced them *to do things to him*, on their knees. Total subservience was essential to a successful relationship between farmer and livestock, owner and the owned. It was just like wrangling the pigs, only with much more force.

The pregnant veal lay on her back upon the bed of barn hay, legs stretched out. At the man's suggestion, the boy had constructed a cage large enough for her to lie down in. Her protruding belly required it. She no longer fit into a regular veal cage, and it would be damaging to her condition to constrict her too much. Even her chains were loose, enabling her to turn on her side. It pissed him off. The bitch was almost as pampered as those high-end cattle he'd read about who were free to graze and got massaged and bathed daily, their stress-free lifestyle resulting in the most beautifully marbled beef. Not that he would ever eat it.

He unlocked the cage and knelt with the dog bowl full of rice and raw vegetables. Extra beans had been added for protein and fiber, another damned luxury. The boy cleared his throat and nudged her.

"Dinnertime," he grumbled. "Wake the hell up."

She didn't even stir. He shoved her harder. If she didn't get up and show some gratitude for the dinner he'd prepared, he would make her pay, pregnant or not.

"Get up and eat or I swear I'll shove a cattle prod against yer goddamned butthole. Ya hear me?"

But perhaps she didn't. The boy leaned in to get a better look at her face. Her eyes were half open, staring up through the bars at nothing. He snapped his fingers in front of them. They didn't blink.

"Dang it."

All that time and effort and the needy bitch up and dies?

He poked her rotund belly. Nothing. He separated the lips of her vagina and shoved in a finger, dry. Still nothing. She was warm inside, but the rest of her body was cool to the touch. There was a chill in the pen, but she'd been given one of the man's old flannels, a pair of panties taken off one of the recent captures, and even a blanket.

The boy went off to tell the man the news. He hoped he wouldn't be too disappointed about losing the baby. The boy certainly wasn't.

"Let's just cut it out."

The boy stared at him. "You wanna *what*?"

The man gazed upon the dead veal's swollen stomach, leaning on his cane to get a closer look. He wet his lips.

"If we're careful, I reckon we can take that baby outta there mostly intact. It's a little underdone, if ya know what I mean, but we can give 'er a taste, see if it's worth doin again."

The boy blinked. "Ya really want us to eat *meat*?"

"I know, I know. But this here's 'bout quality control. Need to see just how flavorful baby meat'll be to know if we can market it as gourmet or not."

"Jeez, Pa." The boy put his hands on his hips, shaking his head. "I dunno. I don't think we should eat anythin come outta a veal that just up 'n died."

The man rubbed his chin. "Aw, hell. I reckon yer right, son. I hate takin a hit on inventory, but choppin her up for steaks is kinda outta the question. Damn shame, but can't risk sellin poison meat to customers."

"Yeah. Wonder what all she died from anyways."

"Guess that flu was worser than we thought."

The man retrieved his flask from the back pocket of his overalls. He took a drink and passed it to the boy. He was developing a taste for whiskey. The boy followed the man out of the pen. Hidden woodland creatures were chattering in the newly forming darkness on the edge of the farm. It was nearing suppertime.

"Once," the man said, "before ya was here, some of the pigs got in a bad way. I lost four of 'em that summer. T'was a bad hit, I tell ya. Vet came on out and told me it were this influenza pigs get. They pass it on by touchin snouts. Dried mucus and what-not. I told ya how cramped pigs get when they're bein transported, and these hogs and sows were fresh off the truck. I'd just bought 'em. I reckon bein mushed together like that, one infected pig done gave 'em all the disease. I had to get myself all sorts of shots after that, 'cause they said people who work with pigs can get this swine flu too."

A tingle ran across the boy's flesh. He thought of the man's necrotizing fasciitis and the near certainty it was caused by his rolling in the mud with the sows, mating with Polly and getting bit by Mr. Buster. He thought of the pregnant veal's ceaseless puking and uncontrollable bladder, of all the nastiness that had come with her illness. For the first time in years, he was a little nervous to be on the farm.

"Makes me wonder 'bout the veal," the man said. "Maybe one of the pigs passed it on to 'em. Maybe ol' Tessie's got the flu and passed it on to the girl with 'er milk."

"Tessie's sick?"

"Well, she's been actin off lately. When it's feeding time, she ain't goin after it like usual. She's been bleary in the eye. Didn't think she was all that bad off but now I wonder. Best get the vet out here soon as we can. Don't want no plague spreadin' through the sounder."

"Right, Pa." The boy put his hands in his pockets and looked across the way to the legion of pigs shifting about in the blue light of dusk. "What'cha wanna do with this here veal then?"

They looked down at the pregnant girl. A cool breeze shook what was left of the browned autumn leaves still clinging to the trees.

The man shrugged. "Reckon we bury her."

THEY ALL DIED SCREAMING

It was similar to all the other holes the boy dug to discard of useless veal parts that remained after a slaughter, only it was longer so he wouldn't have to bother chopping up the girl. The hole was four feet long and three feet deep. He figured he could bend her at the knees to make her fit, ironically putting her into a fetal position. The man always stressed the details of burial when it came to any remains.

"Diggin' a full six feet under's too much of a backbreaker," he'd say, "but ya don't wanna make things easy for anyone who comes snoopin 'round."

As darkness came in full, the boy turned on the floodlights on the side of the barn, though there was abundant moonlight tonight, the sky clear and huge and freckled with stars. A ghostly breeze made the hair on his arms rise. Looking into the shallow grave, he was reminded of one of his earliest memories on the farm, one of his few childhood recollections that hadn't been blacked out by the passage of time.

On that day long ago, the man had been too drunk to dig a hole for a recent kill, so the boy had been handed the shovel. It was a gray afternoon and they'd been toiling in a hell of weeds, poison ivy, and fruitless bramble. He was not yet accustomed to the stench of pig feces, and it dominated every other odor, canceling out the fresh, country scent of the woodland surrounding the farm. On that day, the boy had tossed aside a clump of dirt containing a fat, writhing worm, wanting to save a life—*any* life.

This act of mercy seemed childish to him now. He chuckled at his younger self's silly sense of nobility. He felt no such empathy for this veal carcass. He'd dragged her out of the pen by her ankles, leaving a trail through the dirt and covering her in soot. Not that it mattered, considering where she was headed. Ashes to ashes. Filth to filth. He stuck the shovel into the ground beside him, making it stand in place. Her head hung as he reached for the girl's wrists and pulled her into the earthy abyss. The boy hocked and spit, adjusted his crotch. Then he started burying her. He got her halfway covered, but he was bone weary and ready for dinner. The grave could be finished tomorrow. He switched off the floodlight. That's when he noticed the other light in the distance. He froze, gazing toward the winding path that snaked out of the woods to the farm.

A pair of headlights.

No one ever came down this dirt road. No one. *Ever*. The car was still a distance away, moving slow but coming nonetheless. The house went dark and the man scampered down the porch steps in his robe, the rifle in his hands.

"Who are they, Pa?"

"Don't rightly know."

The man checked the rifle was loaded and the boy started toward the shed for additional weapons. "I'm a get some—"

The man pointed at the open grave. "Cover her up first, dammit!"

In his fear, the boy had already forgotten about the dead body. His mind had been on protecting the farm, the pigs and Pa. He hadn't given the veal a single thought. Out in the world was one thing, but here on the farm he'd gotten so used to using them in whatever way he wished. It seemed strange to think of them as something you weren't supposed to kill. It was a law he could never wrap his head around. Expunging the shovel, he hurriedly began tossing the earth back to where it had come.

"Maybe they's just lost," he said.

The man scowled. "Somehow I don't think so."

The car was getting closer, only a few more acres before it would reach the farm. The trees made an eerie lightshow out of the headlights, but the man and the boy were far enough from the path to stay out of view.

"Get 'er buried quick," the man said. "I'll stall 'em."

"Ya ain't gonna just start shootin are ya, Pa?"

"We'll see."

"But what if it ain't nobody to worry 'bout?"

The man spat. "That's what I'm fixin to find out."

He started toward the opening where the dirt road led to the entrance of the farm, his rot-scarred face tight with anticipation. Looking at the land's openness now, the boy felt terribly exposed. He wished they'd constructed a fence, laid down barbwire and sealed up the place with locks and chains. He kept shoveling, sweat rising from his pores as every muscle pumped. More dirt. The car was closer now, too damn close. His heart rebounded off his ribs. More dirt. The veal was mostly covered. She wasn't fully buried yet but at a passing glance you'd never know she was under all that dirt. He pumped harder, faster, flinging larger amounts. The movement of his swinging hips reminded him of fucking and he fondly remembered the veal's body pre-pregnancy. More dirt. Lights swept over the front of the house as the car approached. Though cloaked in darkness, the boy crouched. But he kept on shoveling. There was a voice then, a woman's voice. He looked toward the approaching car before realizing the sound was coming from below.

The boy froze.

The earth shifted in the grave. A low moaning rose out of the pit, the words muffled and unintelligible.

She's still alive.

He heard the car's engine turn off, but the headlights remained on. Two fingers poked out of the grave and the boy swung the shovelhead down upon them. They writhed and he flung a mound of dirt over the busted hand. He spun, dug and tossed. Spun, dug and tossed. Faster and faster. More dirt. The mound of her swollen belly rose and fell beneath twigs and pebbles. He piled the dirt where the girl's head was, drowning out her muted screams. Now other voices came from the entrance to the farm—stern, male voices. The boy flung more dirt. The grave was shifting less now, the weight of the loose earth pinning the girl down, her sickness and lack of oxygen making her too weak to dig herself out. Sweat ran down his brow and into his eyes. Still he shoveled harder, forced to ignore whatever was going on between the man and their visitors, his entire focus on burying this pregnant bitch alive.

The man's voice boomed. "Ya'll best get the hell offa mah property!"

The other voices were authoritative, but at this distance the boy couldn't make out what they were saying. The grave covered, he patted the earth smooth with the shovel, confident the girl could never escape. He hurried to the barn and put the shovel with the pitchforks and axes.

A gunshot split the night.

Pa!

The boy grabbed the newest axe from the lot. He ran around the back of the barn, his blood pumping like the gears of a runaway freight train. Tears burned down his cheeks. There were more shouts from the clearing. Another gunshot. The man cried out in pain.

Pa . . .

The boy ran so hard he stumbled over an exposed root. The axe flew from his grip and he tumbled down the incline, sobbing now, his whole heart breaking for his father. The harsh beam of a flashlight suddenly blinded him. He looked for the axe, but it was gone, lost somewhere in hopeless dark.

The voice behind the light yelled. "Show me your hands!"

The boy thought if he complied they might not hurt the man anymore, so he got to his knees and put his hands in the air. As the cuffs were snapped onto him, another man appeared, his pistol still in his hand.

"Christ. He's just a kid."

CHAPTER TWENTY-THREE

CHUCK PRESSED THE door of Keisha's apartment closed. Locking it, he put his back to the wall and slid down until he was sitting on the floor beside Brittany. The girl was as pale as the dead. Her eyes were unfocused and her arms were pulled tight against her chest, hands clutched under her chin as if in prayer. But no God would answer.

"You okay?" he asked.

Eventually she nodded.

"Not hurt?"

"No," she managed, "not really. Just a few nicks and scrapes. Are you alright?"

Chuck spied an ashtray on the coffee table. A pack of Newports lay beneath a Zippo. "I am now."

He scooched across the floor and lit up two cigarettes, then handed one to the girl. They puffed several times before speaking again.

"I don't even smoke," Brittany said. "Just weed, never tobacco." She took another drag. "Glad to have this now, though. Thanks."

"Don't mention it."

Smoke flooded Chuck's lungs and the sweet nicotine coursed through him. He went to the kitchen and opened up the cabinets, finding a near-empty bottle of tequila. He unscrewed the cap and took a quick belt from it, sniffed, then finished it off. In the fridge was a box of chardonnay that had hardly been touched.

"I've got a joint," Brittany said. "Last one from that shit you got me."

Chuck took a coffee mug off the counter and poured wine from the spout. He listened for the babies but there was nothing but the sound of little bubbles settling in his drink.

"Wanna spark it?" Brittany asked.

"Now?"

"Sure. I mean, this might be our last chance. We almost . . . almost *died* out there." She sniffled. "Keisha . . . and your friend . . . dead. Both dead. Just like that." She snapped her fingers. "The world's become an awful place."

"It always was."

"So awful we can't mourn it?"

Chuck drank hard and wiped his mouth with the back of his hand. His eyes dropped. "Ain't the world that's goin away. It's us. Mourn for humans if ya want to, but mass extinction's happened to other species. Guess it's just our turn."

"The difference is, if this thing, like, really is caused by global warming—melting ice caps and releasing some ancient virus—then we did this to ourselves, right? We caused our own extinction without even trying. No other species did that, least none I can think of."

"Reckon that's so." Chuck poured another and went to the girl. "You're smart for your age. Smart for any age, really."

"Lotta good it'll do me now." Brittany twirled the joint in her fingers. "Well, I'm getting high."

Chuck thought of what Eugene had said about appreciating every bite of every sandwich, how the whisky was the sweetest he'd ever had because he'd accepted he was not long for this world. Chuck hadn't smoked pot in years. Even a hallucinogen as mild as marijuana tended to screw with his head in ways he didn't appreciate. Even when he was obliterated on booze, he felt more in control of himself than when he was stoned out of his gourd. But a slight buzz might do him good.

"Maybe just a hit or two," he said, hoping it would mellow him. "Gotta make the most of whatever time's left. If this really is the end, might as well smoke 'em if we got 'em, right?"

She smiled, but it was a weak and hopeless smile. She reached for the lighter.

But Chuck had a promise.

"Be right back. Start without me."

Brittany lit up the joint, alternating drags off of it and her cigarette. Her face was blank with gloom, those blue eyes emptied by the horrors she'd seen. Chuck entered the hallway, passing the bathroom, then the linen closet. Still he heard nothing. Not a cry or giggle, none of the innocent melodies of infants.

She killed them, he thought. *Their own grandmother . . .*

The bedroom door was closed, the hallway haunted by abundant shadow. He stubbed out his cigarette butt on the wall and let it fall to the floor, then turned the doorknob and stepped inside, holding his breath in anticipation of the foul stench of gore. He was so used to it by now—that hellish aroma, a mélange of copper and sewage. But he did not detect it here. Sunlight fell through a curtain, revealing a twin bed pressed against one wall. On the other side of the room was a crib.

Behind the wooden bars were two babies, burritoed in white blankets. They were completely still. Chuck moved slowly, afraid and not knowing why. He hovered over the infants when he reached the crib, watching their soft, brown faces, his mind void of all other thought as he took in their simplicity and beauty. He wanted to stamp their image into his mind forever.

One of the babies cooed, head turning to one side as it continued to snooze. Chuck reached down and put his hand on the other one. Its little chest rose and fell with breath and Chuck stood perfectly still.

A little voice. "Chuck?"

He gasped, thinking for a moment it was one of the children. Brittany called to him again and he said he'd be right out. He left the babies to their nap and when he got to the living room Brittany was sitting on the sofa with her feet on the table, one leg flat and the other arched. The apartment had no air conditioning unit and she'd undone several of the buttons on her blouse. He looked, but there was nothing for him to see. He refilled his wine, sat down beside her and took a hit off the joint.

"They're okay," he said.

She sighed with relief. "Oh, thank God. I was too scared to look for them myself. I don't think I could've taken it if they were . . . you know . . ."

"Yeah."

They smoked and drank and sweated.

"Stay here with 'em," he said.

She shook her head. "No, no. I don't wanna be alone."

"I gotta get Leslie some help. You'll be safer here. So will them babies. That's what's important now."

"But . . . are you coming back?"

"Yeah. I promised I'd take care of them kids in there, but right now I need you to do it. I'll be back soon as I can."

"But what if something happens and you *can't* come back?"

Chuck finished his drink in one long pull. "Then it's up to you to take care of 'em."

"Fuck, man. Don't put that on me." Her eyes misted. "I mean, like, I wanna help them, but I just can't handle that. I can never handle *anything*. I'll fuck everything up."

"You'll be fine." He wanted to say more but was no better at assuring others than he was at consoling them. "Just hang in there and I'll be back 'fore ya know it."

They stood. Brittany took him by the wrist with both hands, her palms silken, warm. Chuck wet his lips without thinking about it. The girl opened her mouth to speak but then tucked her chin without a word.

"What is it?" he asked.

She looked at him with dreamy, exhausted eyes. "You really think this is the end of everything?"

Chuck looked away, not wanting to upset her with the truth.

"I think it is too," Brittany said. "It's just a matter of time, right? Either they kill us or we become one of them. It's just not fair. I've only just begun to, like, live the life I've always wanted to live, the life I knew was right for me no matter what my parents said." She took a deep breath. "There's just so many things I never got to do."

Her small hands closed around his large hand and when he glanced down at them he noticed for the first time the slight scars that ran over the insides of her wrists, the faint echo of a failed suicide, or at least a cry for help. A cloud moved across the face of the sun, diming the room. When she bowed her head, he leaned in and smelled her scalp. She pressed into him, shy and hushed.

"Chuck . . . I don't want to die a virgin."

A tingle went up the back of Chuck's neck. Still, he snorted and stepped back.

"Come off it," he said. "You'd say anythin to get me to stay. Ain't no way a girl as hot as you's a virgin."

"I am, though. There's something . . . something you don't understand."

Brittany stepped into him again and this time he didn't move away. Her lips pursed, making them even plumper. Her eyelashes fluttered and she put her hands up on his chest. She was trembling.

"Can I kiss you?" she asked.

He responded by initiating it for her. The girl's mouth opened and he kissed her with all the passion his deadbeat heart could muster. Desire struck him like a fist. Here he was a dirty old man, aging rapidly because he took such poor care of himself, and this angelic, young creature was embracing him, taking him with her arms and tongue. He'd fantasized of this so many times, of having a teenage girl again after all these years, of possessing her even if for just an hour or two. Brittany welcomed him with the same carnal force he could not resist the call of. She moaned inside his mouth and Chuck ran his hands up and down her lithe torso. The memory of the girls he'd had in his youth—those ripe, untarnished, delicious girls—flooded his every sense, making him feel younger and more alive than he would have ever thought possible at this point in his life.

Brittany spoke between kisses. "I really have to tell you something. There's a reason boys don't wanna, like, *do it* with me."

"I don't care."

He ran his fingers through her hair, kissing her cheeks and swan neck. If she had a venereal disease, he still thought it'd be worth it. Even if it was HIV, this was the end of days, so what would it matter considering he had a death sentence anyway? But if she really was a virgin, she would most likely be clean. And if anything, *she* should be the one worried about catching something from *him*. Miraculously, he'd never caught such a disease despite the lifetime of heroin hookers and bar sluts he'd fucked in alleyways and bus station bathrooms. He doubted Brittany, of all people, could give him an STD, but why else would boys her age—teenagers bursting at the sack with pent-up semen—not want to fuck this petite, natural-blonde angel? She was the very pinnacle of beauty, of vibrant life aglow. Chuck ran his hands over her chest, feeling next to nothing beneath the blouse and bra but aching for it anyway. His hands roamed lower, raising the bottom of her shirt, fingertips grazing the velvety stomach and the ring in her belly button. So slender, so tender. His hand went south, gliding over the tight jeans, cupping her lovely ass, and then he reached down to her crotch. He went low and deep, making the girl breathe heavy in his ear.

That's when he felt the lump.

Chuck paused. He pressed his fingers into the lump again, squeezing the unmistakable package of a tucked dick and balls. His mouth left hers as he stepped back, the string of their shared saliva hanging between their lips. Brittany looked away, her face flushed.

"I'm sorry," she said. "I should've told you first."

Chuck's nose and eyebrows scrunched together. "You're . . . a *guy*?"

"No, I'm a *girl*. This," she said, pointing to her crotch, "does not decide my gender. My heart and soul does."

"But how . . . you're so . . . so girly, so pretty."

She crossed her arms. "I've always been cute in a girlish way, and these days I'm getting hormone treatment. I'm on my way to having gender reassignment."

"That's, like, a sex change, huh?"

"Don't say it like that. God, you sound like my parents. They didn't understand either, that's why they sent me out here." She tucked her blonde locks behind her ears. "It's just not fair. Nobody knew me here. I mean the old me—Bentley, not Brittany. My life here was like a do-over. At least it was until this zombie shit happened. I was finally starting to have a real life as the girl I've always been on the inside. And now . . . now I'm gonna die. Dead before I could live."

She hung her head and tears came. As Chuck watched the poor girl his mind went to Barman and what he'd said about atonement, about trying to make up for past sins and doing what was right now that humanity had reached its last stand. Like Leslie, Brittany had a need, one she was asking Chuck to fill. He was her only option now. That was the only reason his miserable old ass even had this shot with her. Whether she was transgender or not made no difference when it came to her loveliness. The small, hidden dick couldn't tarnish her allure any more than the stuffed bra. Despite how most guys may have reacted to the truth about her, she still would have found a young man to love her and take her virginity. It just hadn't happened yet, and now it might never happen at all. The only thing Brittany wanted was to feel the touch of a man. She had not yet fully changed genders, but the act of physical love would change her from a girl into a young woman.

Chuck wrapped his arms around her. Brittany gazed up at him with those dazzling, wet eyes and he leaned in, closing them with a kiss. Their mouths met again, Brittany more passionate this time, resurrected by Chuck's acceptance of who she really was. His hands ran up and down her body, acknowledging her as a female, and she leapt into his embrace. Her legs snaked around his waist and he carried her like the excited youth she was. They moaned as he opened the door to the bedroom and placed her upon the mattress, Brittany bouncing slightly, and together they wiggled her out of her jeans and she turned over onto her stomach, exposing the perfection of her ass beneath the pink, cotton panties. Chuck pulled them down just enough to expose her anus without revealing the taped down genitals he knew she loathed. He performed analingus on her, his tongue alive between her smooth cheeks, probing the virginal rosebud in her backside. She moaned and shuddered. Chuck got harder. He went to the end table by the crib and retrieved the babies' diaper rash cream. He lathered his manhood and entered Brittany gently, whispering to her, telling her how to relax her body to better take him. She whispered back guidance of her own, telling him when to show mercy and when he could pump faster, plunge deeper. He pressed his whole body flat on top of hers, bucking his hips and nibbling her ears, and when she turned her head they kissed away the horrible, horrible world, escaping into something so powerful in its purity and simplicity they forgot that this, much like their lives, wouldn't last forever.

"Look, I gotta go to her," Chuck said. He puffed on the cigarette as he zipped up his fly. "And I gotta go now."

Brittany was lying on the bed in post-coital serenity. Her face was still flushed, her hair a tangle made all the more blonde by the honey sunrays that fell upon her through the window. Sweat glistened on her exposed flesh like a smattering of diamond shavings.

"Thank you," she said.

"Ain't necessary."

"But I know you're . . . " She hesitated. "I know you like women. *Complete* women."

Chuck shook his head. "This weren't no pity fuck."

"Well . . . I think it started that way but became something more for both of us."

Chuck took another drag and looked at the floor, uncomfortable with such tender talk. Everything they had expressed physically was an intense enough outpouring of emotions to last him a lifetime. Like the whisky and the bites of that hypothetical sandwich, knowing this might be his last fuck made it all the sweeter—a coupling of age with youth, experience with innocence, cavalier cynicism with ignorant hope. And he had no remorse or shame, no fears of being a homosexual who'd been in denial. But for lack of a vagina, Brittany truly was a woman, one of the most attractive women he'd ever been with. Many nights he'd gotten wasted and banged women so homely they may as well have been men. Brittany was far more feminine than the majority of women who'd been foolish, desperate, or self-destructive enough to go to bed with him. She was oxygen and white light, a final taste of what might have been if only he'd lived a different, better life. And because she'd been eager to receive his physical love, she even trumped the pretty girls of his youth.

But she wasn't Leslie.

Though there was passion in their lovemaking, Brittany could never know him the way Leslie did. She was too unsoiled, too sweet. Once fully exposed, Chuck's total brokenness would be an ugly, alien thing to her. It would chase her away just as it had chased away all the other women who weren't Leslie. Chuck had shared an enlightening, tender moment with Brittany, one he would always be grateful for, but the connection could never be as solid as the one he had with a woman as deranged as himself. It almost made Chuck believe in soul mates.

"Promise me you'll look after the kids," he said.

Brittany nodded. "I'll do everything I can."

"Thanks. Come on and lock up behind me. Find some weapons and just stay put 'less ya have no choice but to leave. Don't *let nobody* in no matter *what* they fuckin say."

"I won't."

Chuck scratched his head, feeling more protective of Brittany now, like a father sending his daughter out on a first date. This newfound consideration for others was a miracle in and of itself, he thought, wondering if Barman's transformation from misanthrope to antihero had rubbed off on him.

Nah, he decided. *You're just a cockroach dreaming he's a butterfly.*

Chuck went to the bathroom and pocketed antiseptic, cotton balls and gauze. He found an open box of Maxi Pads. Brittany followed him through the living room and he grabbed the box of wine and the second largest knife in the kitchen, leaving the big one for her.

He put his hand around the doorknob and she kissed his cheek.

"I'll do my best," he said.

"To do what?"

"Come back alive."

She nodded. "In that case I'll do my best to be alive when you get back."

They fell silent. Chuck turned the knob slowly, every tick of the tumbler seeming as loud as fireworks.

The bodies in the hall brought such bile to the back of Chuck's throat he was barely able to swallow it. The floor and walls were a cosmos of human waste, the reek of death stinging his nose with its backhand. He moved quickly, stepping over and around the remains. If screamers really were some kind of zombie, they didn't reanimate after death like the ones in the movies. They died just like people died. At least there was some relief in that. The enemy was not invincible or even particular in their mortality. You didn't need a headshot or holy water or silver bullets. Just kill the pricks.

Chuck wished he had a rifle. Maybe he could break into a gun shop or sporting goods place when he and Leslie left. He hadn't fired a gun in decades but now the thought of one left him yearning. For the time being he would have to settle for the knife he held out in front of him.

His ears perked up at the sound of a muffled scream. He looked all around the hall, seeing nothing. A thump turned his head to the apartment door on his right. It was closed but shook as something battered against it from the inside. The scream grew louder, a woman's high, shrill bellow. As he passed by the door, he noticed the number.

209. *Eugene's apartment.*

The many locks and bolts she and her paranoid son had sealed the place with now trapped Eugene's mother. There were sounds of fingernails scraping hard enough to snap, of teeth gnawing at wood in an attempt to break through and get at Chuck. He'd been so quiet. Could they sense people somehow, a side effect of the disease being a heightened sense of smell or something? Whatever it caused, it had stripped Eugene's mom of the cognitive faculties required to unlock her own door. Chuck pressed on, surprised by the hallway's emptiness. He'd thought for sure the noise from earlier would have drawn the shrieking bastards to this floor for more things to kill. Maybe the disease had changed form and they were dying off on their own. Maybe they'd gone back to throwing themselves down stairs and off bridges. He figured it was a false hope, but still a pleasant thought.

He reached Leslie's apartment without incident, but when he went for the doorknob, he found it locked. That made sense given the chaos that had occurred in the hall after he'd left. Eugene must have secured the door for safety, Chuck thought. He knocked.

"Gene, it's Chuck. Let me in." Silence. He knocked again. "Come on, man. It's safe. Open up."

He waited, knocking and repeating the same words. The weight of the midday heat was heavy now and Chuck was exhausted after being up all night. The blood-pump of fear and violence had faded. He longed to nap, but they had to get moving. He'd wasted enough time having sex with Brittany. Well, not wasted, he thought, but burned up. Chuck had been torn between the two women's needs and yet also still driven by his own, perhaps misguidedly and even selfishly. But they both needed him. All these years he hadn't been needed or even wanted by anyone, and suddenly he had to balance the wishes (perhaps *last* wishes) of others against everyone's needs.

He kicked the door. "Gene! Let me in, goddamnit!"

A scream was his reply—a woman's scream. Chuck dropped the box of wine.

Leslie . . .

He battered at the door with his shoulder. Several running shoves and the wood snapped but still it wouldn't open. A strange, electric buzzing crackled from within the apartment, followed by more screams, female and male. Chuck kicked at the knob until it broke off, then reached into the hole and fiddled with the slot until the tumbler shifted. The door came open and he rushed into the living room, seeing no one, and then ran down the hall.

You never should've left her alone with him.

But what if she's got The Scream?

When he reached the bedroom, Chuck came in with the knife held high. His whole body shook with anger as he entered the room. It was in shambles, the bed covered in blood. Eugene was on the floor with his shirt off and his slacks around his ankles, shoes still on. He was turned away from Chuck and the claw marks on his shoulders seeped red. He didn't appear to be breathing.

Leslie was curled up in the corner where the mattress touched the wall. She was still nude and held up the blood-speckled sheet to her chin. Her face was hard, her breaths fierce between clenched teeth. She gazed up at Chuck. She was albino pale and the dark rings under her eyes made her look like a corpse.

"He was raping me," she said.

Chuck sank inward. "Jesus . . . "

"That no-faced-motherfucker was raping me, Chucky. Said he had to. Said I wasn't no virgin, but it was worth a shot." Her face pinched in confusion. "What's that even fuckin *mean*?"

He sat down on the bed and reached for her, but she didn't move.

"He didn't get very far," she said, sneering. "He was drunk and all fumblin with his pants and couldn't get his dick hard with me punchin and kickin him. His skinny ass didn't have much strength to hold me down neither. That miserable cock of his just grazed my pussy; never made it in but it's still fuckin rape, right?"

"Yeah, of course it is." He scooched closer and put his arm around her. "That son of a bitch. I'm so sorry, Les. I didn't—"

"Ain't your fault, Chucky. I told ya to go care for them babies. They ok?"

He nodded, opting not to explain what had happened to their mother.

Leslie went on. "I ain't mad ya left. 'Sides, I handled his ass good."

She moved the sheet aside, revealing the small, black device in her hand. The steel square had a metallic ring on the tip of it.

Chuck blinked. "You had a taser this whole time?"

"Sorry I kept it from ya but, well, *anybody* could turn into a screamer, including you. I didn't use it earlier 'cause I didn't want nobody to know I had it. It's a good thing too." She pointed to the nightstand's open drawer. "Keep it in there. Gave me peace of mind at night. Always knew if somebody broke in I could defend myself. And that's what I did with this bastard. Soon as I could get to the taser, I stuck it into his nut sack and didn't let up. And when he hit the floor, I got on him and shoved the fuckin thing in his mouth. Wanted to cook what was left of his ugly face, ya know? Then I stuck it in his ribs until he stopped twitchin."

Chuck leaned over and got a look a Eugene's corpse. Black burn lines underscored the huge, purple bruise on his chest where he'd been shocked to death.

Leslie said, "Taser can stop your fuckin heart, ya know. Think he went into cardiac arrest."

"Good."

"It's cool, right? I mean, it's okay, ain't it? He wasn't a screamer, but I murdered his fuckin ass anyway. Maybe I coulda stopped him without killin him but . . . fuck . . . I dunno. Just tell me it's alright, Chucky."

"It is, Les. Even a world this shitty is better off without the likes of him." He looked at the sopping, red mattress. "Did the taser make him bleed too?"

"Nah," she said, her voice dropping. "That's my blood. I been tryin to plug my asshole with the sheets. It just keeps on bleedin."

The violence had gotten her fur up, but now that her adrenaline was fizzling Chuck could see the rapid blood loss weighing down on Leslie. All the life had fled from her face, leaving only a ghost of a woman.

"I've got some cotton balls and period pads," he said. "Let's patch ya up as best we can and get ya dressed. We gotta get ya to a doctor."

Leslie snorted a laugh. "Ain't no doctors out there to help nobody now."

"I think we can get to a hospital if we try."

Leslie turned to the window and motioned with her head toward the outside world. Chuck went to it and looked outside. Fires were raging, increasing the summer heat and diminishing the city's already poor air quality with the choke of black smoke. Everywhere widows were shattered and doors were off their hinges. Cars were crashed into buildings and abandoned in the middle of the streets. Bicycles were discarded, food carts abandoned. Trash and debris flew down the streets like autumn leaves. Far down the end of the avenue, a tank was on fire—*a fucking tank*. Everyone in plain sight, military or otherwise, was either fighting or fleeing or chasing or screaming. So much screaming. Guns popping, crowbars wielding, bones breaking, lives ending. The streets were polluted; not just with the mountains of trash that had piled up since the strike, but with the fallen victims of this epidemic—dead civilians stacked alongside the soldiers, police and firefighters who'd tried in vain to defuse the situation. Mangled remains were so widespread it was hard for Chuck to tell which severed body parts belonged to which crudely amputated torsos. Limbs and heads were scattered about like the aftermath of a dirty bomb. Chuck realized the sound of all this anarchy had been so constant it had become nothing more than background noise to him. Now he heard it in full—the true, blackened call of madness, a chorus of hundreds of thousands of screamers whom had overrun the city.

"There's nowhere to go, babe," Leslie said. "All we can do is hide. Bide our time . . . then try and die in peace."

She was right, but part of him still held on to that desperate fantasy of escape, of medical care and Leslie surviving another day.

He said, "But we have to try and—"

She touched his lips to shush him. "Look, if I gotta die today, I don't wanna go out gettin ripped apart while watchin *you* get ripped apart too. The plan was to ride out the apocalypse right here. So just patch me up best ya can, Chucky . . . and, more importantly, get me a drink."

After some first aid, Leslie put on panties to keep the pad and bandaging secure, and opted for a faded *Invasion of the Blood Farmers* shirt that was too big and covered half her thighs, another remnant from her ex. Rather than wasting time changing the sheets and disposing of Eugene, Chuck carried her out to the living room and placed her upon the couch. All the remaining booze and cigarettes were spread out on the coffee table, a drunk's party platter.

"I'm cold," she said.

The room was well over ninety degrees. Chuck got her a blanket from the closet and had her cuddle up to him. Her flesh squished against his, arctic to the touch. He made Leslie a cocktail and poured himself a whiskey.

She held up her glass. "This and you will warm me up."

"Anythin else I can get ya? Hungry at all?"

"Nah. Don't feel like eatin. It's funny not to want to. All these years I just wanted to feel full. Now I don't want no food or dick or anything else. Guess I understand it now. Ya can fill up all the holes in your body, but ya can never fill up that *big* hole. It's just an endless void, Chucky. Once that hole opens up inside ya, it never closes again. It can't be filled. Nothing's ever gonna be good enough for it . . . or for you."

Leslie sighed and turned on the television. The first six channels offered only dead air. She found one with an emergency broadcast alert, just a silent, blue screen and flashing yellow print.

—all emergency services have been suspended. Stay indoors. Do not attempt to evacuate—

The same information, but someone behind the broadcast had added something of their own, a single word.

PRAY.

"I love this show," Leslie said and handed Chuck her empty glass. He poured her another. "This is the best show ever, man. A real riot. Guess it's the final episode though, huh?" She laughed and sipped. "It all happened so fast, Chucky. That's what blows my fuckin mind. I mean, ya think about all the years people worried about nuclear bombs and terrorists and fuckin World War III and shit like that, and then some whack disease drops and we're all executed in a snap.

In twenty-four hours, this whole fuckin city became hell on earth. The world ain't never goin back to the way it was before all this. Never. It just ain't possible."

"Reckon your right."

She snorted a laugh. "*Reckon*? God, you talk like a hick sometimes. Ya grow up in a barn or somethin?"

Chuck forced a smile. He held Leslie closer, running his hand up and down her arm as she pressed her head into his chest.

"Kinda nice though," she continued. "The end of the world, I mean. Ya ain't gonna have to worry 'bout findin no fuckin job now, Chucky. And I don't have to go back to mine. Never have to serve samples to those disgusting, entitled customers no more. I wonder how many of the store's nasty regulars are dead already. Most of 'em, I hope. Probably ain't supposed to say somethin like that—wishin people dead and all —but you understand, don'tcha?"

"I do."

"They've all got it comin. '*Oh, whatta we have here?*' Death, you buncha assholes." She took a deep breath, wheezing a little. "Chucky?"

"Yeah?"

"Whadda ya think death is like?"

He took a few seconds to reply. "It's nothin."

"What'cha mean *nothin*?"

"It's the opposite of anythin at all."

"So no heaven or hell, just, like, *darkness*?"

"Darkness is the absence of light. Darkness is still somethin. You're aware of darkness. With death, you ain't aware of a damn thing. You're just gone. No consciousness whatsoever. Least that's what I think."

She sighed. "Like a sleep ya don't wake up from?"

"Like that, but without dreams."

"And without nightmares." She hugged him, burying her face in him. "Death sounds wonderful."

They didn't speak much after that.

Soon she never would again.

CHAPTER TWENTY-FOUR

THE **BOY WAS** a victim. That's what the man convinced the police of anyway. They had no reason to disbelieve it. The boy hadn't been seen participating in any of the abhorrent crimes that had taken place on the farm, and there were no live veal in the pen to accuse him. The last of the herd had been buried alive in the nick of time. The man immediately confessed to kidnapping the boy over seven years ago and told them where they could find the school I.D. card. The boy was touched the man had held onto it all this time. It made their separation all the more heart wrenching.

The female officer sat at her desk across from the boy. She wasn't one of the officers who'd arrested the man. The boy could tell she was above that sort of duty. Her white, button-up shirt made that distinction clear even before he read the sign on her desk: *Chief Jackie Harriett.*

The chief had dark eyes that, while hardened from years of police work, had yielded under the sorrow of the case. She smiled at him, a somber smile of reassurance, a mother comforting her child after a monster in the closet. The boy wondered if she had kids of her own.

"We've contacted your mother," the chief said.

The boy nodded. He hadn't given them any information, faking mild amnesia. He didn't want to incriminate his Pa any further.

"Sergeant Hitchenson says you didn't want to speak to your mother when he called."

The boy didn't say anything.

"She's on a flight now," the chief added. "Should be here in just a few hours."

He blinked in confusion. "A flight?"

"She moved out of state a few years ago. She lives in Milwaukee now."

The boy rubbed his neck, recalling a blurry image of someone else who'd once raised him.

"What about my . . . " It pained the boy to call another man this. "My dad?"

Chief Harriett crossed her hands upon the desk. "We're still trying to reach him."

Somehow the boy didn't believe her. Why would his "mom and dad" not be coming together? Wouldn't his mother tell his father right away?

"Everything's going to be okay now," she assured. "This whole ordeal is over. I can't imagine what you went through on that farm, but it's over now. Quaid Crews is never going to hurt you or anyone else ever again."

They knew the man's name. The boy shuddered.

Harriett said, "But I have to ask you some things about him, okay?"

The boy nodded, more emphatically this time. This was his chance to clear Pa of any wrongdoing.

"How long was he using the . . . *alternative* meat?"

"That why ya'll arrested him? Just 'cause of beef?" the boy shook his head in disbelief. "Come on now. It's good meat. Best in town. Everybody says so."

The chief shifted in her chair. "He was selling meat without the proper certification and licensing. He used fraudulent stamps and documents."

The boy swallowed, a soft relief drifting through his fear like smoke. Maybe they didn't know the extent of things yet.

"That's what brought us to the farm with the warrant," Harriett continued. "His violent resistance was quite a surprise to the arresting officers. Do you know why he would react that way?"

The boy didn't answer.

"Any reason at all?" the chief asked.

"It ain't right—steppin on another man's property when yas ain't invited. We don't take kindly to it."

"We?"

"Yeah. Me and Pa."

She took a breath. "My officers did tell me you kept on calling Mr. Crews that. *Pa.* Is that what he wanted you to address him as?"

"That's what he *is*."

"Maybe he has you thinking otherwise, but he's not your kin. He kidnapped you from a shopping mall. You've been a missing child since 1987."

"He took me in when my mama abandoned me at the mall. He's a good man! He may not be my blood but he's more kin to me than my blood relations ever were. I've been his son almost half my life."

"But you weren't abandoned, you were abducted. Your mother has been searching for you all these years. You were *kidnapped* by Crews, not rescued. You're not his child. You're his *hostage*." She lifted the plastic evidence bag and held it out so he could read the identification card. "This is who you are."

The boy looked away, hating that smiling little face from yesterday, a reflection of a past he hardly believed was real.

"I don't know him," the boy said, and it was almost true.

"You're a perfect match to his fingerprints."

The boy's face scrunched. "My *fingerprints*? I ain't been brought in by police never before."

"Your parents had you printed as a baby. Lots of people do it for safety reasons." She leaned forward across the desk, trying to make eye contact, but the boy still looked at the floor. "Quaid Crews has brainwashed you into thinking better of him than you should."

"That ain't true!"

"I promise you it is. I think you have what's called Stockholm's syndrome. You're a captive who's come to identify with his captor, even sympathize with him. Given all the years you were with Crews I can underst—"

"It ain't like that. Not like you say."

A brief silence hung between them like a veil. The boy wished it would never lift.

"How long?" the chief asked again. "How long was he selling this meat?"

The boy could only shrug, not wanting to commit to anything, nor contribute to his Pa's degradation. This police chief was flat out insulting the only family that mattered to him, making every effort to screw with his head just to get dirt on the man.

Chief Harriett straightened in her chair. "The tests came back from the lab. We know now what kind of meat this is. Do you?"

Slowly the boy nodded. "It's the best meat in town."

There was a knock at the door. The chief welcomed in a tall, bald man with a friendly smile. He wore spectacles, kakis and a V-Neck sweater, a much more relaxed, informal appearance than the others at the station. He shared a hello with the chief and she introduced them.

"Oliver is a psychologist," she explained. "He'd just like to talk to you for a little bit, okay?"

A mean heat rose from the boy's chest, flushing his cheeks.

"I ain't crazy," he said.

Oliver sat in the chair beside him, still all smiles. "I'm certainly not here to say that."

"You've had a harrowing experience," Harriett added. "We don't want to push you. If you're not ready to talk right now, we understand. But I really think it'd do you a world of good to get some things off your chest. Wouldn't you agree, Oliver?"

Without taking his eyes off the boy, Oliver said, "I certainly do; one hundred percent. I'm here to help."

"Ya'll just wanna mix me up," the boy said. "You're tryin to make me say things I don't mean. Stuff that ain't true 'bout my Pa."

The chief and psychologist shared a concerned glance. She slid the plastic bag containing the identification card to Oliver and he picked it up, looking it over.

He smiled. "You certainly looked happier then, son."

"Only Pa calls me son."

"Alright then." Just like the chief had, Oliver held out the card for the boy to see. "Do you prefer Charles, or do you go by Charlie?"

"It's a miracle this young man hasn't contracted a disease," the doctor said.

The farm the boy called home was referred to as a squalid death camp. They told him Quaid Crews was officially diagnosed with necrotizing fasciitis, but there was more to his skin lesions than that. Judging by the boils and hypopigmented macules (flat and pasty white spots on the man's body), the hospital also diagnosed Crews with borderline lempromatous leprosy. They attributed this to his self-proclaimed status as a pig-man, one who lived among the swine and relished in their muddy pits as if he too were a hog. It had sickened them to hear him explain he'd even committed himself to a female pig "romantically", engaging in frequent bestiality.

And the pigs were sick too.

After the raid on the farm, the complete litter and sounder were declared infected with swine influenza and were quarantined for medical rehabilitation or euthanized depending on the severity of their individual conditions.

"He never got sick, not even as a baby."

The woman speaking was nearly unrecognizable to him. Her hair had gone gray and fine, and she was thin enough to seem sickly herself. The mental image he'd retained of her was vibrant and colorful. The lady sitting by his bedside was wan and crippled by the grief of lost time—an alien by comparison. The hand that held his felt like a skeleton's draped in cheesecloth.

"My baby," she said, eyes just as wet as they'd been when she'd first seen him at the station. "My sweet, little Chucky. You're okay now. Mommy's here."

The boy's stomach boiled. It was weird enough for a woman to refer to herself as Mommy with her teenage son, but weirder for her to still consider herself his mother after all that had happened. She was a ridiculous woman. Just another piece of veal in his book. But he knew what was expected of him now. The past few days had been a hard learning experience. This whole charade was their game, but he had to play along if he wanted to exonerate Pa. All the boy's objections to their warped version of reality only made the psychologists, cops, and doctors treat him like he was fucked in the head, and they wouldn't listen to him if they believed he was insane, that he had this Stockholm's bullshit they kept talking about. In their mind, this crazy, blubbering woman was his mother, so if he reacted to her affection in kind, they might think they'd convinced him he was another one of Quaid Crew's victims, the only one lucky enough to survive.

Despite the grim state of things, he wanted to hold out hope for Pa. His *real* Pa, not that virtual stranger who'd come to see him. It was interesting that this mom and dad wouldn't even be in the same room together. Teary-eyed, she later explained his "dad" still blamed her for what had happened. Their marriage had been a failure. The boy supposed they were no better spouses than they were parents.

He wanted his real and only parent back. He wished he could explain to everyone who Quaid Crews really was. He certainly wasn't the ghoul they made him out to be on the news. The boy had refused to talk to any of these despicable, slanderous reporters, but they kept on telling *his* story anyway, how little Chucky was imprisoned on the farm far longer than any of the other victims of the diabolical Crews, a man they were calling America's worst serial killer since some guy named Ted Bundy. They even labeled Crews a cannibal! The nerve! Just because Pa sold meat didn't mean he ate it. Other than the occasional taste test for quality assurance, they were strict vegetarians. But the press leaned heavily on this cannibal thread, all while the police were being hailed for their discovery. They'd only come to the farm to arrest Crews for forging USDA documents and selling meat illegally. They'd come to clear out his abbitoir, unaware of just what kind of meat they would find. After the test results came back, they returned to the farm with twenty officers and half as many cadaver dogs. More veal parts were found in the meat shack and the skinned limbs of others were found packaged up inside the coffin-sized freezer behind the house. And then there were the bones and other remains found buried all over the property, initiating a full excavation of the farm.

The first body the police discovered was in a shallow grave packed down with freshly dug earth, a twenty-two-year-old woman named Christine Lauter. Having not decomposed yet, she was easiest to identify. This was considered a most heinous murder due to the young woman being pregnant, and the coroner's report stated that though Lauter had a severe case of influenza, she had died from suffocation. The dirt found in her lungs confirmed she'd been buried alive.

Day by day, the grisly details mounted, further condemning Pa. But what made matters worse was Pa was *confessing* to everything! He'd even accompanied the police to the farm and guided them to the other burial sights and explained the entire process of conditioning the meat in the pen with chains and low-iron diets, giving away the family secret. Plus, he took credit for *everything*, never mentioning all the hard work the boy had put into the veal and the farm and nursing the man back to some semblance of health. The boy felt betrayed. He couldn't believe Pa was folding so easily. And worst of all, Pa laughed right into the camera when he was asked about his relationship with him.

"*Relationship*?" he'd said. "That lil' bastard weren't nothin but a slave. Free labor. And if I hadn't been sick, I woulda killed him too."

The boy cried often. He knew he wasn't crazy, but he was deeply depressed. A stay in this mental hospital might be good for him after all, especially if it kept him from going to the place his mother kept referring to as "home", even though Chuck had never been to Milwaukee, or even Wisconsin for that matter. The thought of living with this emotionally needy old hag depressed him all the more.

Though he tried to convince everyone of his sanity, he found his sadness too powerful to conceal, and then there were Rorschach tests and prescription pills and seemingly endless one-on-one sessions with specialists. Though designed to improve his mental and emotional state, they had the opposite effect. The psychiatrist listened when the boy spoke fondly of Quaid Crews, but never agreed or advised. He clearly wanted their little Chucky to come out of some kind of spell, as if Pa was a hypnotist who'd scrambled and deprogrammed his brain. If anyone was trying to scramble his brain it was these damned doctors and their pills! It was as if he were being poisoned.

Soon he didn't want to talk to the shrinks anymore than the press or the police. He found he had nothing to say to his so-called parents. He was sinking inward. There was only one person he wanted to talk to, the only person in the world who had ever mattered.

It took a lot of convincing. If he hadn't paid close attention to the psychobabble these nitwits had been preaching these past eight months in the mental hospital, the boy may not have come up with a good cover. He used their own terms and theories against them, saying it would be *cathartic* and give him *closure*. He told them he had to *face his fears* to *face reality*. To sweeten the deal, he said he was struggling to recall important details that could help the police with their case, who were still facing strong public demand to identify more bodies. A multitude of parents and loved ones of missing young women and girls had inundated the department with enquiries and were squawking to every newsperson who'd listen. Elected officials were sweating. The boy had been told time and again how invaluable anything he could remember would be. It was time to put a price on it.

Pa refused to see him at first, twisting the knife of rejection deeper into the boy's heart. Persisting, he asked the police to approach Pa again, getting the prison warden to offer some special amenities in exchange for the visitation. Finally, Crews agreed. When the boy found out he'd be seeing his Pa for the first time since the awful night those fucking cops tore his family apart, the influx of emotions made him crawl into his cot and sob while smiling.

It was miserably hot. Somehow, he had always imagined prisons being cold, the hard concrete and steel bars creating an arctic hell. But the visitation room was moist and stuffy. It stank of the collective body odor of convicts and their cigarettes. The boy sat at the booth, holding the phone receiver in his hand even though Pa hadn't shown up yet. The boy's reflection gazed back at him from the safety glass divider. He tapped on it, wondering how thick.

His mother wanted to come with him, but he insisted on doing this on his own. He'd even convinced the shrink it'd be better this way, that he could confront his demons on his own terms as long as he was brave enough to confront them at all. But of course the boy knew this wasn't a demon he was going to see. It was *Pa*, his whole world.

The sound of a steel door coming open caused his heart to drop into his belly. He sat up straight. There was a shadow and the distinct rattle of chains. Quaid Crews stepped before the stool, looking down at him with a blank expression. He waited until the guard walked away before sitting down. Then he picked up the phone.

"Whatta ya want, kid?" he said, monotone.

The boy struggled not to show the hurt. "I wanted to see you. I *had* to see you."

There was a sudden gleam in the man's eyes. They'd gone wet. A warm tingle went through the boy and he licked his lips with cautious hope.

"Well," Crews said, "you've seen me."

"I wanted to . . . to tell you . . . tell you how much I—"

The man cut him off. "Ya don't need to tell me nothin, Chuck."

Chuck was trying to say he loved him, but kept suffocating on his own words, his chest too tight with the dual choke of affection and sorrow. But he knew Pa understood. He knew what Chuck felt and Chuck could tell by the warmth in Pa's eyes that he felt the same, but he turned the conversation in another direction.

"Guess ya feel bad 'bout all this," Pa said. "What with ya bein the only one I didn't kill. Guess ya feel what they call 'survivor's guilt', huh? Well, you're only breathin 'cause I needed work done at that farm." The man cleared his throat in an effort to take the tremble out of it. His eyes remained wet, but he didn't allow a tear to fall. "I was busy snatchin them girls off the street and killin 'em and choppin 'em up. I needed ya to do all the chores so I could do my crimes. Reckon ya did alright sloppin the hogs and tendin to the fences and what not, but I sure as shit couldn't trust ya to help me with them girls! Ya was always tryin to get me to let 'em go, ya lil' crybaby."

Pa's eyes never left Chuck's, saying what his words weren't. Chuck swallowed back tears too. He understood now, understood it all.

"*They* sent ya here, didn't they?" Pa asked. "Them coppers thought I might feel remorse for what I done to ya, 'specially 'cause ya been all messed up with that Stockholm's shit, thinkin I ever gave a flyin fuck 'bout ya. Them coppers think ya might get somethin outta me, huh? Christ, don't matter how much I give 'em. They're always lookin for more dirt, always trying to get me to talk," his eyes widdened "always *listenin*, ya know?"

Chuck did know. He grasped the meaning completely.

"But you and me know ya can't tell 'em anymore than I already have, kid. Ya don't know nothin 'bout what I did to them girls 'cause I took care of 'em all myself. Every one of 'em. They were my bitches! *Mine*! I'd never let the likes of you or anybody else get near my bitches. Closest ya ever came to 'em was when I got sick and had ya make deliveries of their meat. By then I had yer sorry ass so whipped and scared I didn't even worry you'd turn me in." He started sniffling again, so he faked a laugh to cover it. "You were too chicken-livered after all I'd done to ya. Ain't that right, boy?"

Chuck took a deep breath. "I was just another victim. I see that now."

"Good."

A flood of affection emanated through the divider, undetectable to anyone other than the man and the boy.

"Glad we finally gots that through yer thick skull," Pa said. He leaned in close, his nose nearly touching the glass. "T'was kinda fun to see ya one more time, ya little turd, but don't come back here no more. Got me?"

Chuck nodded. His soul ached. This would be the last time he'd see his father, but it had to be this way. It was all clear now, this new truth. Though their visitation time was nowhere near up, Pa stood, hung up the phone, and walked away from the booth, sneering for the guard to see, as if he'd been annoyed by the boy's visit.

CHAPTER TWENTY-FIVE

CHUCK **COVERED LESLIE'S** body with the blanket. He hadn't felt this kind of grief since the day they'd strapped Quaid Crews into the electric chair.

She was gone.

Leslie had taught him the one thing Pa had been wrong about. Not *all* women were veal. Chuck had already known this to some extent, but Leslie had pushed this fact deep into his consciousness just by being who she was. A kindred spirit to his own lost one, a soul mate though he had no soul. Some women were human, odd as that may seem, given how different they were from men. But some males were also different from men and closer to being women, such as Brittany, formerly Bentley.

Chuck thought about how Eugene had tried to rape Leslie and wondered if he'd ever raped anyone else. Perhaps it was the only way a freak like him could 'get' a woman. Chuck thought of Barman's soul-crushing guilt over being a rapist. Should Chuck feel that same guilt for what he'd done on the farm? Was he capable of it? Should he try to force it somehow? He'd raped far more women than Barman had confessed to, and in much worse ways. He'd also done things far more heinous than sexual assault. But just like him, Eugene and Barman had treated women like veal. Did it matter if it was today or thirty years ago? Did it matter if they were remorseful or not? What would it change? Chuck didn't know.

He glowered at the bitter realization. Three rapists and a crippled hobo had been the last hope for a young mother, a hooker, a teenager, and a lush. In a world full of monsters, even heroes have fangs.

Chuck hadn't raped anyone since his days on the pig farm. For one thing, doing so would have seemed like an insult to what Pa had done for him, keeping Chuck free while he went on to death row by claiming all responsibility. He didn't want to go to prison after Pa's great efforts to protect him from such a horrible place. More than that, Chuck didn't have any desire to rape and certainly didn't want to go through the tiring effort of keeping women in chains, whether they be veal or not. Chuck also hadn't killed anyone since his years with Pa, not until this screamer chaos had unfolded and he'd been given no choice. His mindset had simply changed as he'd matured. Rape and murder had been replaced by alcohol, degeneracy, and a low-level madness.

He had long stopped making people suffer and die.

But dying hardly seemed the worst fate in a world this toxic and dreadful. In the end, Leslie had even looked brightly upon the complete annihilation of her own consciousness. The great, white skull of death had smiled upon her, and she just smiled back. She'd danced with the reaper too long to be afraid. Chuck wondered if he would go as gracefully. Leslie was so beatific in her moment of dying, so serene as she went septic from infection. As the world fell to ashes, she snuggled up to him on the couch like they were an old married couple watching a crackling fire. He smelled her hair, tasting the sweat even as she shivered, her body going cold from blood loss and sickness. Their fingers interlinked and they held hands until hers went slack. He briefly thought of making love to her one last time—not fucking her, but *making love* to her, of fisting her sweetly, pleasing her body though her spirit was gone. But he decided against it. Not because of the perversity, but because he couldn't muster the fortitude to do so while strangled by the noose of grief.

Having appeared like a wraith, Leslie's cat pushed against his thigh and Chuck opened the front door to free him. The cat, whatever his damn name was, was no longer an inside cat. Let him enjoy a newfound freedom. Nothing still living should be in this apartment, Chuck thought. It was Leslie's mausoleum now. He had even struggled to get Eugene's skinny ass out the goddamn window just so she'd have the place to herself again.

Chuck put the taser into his front pocket and slid the butcher knife under his belt. He stuffed the bottle of Scotch into his back pocket, put the vodka in the crook of his arm, and carried the two, half empty bottles of whiskey in his hands as he left the apartment. He needed every drop of booze to regard the end. He looked upon this great holocaust with the utmost respect and wanted to toast it. This plague was the great leveler. There was no bottom rung, no upper one percent. No men or women or in between. There was only veal. Just human meat struggling with the curse of their own awareness as they shuffled toward an abhorrent, screaming death. There would be no eyes of history to reflect upon this cataclysm, and therefore no lesson to be learned. Chuck admired the apocalypse for its sheer pointlessness. It made him chuckle. All those people who'd always told him everything happened for a reason had some serious fucking explaining to do.

Passing by Eugene's apartment, he heard the shrieking mother bashing into the locked door with such force he thought she might just break through given enough time. Chuck thought of his own mother, the woman he had never accepted, much to her dismay. He thought of his birth father and the general apathy the man had shown to his weird son's return once the news cameras found another tragedy to milk and moved on. Most of all he thought of Pa now and wondered what he would make of this final, gore-spattered circus. Chuck figured he'd be relieved by the termination of humanity for the sake of the animals. They could have the world back. They deserved it more than we did. The coyotes, the fawns, the swallows, the foxes and the owls had treated the earth better than humans had. Dogs and cats would be better off without us. The dogs wouldn't have to spend all day bored and alone while their owners worked, and the cats, much like Leslie's furry friend, could roam the wild like the tiny tigers they were. And pigs, at long last, would no longer be the innocent victims of knives and forks and hungry mouths.

Pa would have liked that.

When he reached Keisha's apartment, he knocked before realizing the door was slightly ajar. *The dumb kid left it open?* Chuck entered, placing his bottles on the end table by the door. He closed and locked it, eyes struggling with the dimness, the beginning of a sunset muted by drawn curtains.

"Brittany?"

Silence.

His eyes adjusted.

The apartment was in ruin. Stuffing had been torn out of the sofa, exposing springs. The television was smashed in and the coffee table overturned. Holes had been made in the wall—fist-sized holes, shoe-sized holes. Plates and glasses had been pulled from cabinets and lay in shards upon the kitchen tile.

She's fucking turned, he thought. *She's out there somewhere, screaming.*

Suddenly the silence became all the more grievous.

The babies.

One last wish. Leslie had asked him to do one simple thing before she'd died, and he'd failed to do it. Like everything in his life that had happened since leaving the farm, Chuck had fucked it up. He'd only wanted to be by her side. He'd only wanted to hold her in his arms as she left this wretched earth. He'd let her believe the babies were okay, tacitly implying they were with their mother, but was that enough? It had eased Leslie's mind, but it was far from the truth and even further from keeping his vow. If he'd just taken the babies back to the apartment, maybe—

There was a sudden wail from the bedroom. Chuck's heart sped up. The wail rose into a scream, and then there was crying, infant voices expressing unhappiness. They might not have been happy, but they were alive. Brittany hadn't murdered them in an infected rage. Just like the grandmother, she'd left them untouched. It made him think of Eugene's mom and the door she couldn't unlock. Was this similar? Brittany had opened the front door of the apartment. He wondered if, in her screaming mad state, she'd even remembered the babies were back there sleeping.

As Chuck moved down the hall, he was struck by the notion that Brittany might still be somewhere in the apartment, and he drew the taser from his pocket and kicked the bathroom door all the way open, finding no one. He zeroed in on the bedroom, turned the doorknob, and stepped inside. Here the orange glow of early evening was all encompassing. It filled the room, illuminating the fresh lives within the crib. The wailing and screeching of both babies did nothing to diminish the serene wholesomeness, not until he walked up to the edge of the crib.

The baby in blue was screaming and clawing at the face of the crying baby in pink, the infant's tiny, razor-sharp fingernails working like switchblades. Blood poured down the crier's cheeks. The screaming baby head-butted his sibling and tore the little bow out of her fine hair. He repeatedly kicked her in the ribs, all the while screeching and frothing like a rabid animal. The crier wiggled, but the confines of the crib gave her nowhere to escape to.

Chuck snatched up the screamer and the infant's little eyes opened. They were bloodshot and feral with bits of pus in the corners. His skin was changing color, the brown going beige as the jaundice set in. There was no mercy in the baby's stare. His drooling mouth opened and closed, trying to bite Chuck with what few teeth he had. Chuck glanced back at the baby girl still weeping and writhing from her brother's assault, and then returned his attention to the baby boy squirming in his outstretched arms.

Another male abusing of a female, Chuck thought with a small amount of disgust. The baby boy shook in his hands, almost convulsing with the desire to destroy. *What do you want me to do now, Leslie?* He placed the infant on his mother's bed, watching him strive to turn onto his stomach. Though it seemed too young to be able to do so, the infant began to crawl, coming at Chuck.

Chuck took the taser from his pocket.

It would be better than the knife, better than dropping the baby from the open window and into the street. The child was so small and fragile it would likely stop his heart instantly.

There was a time when the most humane form of executing a condemned man was via electricity. Pa had died that way, so why not this hopelessly infected infant? There was no way to protect the girl without getting rid of the boy. Chuck realized this had always been true with boys and girls, even before the scream.

As the small bolts of blue lightening reflected off the emptiness in the screaming baby's eyes, Chuck remembered the cattle prod, and how the veal's cries had echoed through the woods, raising birds from branches and riling up the pigs.

After wrapping her brother's corpse in a towel, Chuck took the little girl in his arms and cradled her. Her soft flesh was torn and already starting to bruise, so he tended to her abrasions with cotton balls and sterilized them with vodka which only made her wail even louder. He worried the cries would summon more screamers, but there was nothing he could do about it. He could only rock her gently and try to hush her with calming coos, the sort of nurturing he'd only seen others do.

He finished off the scotch first, wanting to save the whisky for last, it being his favorite. The booze made the baby girl's screeching a little more tolerable, but the sudden stench coming off of her was not. He'd never changed a diaper before and didn't want to now. But he'd promised Leslie. Chuck took off the infant's onesie and removed the loaded diaper and tossed it in the trash. He cleaned her with wet paper towels, found a fresh diaper and put it on her. It looked wrongly assembled, but it held.

Still the child screeched, its cry going through his head like an aneurism.

Chuck carried her to the fridge, stepping around the broken dishes and debris. There were three bottles in the fridge, all marked *breast milk*. He warmed one up in the microwave, just as he'd used to when feeding the veal their low iron shakes. Before giving it to the baby, he took a few good swigs of the creamy substance, reflecting on the nursing mother they'd kept alive for a while. Pa had so loved titty milk. The baby spat out the rubber nipple, refusing the bottle, still crying. Chuck squirted some of the breast milk into his glass of vodka and sat down on the couch with the baby in one arm, pressed into his chest just as Leslie had been.

What the fuck am I gonna do now?

There seemed nothing else *to* do. Just watch the sun fall down and the stars appear out of the cosmos. Just sit and listen to the world die. He lit a cigarette. What did smoke matter to the baby's health when there was no way she was going to see another birthday. He drank but the drunkenness he craved was still far away. Suddenly the light in the kitchen went out and the oscillating fan in the corner whirred to a stop. They'd finally lost power.

The baby cried and cried and cried. Loud and shrill and terrible. Was she shrieking because that's just what babies did, or was she becoming a screamer? She wasn't attacking him—yet. Another grim thought punched into his mind like a hammer to the skull.

What if I turn into one?

It was something he genuinely hadn't been afraid of until now. He'd never been susceptible to illness. Not a cough or a stuffy nose in all his life. The threat of flu had never caused him worry. Perhaps it was arrogant, but Chuck considered himself immune to such things. If he were immune to The Scream, he might just end up being the last man on earth. The thought was absurd to him.

One man left on earth and he's a scumbag.

But what if he wasn't impervious? What if he turned into one of those yellow monstrosities and ripped this baby girl into scraps?

Promise me you'll take care of them, Chucky.

He couldn't leave her. The baby would starve to death. Plus, if he left her alone in the apartment, another screamer might get to her, defeating the purpose.

The taser in his pocket felt suddenly very heavy.

Taking care of the baby took on a different meaning. There was little hope for life, but there was always mercy.

He'd failed to show mercy to so many young girls. He'd been a child himself then. Everyone had told him he too was a victim, just like the girls whose killings had been solely attributed to Quaid Crews. Chuck's birth parents and shrinks had reminded him of his supposed victimhood until he was old enough to get away from them for good. While he didn't believe it, he had hazy memories of being in that dog cage in the basement. Things had been different between he and the man then. It was the women—the veal—who had brought them closer together. Man and boy bonding through dehumanizing, defiling, and murdering the innocent. Chuck would not stoop to thinking of it as a wrong that had been done to him by Crews. Chuck had *wanted* to use the veal to fulfill his own needs, be they for sex, profit, or his initiation into manhood via slaughter. He'd had no remorse back then and no real remorse had come to haunt him later in life. Their deaths had just seemed right at the time, even the death of the inutero veal, the *gourmet*, as Pa had called it.

Looking down at the crying infant in his arms, a baby's death seemed right again.

He thought of Leslie's story about her husband killing himself and their children. Keisha's babies would be the loss of two more. They were the last children Leslie's maternal instincts had reacted to with such light. So, for Leslie, he let the baby cry as night fell in full. As the darkness wrapped itself around them, the sweet numbness of the alcohol settled in, and the baby stopped crying so gradually he hardly noticed. The silence grew so loud he wondered if he'd gone deaf. Carrying the baby with him, he went to the window and stared out at a city without hope. The sirens had died down. The only screams were so distant they were mere echoes. And under the smell of ashes was an odor not unlike pig feces. Probably dead bodies, Chuck thought. The block was eerily calm, peaceful in the worst possible way. The sky offered no moon, no stars. Every window in every building was black. There wasn't even the tangerine glow of fires anymore. There was no longer light in this world, only a swarming, suffocating darkness with no end.

He would give the baby one more night to dream in, and then he would kill her too. It would be mercy killing, unlike all the others he'd done, but it would be just as easy, because even if humanity wasn't doomed, the odds were good the infant wasn't the sort of girl who could grow up to be a real woman like Leslie.

It was far more likely she was just another veal.

ACKNOWLEDGEMENTS

Thanks to Marc Ciccarone and Joe Spagnola and everyone at Blood Bound Books. Also thanks to my good pals, instigators, and enablers, including John Wayne Comunale, Tangie Silva, Ryan Harding, Josh Doherty, Brian Keene, Christine Morgan, Bernard DeBenedictis, Gregg Kirby, Nicole Amburgey, Mary Sangiovanni, Wesley Southard, Bryan Smith, and Jack Ketchum (RIP).

Biggest of thanks to Bear, the best assistant editor and such a good girl.

And special thanks to Tom Mumme—always.

ABOUT THE AUTHOR

Kristopher Triana is the Splatterpunk Award-winning author of *Full Brutal, Gone to See the River Man, Blood Relations, Body Art* and many other terrifying books. He is also the author of the crime thrillers *The Ruin Season* and *Shepherd of the Black Sheep*. His work has been published in multiple languages and has drawn praise from the likes of Publisher's Weekly, Rue Morgue Magazine, Cemetery Dance, Scream Magazine, The Horror Fiction Review and many more.

He is also the co-host of the podcast *Vital Social Issues 'N Stuff with Kris and John Wayne.*

Incredibly, Triana finished the rough draft of *They All Died Screaming* in February of 2020, just before Covid-19 hit.

He lives somewhere in New England.

Visit him at:

Kristophertriana.com
Twitter: Koyotekris
Facebook: Kristopher Triana
Instagram: Kristopher_Triana
Podcast: krisandjohnwayne.com

Printed in Great Britain
by Amazon

18336902R00130